RYOHGO NARITA
ILLUSTRATION BY
SUZUHITO YASUDA

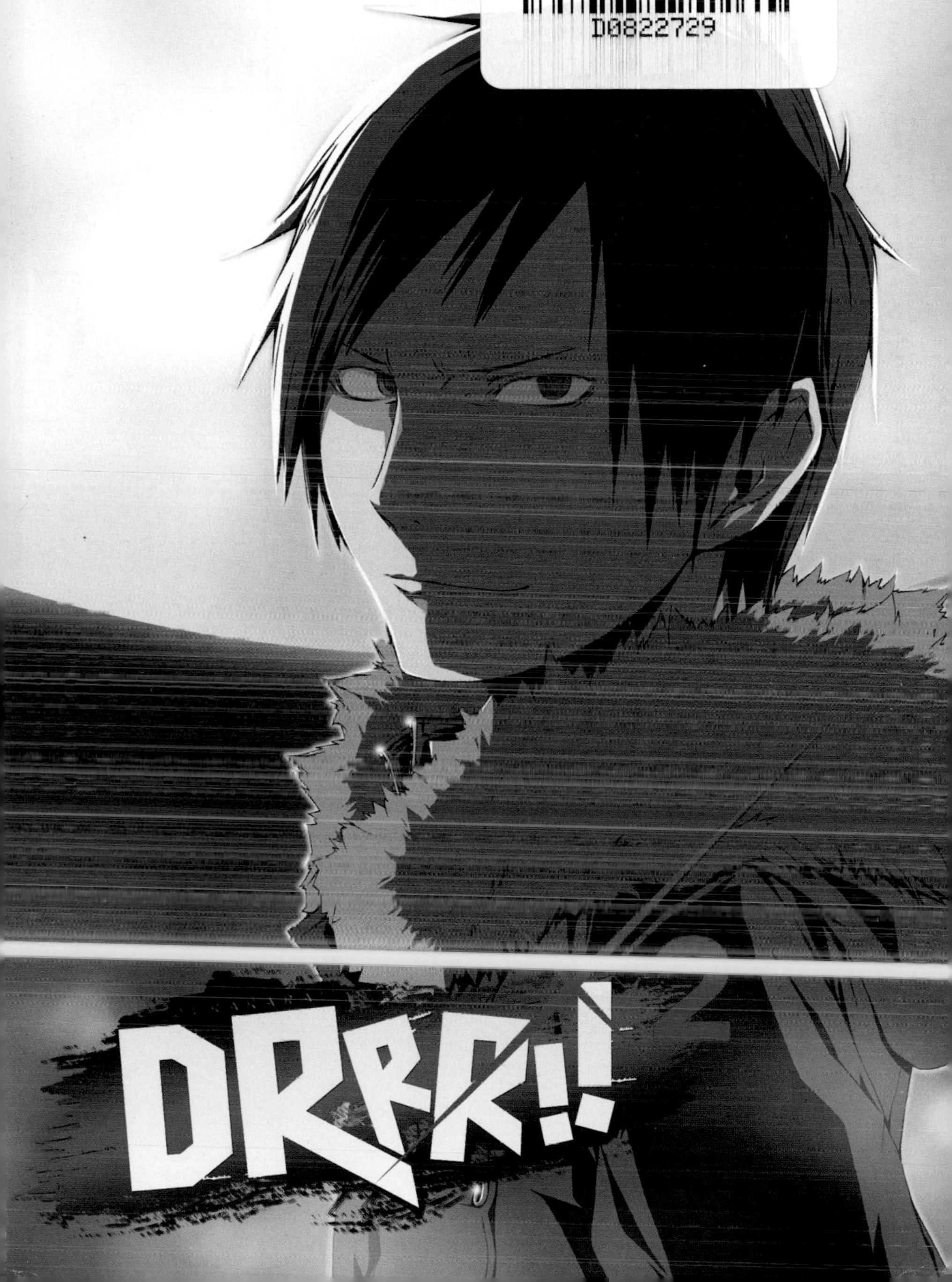
DRRR!!

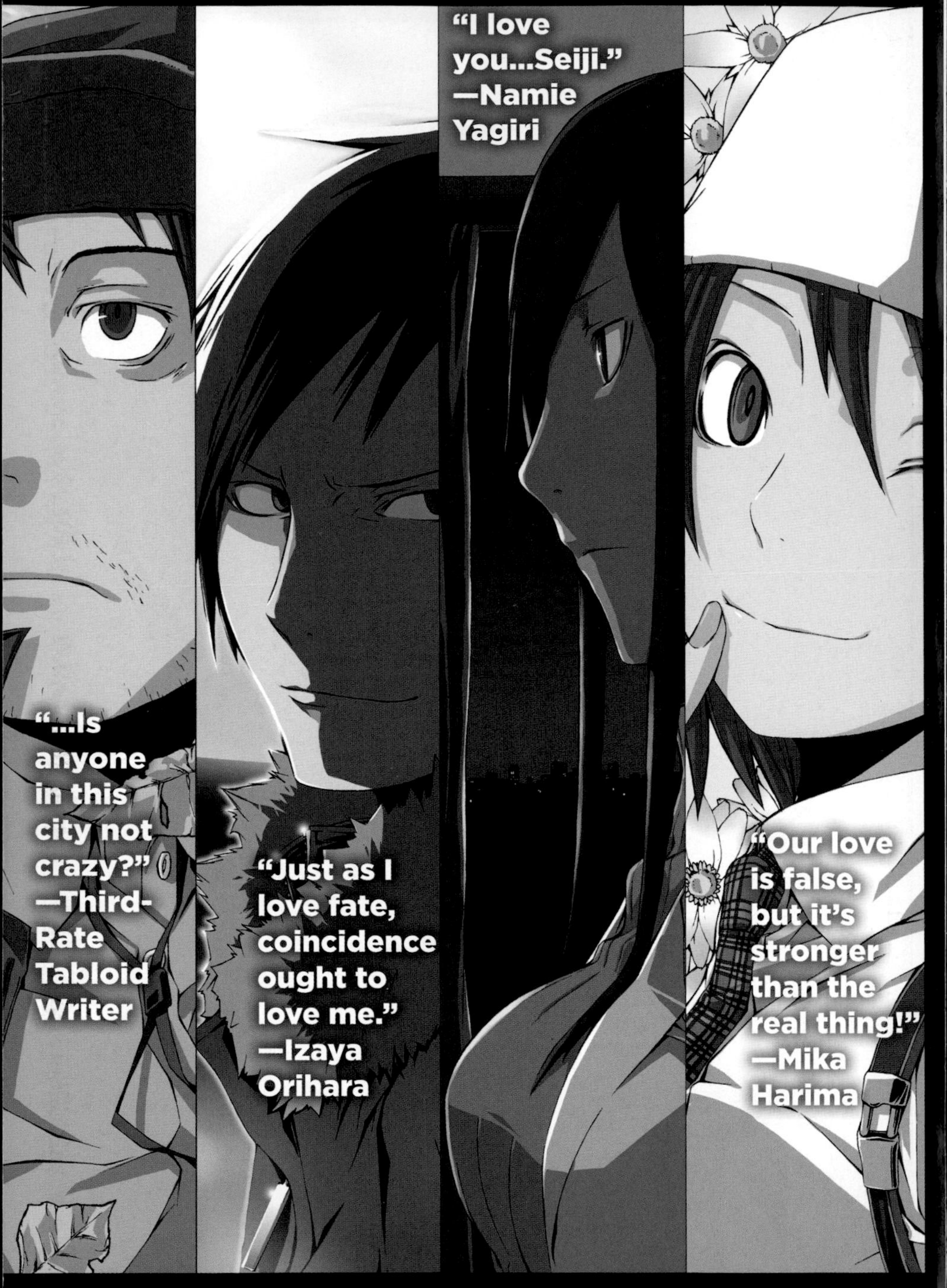
"I love you...Seiji."
—Namie Yagiri
"...Is anyone in this city not crazy?"
—Third-Rate Tabloid Writer
"Just as I love fate, coincidence ought to love me."
—Izaya Orihara
"Our love is false, but it's stronger than the real thing!"
—Mika Harima

"Everything about our love is false."
—Seiji Yagiri

"Every time you come home, it's like the footfalls of a visitor to the lonely valley of my heart."
—Shinra Kishitani

"..."
—Celty Sturluson

"You want me to crush every last inch of you starting with the fingernails?"
—Shizuo Heiwajima

"It's another peaceful day in the neighborhood... right?"
—Mikado Ryuugamine

"Umm...I'm not sure what to say to that..."
—Anri Sonohara

"I'm always on the side of whoever has my back."
—Masaomi Kida

"The most tiresome thing is complaining that you're tired."
—Kyouhei Kadota

"When I die, I want to go to two-dimensional heaven."
—Walker Yumasaki

"I hope to die under a mountain of books."
—Erika Karisawa

"Our sushi, very fresh. Just opened can of fish this morning."
—Simon Brezhnev

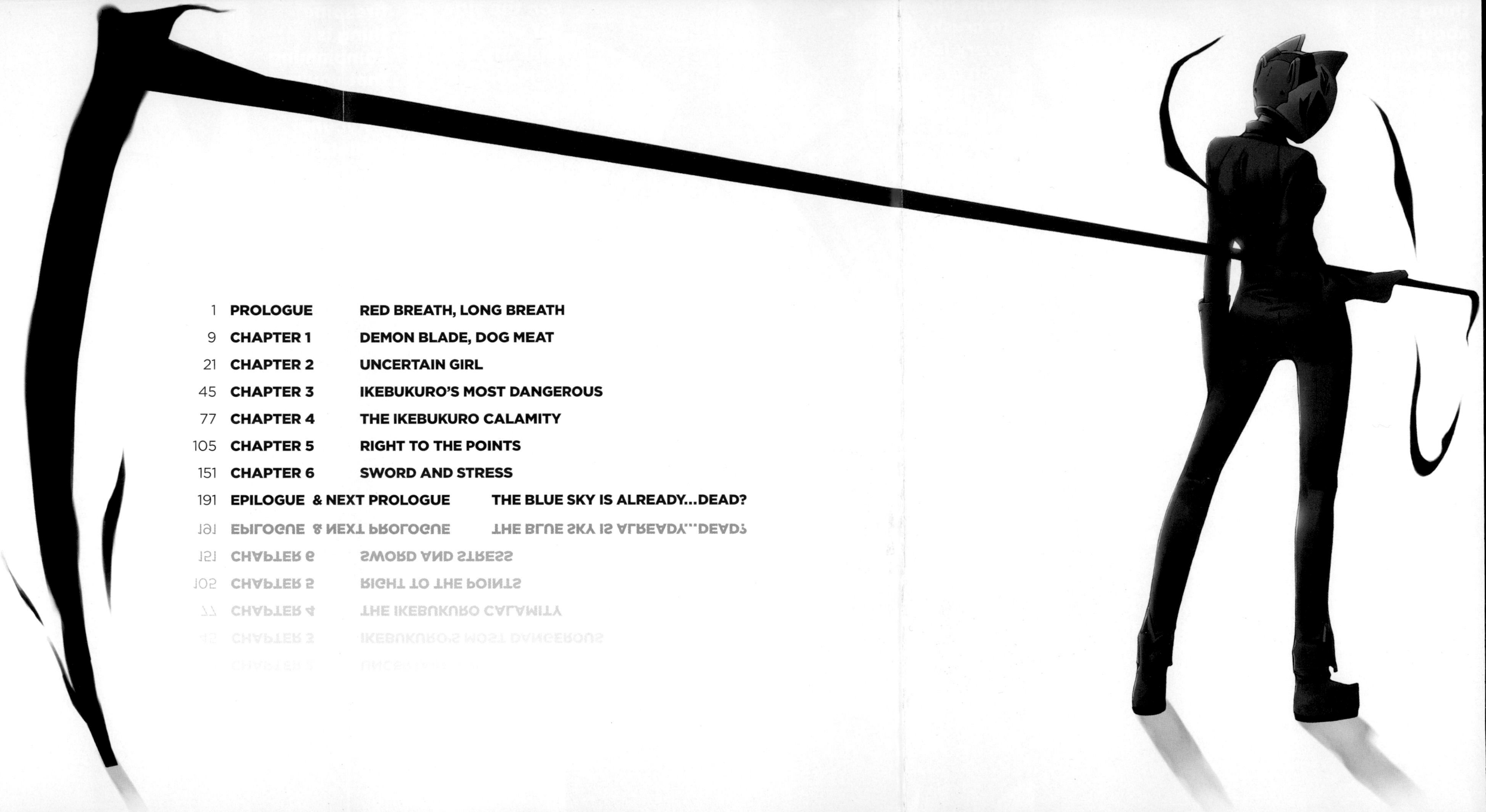

DURARARA!!

VOLUME 2

Ryohgo Narita
ILLUSTRATION BY **Suzuhito Yasuda**

YEN
ON

NEW YORK

DURARARA!!, Volume 2
RYOHGO NARITA,
ILLUSTRATION BY SUZUHITO YASUDA

Translation by Stephen Paul

DURARARA!!
© RYOHGO NARITA 2005
All rights reserved.
Edited by ASCII MEDIA WORKS
First published in 2005 by KADOKAWA
CORPORATION, Tokyo.
English translation rights arranged with
KADOKAWA CORPORATION, Tokyo, through
Tuttle-Mori Agency, Inc., Tokyo.

Yen On
Hachette Book Group
1290 Avenue of the Americas
New York, NY 10104
www.hachettebookgroup.com
www.yenpress.com

Yen On is an imprint of Hachette Book Group, Inc. The Yen On name and logo are trademarks of Hachette Book Group, Inc.

First Yen On edition: November 2015

ISBN: 978-0-316-30476-4

10 9 8 7 6 5 4 3 2 1

RRD-C

Printed in the United States of America

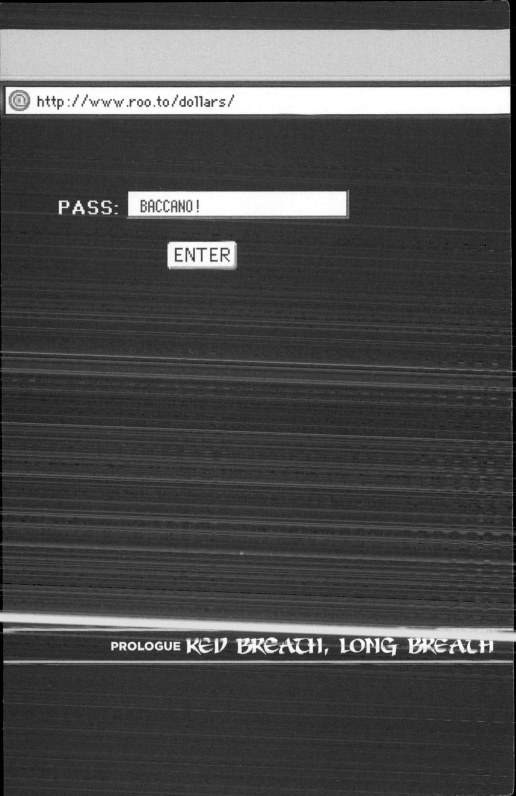

http://www.roo.to/dollars/

PASS: BACCANO!

ENTER

PROLOGUE RED BREATH, LONG BREATH

Her love was so unbearably creaky,

so unsalvageably rusted,

and while so apparently deep in its fixation—

it was in fact ignorant, foolish, and shallow in the extreme.

I love people.
Whom do I love? No, not whom! I love all human beings!
What do I love about them? Don't ask silly questions! Everything, I love everything!
I love the hot blood that goes from bright to filthy black as it races through their bodies!
I love their sinewy muscles, so tough yet soft, that tear right apart!
I love their bone, slender and ~~~~ ~~~~ and rough!
I love their cartilage, trembling soft and clinging wetly and smoothly!
I love their throats, chirping and screaming sounds of love when I touch them!
I love their eyes, dripping tears in response to my love!
Most of all, when my love has peaked...and the cross section of split flesh appears.

I love anything and everything about them. You get it?
Yes, I love you, too, of course. But I cannot "love" you.

But you should love me.

Yes, it's entirely one-sided.
In exchange for your love of me, I will love all other humans.
A rather twisted triangle.
Will you abandon me? Hate me? Use me ragged like an old cloth and
throw me away?
But you can't not love me, can you?
You can't not love my power, can you?
It's fine to love me. That's up to you.
But I won't love you. In fact, I can't.
As long as you're gripping me, I can only love those you wish to cut.

And don't you dare think about seppuku.
It will be hard to search for another person to love me...

Her love was so unbearably straight,

so smooth and sharp,

reflecting the figures of those she loved within her body

and tearing everything apart.

Chat room

【Demon blade?】
《That's right! Did you know about that, Tarou?》
【How would I have known about that? Setton, isn't that your forte?】
[A demon blade... Like Muramasa, you mean?]
《No, Setton! That's more of a cursed blade, the kind that brings you misfortune just for having it. This is a different thing! It's more like something out of a manga, where it controls your mind and makes you slice people!》
[But...I thought most of those were just called Muramasa.]
【Like a Muramasa Blade?】
["You decapitated your foe!"]
【That's from *Wizardry*, right? I didn't realize you were a gamer, Setton.】
《Hey, stop going off on tangents!》
[Oh, sorry.]
【Sorry, Kanra.】
《Well, listen up! Ikebukuro's buzzing over this demon blade! There's a mysterious murderer who appears in the back alleys late at night, swinging the deadly weapon! There are no fatalities yet, but whoever it is has been going hog wild with a katana on their victims!》
【That kind of sounds like it should be fatal...】
《Apparently they go just shallow enough not to kill! Some of the victims have had their arms cut and stuff!》
[It just sounds like your average crime spree to me.]
《No, you don't get it! This is a katana we're talking about! Whoever it is just slips in and slices the victim before they can escape, with these eerie inhuman moves! Whoever's responsible must not be human!》
[But why does that make it a demon blade?]
《Heh-heh, well, just between us...one of the victims got a look at the face of whoever slashed them, and it was apparently totally wild.》
【What do you mean, wild?】
《Like, with glowing red eyes, as if they were under some kind of hypnosis. Like they'd been bitten by a vampire and put under his control!》
[Okay, so it's a vampire, then. lol]
《No, Setton, that's silly! There's no such thing as vampires, obviously!》
[...]

《Oh, I'm only kidding!☆ Don't be mad, Setton!》
[But I'm not mad (grr!)]
【Yes, you are, yes, you are! lol】
【But we already know there's a headless rider, so there could be a demon blade, too.】
[The headless rider... They were just doing a TV report on that one.]
【Yes, along with a segment on a flying girl with green skin. One of those paranormal shows.】
《And Setton always makes sure to watch any TV show about the headless rider!》
【Are you a fan?】
[No...I wouldn't say that. But my partner, the man I live with, certainly is.]
【Partner? Wait, Setton, are you married?】
[No, not yet...]
《But you live together?! Eeek!》
[Why does being a partner make him my lover? And wait...do you know my gender?]
【Um, you're...a woman, right?】
《It's really obvious from the way you talk. It's feminine, but not over the top enough to be a guy pretending to be one.》
[Did you think we'd never noticed before this?]
[Oh my, look at the time. I've got an early morning tomorrow, so good night.]

—SETTON HAS LEFT THE CHAT—

【Oh, she ran away.】
《She certainly did.》
<Private Mode> [...Are you just poking fun at yourself when you talk about people pretending to be effeminate online, Izaya?]
《Eeeeek! Tarou's harassing me with PMs!》
【No, that's not it! It's not like that!】
<Private Mode> [No, but seriously, who is Setton?]
<Private Mode> [Is she someone I know? Karisawa, maybe?]
<Private Mode> 《Hmm. It's a secret.》
《Well, I should be logging off now. Careful not to get taken over by the demon blade!☆ 》

* * *

—KANRA HAS LEFT THE CHAT—

【Okay, good night.】
【...And really, it wasn't like that! There was no sexual harassment going on!】

—TAROU TANAKA HAS LEFT THE CHAT—

—THE CHAT ROOM IS CURRENTLY EMPTY—
—THE CHAT ROOM IS CURRENTLY EMPTY—
—THE CHAT ROOM IS CURRENTLY EMPTY—
—THE CHAT ROOM IS CURRENTLY EMPTY—
—THE CHAT ROOM IS CURRENTLY EMPTY—
—THE CHAT ROOM IS CURRENTLY EMPTY—
—THE CHAT ROOM IS CURRENTLY EMPTY—
—THE CHAT ROOM IS CURRENTLY EMPTY—
—THE CHAT ROOM IS CURRENTLY EMPTY—
—THE CHAT ROOM IS CURRENTLY EMPTY—
—THE CHAT ROOM IS CURRENTLY EMPTY—
—THE CHAT ROOM IS CURRENTLY EMPTY—
—THE CHAT ROOM IS CURRENTLY EMPTY—
—THE CHAT ROOM IS CURRENTLY EMPTY—
—THE CHAT ROOM IS CURRENTLY EMPTY—
—THE CHAT ROOM IS CURRENTLY EMPTY—
—THE CHAT ROOM IS CURRENTLY EMPTY—
—THE CHAT ROOM IS CURRENTLY EMPTY—
—THE CHAT ROOM IS CURRENTLY EMPTY—
—THE CHAT ROOM IS CURRENTLY EMPTY—
—THE CHAT ROOM IS CURRENTLY EMPTY—
—THE CHAT ROOM IS CURRENTLY EMPTY—
—THE CHAT ROOM IS CURRENTLY EMPTY—
—THE CHAT ROOM IS CURRENTLY EMPTY—
—THE CHAT ROOM IS CURRENTLY EMPTY—
—THE CHAT ROOM IS CURRENTLY EMPTY—
—THE CHAT ROOM IS CURRENTLY EMPTY—
—SAIKA HAS ENTERED THE CHAT—

|person|
|love|
|not|
|weak|
|want|
|love|
|want|
|want|

—SAIKA HAS LEFT THE CHAT—
—THE CHAT ROOM IS CURRENTLY EMPTY—
—THE CHAT ROOM IS CURRENTLY EMPTY—
—THE CHAT ROOM IS CURRENTLY EMPTY—
—THE CHAT ROOM IS CURRENTLY EMPTY—
—THE CHAT ROOM IS CURRENTLY EMPTY—
—THE CHAT ROOM IS CURRENTLY EMPTY—
—THE CHAT ROOM IS CURRENTLY EMPTY—
—THE CHAT ROOM IS CURRENTLY EMPTY—
—THE CHAT ROOM IS CURRENTLY EMPTY—
—THE CHAT ROOM IS CURRENTLY EMPTY—
—THE CHAT ROOM IS CURRENTLY EMPTY—
—THE CHAT ROOM IS CURRENTLY EMPTY—
—THE CHAT ROOM IS CURRENTLY EMPTY—
—THE CHAT ROOM IS CURRENTLY EMPTY—
—THE CHAT ROOM IS CURRENTLY EMPTY—
—THE CHAT ROOM IS CURRENTLY EMPTY—
—THE CHAT ROOM IS CURRENTLY EMPTY—
—THE CHAT ROOM IS CURRENTLY EMPTY—
—THE CHAT ROOM IS CURRENTLY EMPTY—
—THE CHAT ROOM IS CURRENTLY EMPTY—
—THE CHAT ROOM IS CURRENTLY EMPTY—
—THE CHAT ROOM IS CURRENTLY EMPTY—
—THE CHAT ROOM IS CURRENTLY EMPTY—
—THE CHAT ROOM IS CURRENTLY EMPTY—
—THE CHAT ROOM IS CURRENTLY EMPTY—

.

CHAPTER 1 DEMON BLADE, DOG MEAT

- On a news program:

"Today we pick up where we left off in the ongoing story of the serial attacks in Ikebukuro.

"As you see, the total number of victims has risen to fifteen as of now. As the attacks have all occurred at night, eyewitness details are scarce, and most of the victims' reports are vague…

"Furthermore, a number of similar incidents happened five years ago, and as no culprit was ever identified, the police are investigating the possibility that the same person is responsible…

"There's also the case of the so-called Headless Rider in Ikebukuro since last year, a figure running wild with a massive weapon, whom some citizens are saying could be involved."

—On a different paranormal-related program:

"The Slit-Mouthed Woman, the Man-Faced Dog, the Woman in the Wall—Ikebukuro's Headless Rider was nothing more than another of these fanciful urban legends. But ever since last spring, this legendary figure has begun to feel all too real!

"The first sighting was more than ten years ago. So how did some segments of the media finally start reporting this story? It all starts from this footage.

"In the middle of filming this station's program *Caught on Tape! 24 Hours in Ikebukuro*, our staff member riding in a police vehicle incidentally captured this image…"

"Oh my God, what is that?"

"Huh? Wait, look at that black scythe… Is it getting bigger over the course of the shot?"

"The hell is this? That movement shouldn't be physically possible."

"But it's rumored that black motorcycle is related to the recent attacks—"

(after commercial break)

"We apologize for some inappropriate statements made earlier on this program…"

—Headlines from a weekly magazine:

"Eerie News! The Creepy Relationship Between the Headless Rider and the Street Attacks"

"Is It the Same Culprit As Five Years Ago?"

"Why the Police Haven't Caught the Serial Slasher"

"A Modern-Day *Tsujigiri*? The Madness of the Katana"

"Evil Spirit? Motorcycle Gangster? Performer? Examining the Headless Rider's Identity"

♂♀

Night, Ikebukuro, late February

Damn, the shadow thought quietly beneath the girder bridge a short distance away from Ikebukuro Station.

That wasn't a figure of speech—she actually *was* a shadow.

Clad in a pitch-black riding suit, astride a motorcycle enveloped in darkness.

The headlight-less bike was completely black in every way, from its engine to its driveshaft to its license plate. The coloring made it look like someone had simply dumped black paint on a plastic model of a motorcycle. The black riding suit matched the color as well.

It was only the outline of the lights from the bridge overhead that cast her and her bike into profile and made them visible.

Damn, dammit.

The black rider, Celty Sturluson, was faced with a single street punk who trembled in terror.

The thug looked to be in his late thirties. But there was no hint of the dignity or presence that age should have given him. Celty had been in the presence of yakuza officers around the same age as this man, and it was a keen reminder that even after living the same number of years, individual human beings could be extremely different in nature.

Celty was a courier making her home in Ikebukuro.

She wasn't able to advertise her services, given her lack of a license, but her skill and speed at handling illegal and/or dangerous payload, plus the benefit of leaving no traces on the off chance that she was actually caught—there was no official record of her presence in Japan—meant that she didn't have clients. At times, she got benign, upstanding offers like delivering a manga artist's finished draft to the printer, but given that her partner, Shinra Kishitani, was a black-market doctor, most of her jobs ended up being through his unsavory contacts.

She wasn't strictly a courier, either; she took on requests to find runaway children and runaway debtors as well.

This particular case was another one of these "outside-the-bounds" jobs.

A thug terrified into paralysis. All she had to do was collect the money this poor slob ran off with. That was all she had to do, and it should have ended at that.

Damn, damn, damn, she groaned to herself.

The thug was already on the ground. All she had to do was pick up the bag containing the money and that was it.

She had a giant black scythe and the thug had completely lost all intent to fight, over nothing more than a tear in his clothes. She just had to get off the bike and pick up the bag. She'd received no orders about the man's custody. She could take him back with her, but she didn't want more trouble, and she also didn't want the risk of a face-to-face confrontation with the client leading to a possible murder.

One of her ironclad tenets was not to take any jobs involving killing. Part of it was the emotional toll of knowing that someone had died on account of her, but on a more practical level, she was getting by fine without resorting to murder.

She didn't have to worry about living costs to begin with, thanks to the wealth of her partner, Shinra, but Celty always paid him her share of the rent. She didn't want to owe him for something like that.

On top of that, this job should have earned her enough for this month's rent.

It's a simple job, she'd thought.

But Celty was frozen still. She couldn't get down off the motorcycle.

The reason was extremely simple.

A blade.

Without warning, a silver blade grew out of the arm that held her scythe.

At first there was just a physical shock. The pain followed.

For the first moment that she saw the gleam of steel protruding from her arm, Celty didn't understand what happened—but her experience and instinct soon told her that someone had stabbed her from behind.

"A...*aiiee!*"

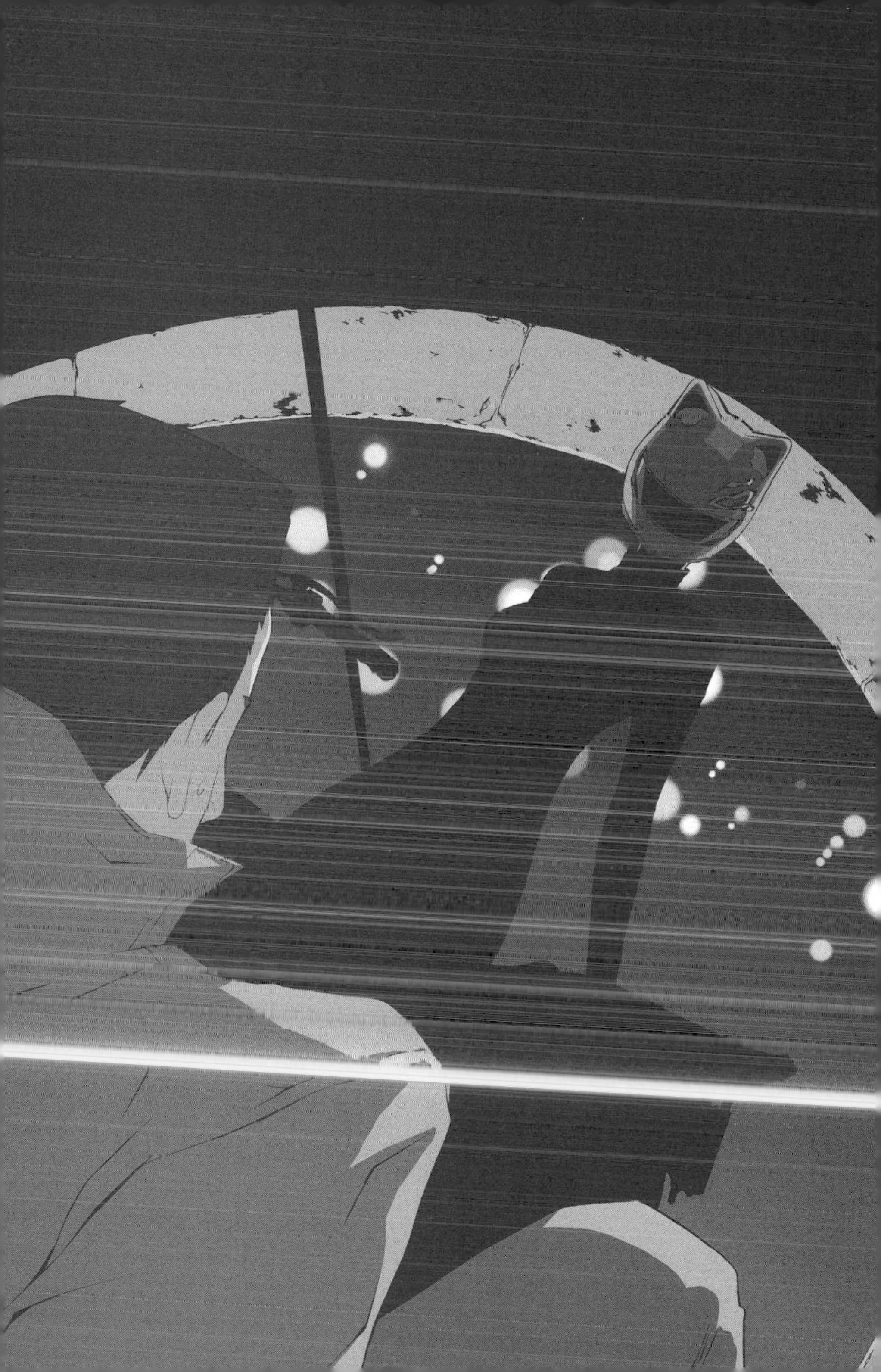

The thug seemed to have grasped the situation quicker than Celty did. He wailed pitifully as he stared over her shoulder.

Damn, dammit, damn.

Someone was behind her, piercing her arm all the way through with the blade.

Normally, she would spin around on instinct, but Celty's sense of pain was much duller than most. More than the pain, it was the distraction of the katana erupting from her arm that kept her from turning around at once.

Surprisingly calm about the situation, Celty wasn't sure whether or not to take her eyes off the thug before her, and that hesitation was what cost her.

Determining that the thug wasn't capable of getting up and running off immediately, she spun the bike around. The moment she squeezed the handlebar, the motorcycle's engine brayed like an organic creature, and it made a completely *in*organic 180-degree turn in place without rolling its wheels.

The next instant, the vein of light flashed.

The katana's long blade reflected the light from above with a beautiful arc, and the glowing circle passed right through Celty's neck.

In total silence, Celty's helmet flew through the air, leaving only unspeaking darkness swirling above the neck of her riding suit.

"Ahyaaaaaaa! Hya! Hyaiii!" screamed the seated, terrified man.

The rider of the black motorcycle who had been trying to kill him (at least, in his mind) was abruptly beheaded by a new figure that had appeared from behind.

Though he couldn't see it from his vantage point, the new figure struck as quick as lightning. It pulled the blade out of the rider's arm as the bike rotated and swung in the reverse direction to catch her on the way around.

Like interlocking gears, the two rotations met up again, and in the next instant, the rider's head was off her shoulders.

The slasher of Ikebukuro.

Both Celty and the street tough remembered the tabloid-fodder story and turned to the new figure.

"*Gweah!*" came an unnatural squawk as Celty tried to tell who this new attacker was.

What was that?! she thought. *Yet another—*

But when she cast her "gaze" back toward the seated man, he was staring at her, goggle-eyed.

"S-st-still m-m-moving?!"

Oh.

"N-n-n-n-n-no h-hea—head."

And then Celty remembered.

She was the Headless Rider.

Celty Sturluson was not human.

She was a type of fairy residing in Ireland called a dullahan, a spirit that visited the homes of those who were soon to die, to warn them of their impending demise.

A dullahan carried its own severed head under its arm and rode on a two-wheeled carriage called a Coiste Bodhar drawn by a headless horse. If anyone at the home of the soon to be dead was foolish enough to open their door to the dullahan, they would receive a basin full of blood splashed over them. Thus, the dullahan, like the banshee, made its name as a herald of ill fortune throughout European folklore.

One theory claimed that the dullahan bore a strong resemblance to the Norse Valkyrie, but Celty had no way of knowing if this was true.

It wasn't that she *didn't* know. More accurately, she just couldn't remember.

When someone back in her homeland stole her head, she lost her memories of what she was. It was the search for the faint trail of her head that had brought her here to Ikebukuro.

Now, with a motorcycle instead of a headless horse and a riding suit instead of armor, she had wandered the streets of this neighborhood for decades.

But ultimately, she had not succeeded at retrieving her head, and now she had partially given up and accepted her new life here.

Celty understood that society would never accept her for what she was, and in her heart, she yelled back, *So what?*

Society might not be able to accept her, but there were some people who did—and that was the lonely, lively life of the headless woman, Celty Sturluson, in a nutshell.

The man's scream brought her back to her senses, reminding Celty that she was just as odd a being as the slasher—if not more so—but she didn't have time to calm the man down now. Not to mention that there was no *need* for her to calm him down.

In less than a second, she was back to her normal wits, and she turned to the shadowy figure.

Suddenly, the fluorescent light illuminating the underside of the girder bridge popped and went out.

?!

For an instant, Celty was disoriented, until she decided that the figure must have thrown something at the light to break it. Her sense of vision went black, but that vision wasn't passing through eyeballs. Celty "saw" the world through a different means than human beings did, and her night vision was much better as a result.

But by the time she had adjusted to the darkness, the figure was already out of sight. It must have escaped while she was distracted by the light. Even with the distraction, it was clear that the figure had moved with abnormal speed.

Damn. Disadvantaged by my own toughness.

If Celty were a normal human, then even before the blow to her head, she'd have spun around instantly to keep an eye on the "enemy" or source of "fear" that was trying to take her life—and never taken her gaze off of it. But because Celty knew she was very unlikely to die here, she allowed her attention to be distracted by other things, and now the attacker had gotten away.

All that was left under the darkened bridge was an unconscious thug and a headless motorcycle rider.

Celty felt a strong *alien* sensation about her abrupt attacker. Not fear—something alien.

The instant the blade pierced her, it felt like some eerie presence was trying to get inside of Celty.

If the attacker wasn't human but another kind of fairy or monster, she would have sensed it before being stabbed. Possibly it *was* such a creature, just one that had learned to extinguish its presence, but Celty dismissed that as unlikely.

So what was *that shadow, then?*

The fight was so brief that she wasn't able to identify the attacker's features or even height, but there was one thing, one powerful memory that stuck out in her mind.

Just before the fluorescent light shattered, she saw the attacker's eyes.

Unnaturally large, bloodred, distorting the light they reflected,

Remembering the inhumanly large, glowing red circles, the dullahan couldn't contain a little shiver.

She remembered the eerie images of the little gray aliens she'd seen on the TV.

What if it was an actual alien?

The headless knight, a symbol of terror for humanity, imagined a cheesy Adamski-model UFO emitting some mysterious beam technology that split the earth in two and shivered.

♂♀

Chat room

—THE CHAT ROOM IS CURRENTLY EMPTY—
—THE CHAT ROOM IS CURRENTLY EMPTY—
—THE CHAT ROOM IS CURRENTLY EMPTY—
—SAIKA HAS ENTERED THE CHAT—

|human|
|strong|
|want|
|love|
|wantlovehuman|
|wanthumanlovestrong|
|want love strong so human|
|love want strong human yes|
|yes so want|

|,|
|so, so, so, so|
|I|
|I, so, want|
|I, so, want, , ,|
|strong, yes, is, human|
|strong, human, want, I, love|

—SAIKA HAS LEFT THE CHAT—
—THE CHAT ROOM IS CURRENTLY EMPTY—
—THE CHAT ROOM IS CURRENTLY EMPTY—
—THE CHAT ROOM IS CURRENTLY EMPTY—
—THE CHAT ROOM IS CURRENTLY EMPTY—
—SETTON HAS ENTERED THE CHAT—

[...]
[What is this?]
[A troll?]
[...That's scary.]
[It sounds like an alien.]
[...Now, I just made myself scared.]
[Um, not that I'm saying I'm scared of aliens or anything!]

—SETTON HAS LEFT THE CHAT—

CHAPTER 2 UNCERTAIN GIRL

After school, Raira Academy, Ikebukuro

What is it that I'm missing? Anri Sonohara wondered as she walked down the long hallway, lit by the western sun.

It was nearly a year since she had come to Raira Academy.

She became the student representative of Class 1-A and made friends with the male representative, Mikado Ryuugamine, and Masaomi Kida from the adjacent class.

It was the first time she'd been friends with boys, and it felt a little awkward figuring out how to act around them, but everything was going essentially fine.

Yet she still found that she couldn't find her "standing" within the school.

In middle school, she had a clearly defined standing: Mika Harima's foil.

Her slightly older but pretty and smart childhood friend kept the plain, unremarkable Anri around to make her look better. It was a classic lopsided, parasitic friendship.

Anri didn't particularly object to this relationship. In fact, she found it comfortable.

Regardless of the form it took, someone needed her. Knowing that meant she didn't have to worry about finding a meaning in her life.

Just as she was thinking about her past, Mika herself walked by.

But it was not Anri at her side this time. She was practically glued to the side of tall Seiji Yagiri, the boy she'd been going out with since the start of school—in fact, they were firmly pressed together as they walked. They were making sure the nature of their relationship was seen and understood by everyone around them.

Mika noticed Anri watching and gave a little smile and a wave.

"Hey, Anri. See you tomorrow."

"Y-yeah..."

An empty exchange. To Mika, that was all Anri was anymore. She had no need for a foil. Mika had found her own place in the world within Seiji Yagiri. Therefore, there was no more reason for her and Anri to prop each other up.

This was because Seiji deeply loved Mika, regardless of if she had someone to make her look better. Even Anri, who knew nothing about romance, could tell that they were bound by deep love. It felt as though there was a sheen of insincerity around it, but Anri dismissed that as an illusion created by her own jealousy.

At the moment, Anri was *just sort of* living her life.

She was letting the days pass by, maintaining a distance from her few friends that wasn't too close, wasn't too far. And a part of her felt that the other part of her that was satisfied with that was wrong.

But she didn't even let those two conflicting thoughts fight in her mind. It felt like allowing her consciousness to grapple over different ideas might destroy the peaceful life she had going now.

Mika, Seiji, Mikado, and Masaomi all seemed to be leading fulfilling lives. If they were missing anything, they knew what it was and displayed a hunger leading them in the proper direction.

So what am I missing?

The organized tests at the end of the year were coming, and barely anyone could be seen in the building after school, carrying out their class duties. As she walked the empty halls, Anri was suddenly taken with a feeling of incredible loss.

She was trapped in her own naive thoughts about her existence.

At the start of her adolescence, the usual time for this soul-searching, Mika's presence had meant she didn't need to worry about this.

I don't understand.

Perhaps she was actually completely fulfilled at this moment, and the anxiety was nothing but an illusion. But there was no way for her to be sure of this.

I don't even know what I should want...

"What's up, Sonohara? You haven't left yet?"

The voice caught her off guard as she wandered along the hall. Anri tensed.

"Ah..."

"Why are you so surprised?"

She turned around and saw an imposing-looking teacher in a suit. She remembered that he was the teacher for Class 1-C, but his name didn't pop into her head immediately. Yet that wasn't for the lack of an impression.

"What's wrong? Hmm? Not feeling well? Need me to escort you to the nurse's office?"

His greedy gaze locked onto Anri's body. That unpleasant stare was extremely familiar to her. Perhaps that was why her mind actively resisted remembering his name.

"N-no, I'll be fine."

"You sure?"

At first, she had thought it was just her usual persecution complex speaking.

"Need me to escort you home?"

"Ha...ha-ha..."

"I'm only kidding, of course...ha-ha."

She tried to brush his comment past with a vague smile and laugh, but Anri knew that the teacher wasn't joking around—he was 80 percent serious about that. At this point in time, Anri was perfectly aware of the meaning of the gazes he was giving her.

"He's been with several ~~students~~ ... ~~he's known to use~~ that fact to keep them close after graduation."

"He harasses them, then threatens them to keep them quiet."

"I heard he uses their grades to pressure them into sleeping with him."

The rumors were fairly typical, but they swirled around him, and his atypical looks (for a teacher) helped burn the image into her head.

She started hearing the stories soon after she joined the school, and they said that multiple girls had suffered nearly indecent behavior at his hands. For that reason, most of the female students kept an eye out for him around the school.

But Anri did not treat this teacher any different from the others. She'd never met any girls who had been his victims. To her, it seemed like a different kind of predictable behavior: the teacher with the distinct looks who served as a convenient scapegoat for school frustrations, a "sacrifice" who would bear the unfair brunt of the girls' unhappiness.

So Anri neither avoided his presence nor sought to get in his good graces. She simply treated him as any other teacher while in the process of carrying out her class representative duties.

But toward the end of the second semester, the girls around her—more than strangers, less than friends—began to butt into Anri's business with warnings.

"I think he's got his eye on you, Sonohara."

"Be careful. If you keep sucking up to him, he'll get the wrong idea."

Not that I was sucking up to him...

"I'm saying that the fact you're not ignoring him completely means he interprets that as sucking up! See how all of the girls ignore him? You're the only one who talks to him normally, so he sees that as his opening."

"The way he looks at you, it's just wrong."

But still, she thought that was just everyone else getting the wrong idea. One day, even the increasingly distant Mika said, *"Anri, you should be careful around him. The way he looks at you, it's not love, it's more like overflowing lust."*

At that point, Anri finally understood the gravity of her situation. Mika's words carried far more weight than those of a hundred acquaintances, and that trust was still strong, even now that they had drifted apart.

All I want is to live peacefully and not rock the boat, she thought and began to ignore the teacher along with the other girls...

"Say, Sonohara. Are you getting along with the other girls these days?"

"Well enough."

"Really? Are you sure? Nothing more like what happened that other time?"

"…Yes. I'm fine."

She shrugged off his probing questions with noncommittal answers. The events of a month earlier came back to her mind.

Since bad timing always had to happen in coincidence, Anri found herself the target of some girls she didn't get along with, right at the moment she began ignoring the teacher. She'd been around the girls since middle school, and they didn't like that she had been a barnacle stuck to Mika's side.

They'd tried messing with her just at the start of the school year, but a fortunate passing encounter with Mikado and an odd man wearing black had scared them into leaving her alone since then.

Coincidentally, she wound up meeting them after school while doing her duties, where they proceeded to bother her again— until this heavy-faced teacher happened by.

Thanks to his presence, she escaped trouble, but since then it became clear that he thought she owed him something.

What if he'd been watching her from the very start, just waiting for the right moment to step in and help her? Could he actually have planned this out with those girls so that the situation happened just as he wanted?

Anri thought that was getting paranoid, but she couldn't discount the possibility entirely. Ever since then, he used every opportunity he could to bring it up.

"Listen, Sonohara. If there's ever any trouble, I want you to come and talk to me. I can *help you* again, just like the other day."

You mean the "other day" well over a month ago? she thought bitterly but didn't say aloud.

"Ahh…"

"Look, I'm a teacher. I . . . . my students. But if that's going to happen, you need to trust me first."

Usually, it goes the other way around, she thought to herself again. Anri didn't want to make waves; her ideal outcome was to sit still and wait for him to get bored of her. She didn't want to set him off and make him even more persistent.

"I've seen a lot of students here at this school, but you make me worried for you, Sonohara... You know?"

The teacher, Takashi Nasujima, placed a hand forcefully on her shoulder, gazing into her face with a look of concern. But only he thought it was a "look of concern."

"You're always looking downcast. As a teacher, it worries me. I know how your homeroom teacher, Mr. Kitagoma, can be tough on you, and Satou in Class B prefers not to get involved with the students' affairs, not to mention Class D..."

—?

Anri finally realized what was bothering her.

As he spoke faster and faster, a clammy sensation spread along her back.

Nasujima was bringing up all of the other teachers in turn, putting them down to show her how trustworthy he was in comparison. It was like he was trying to corner her—there was a note of haste in his eyes now.

There was no sign of anyone else around. That was no doubt increasing his boldness.

Or else...

Just as Anri began to explore other possibilities for his actions—

"What's up, Mr. Nasujima? You harassin' her or something?"

The cheerful voice echoed down the hallway, and Nasujima went violently still.

"Ah..."

Anri couldn't stifle the gasp when the hand clutching her shoulder squeezed forcefully.

"Wow, even forcing the poor bespectacled class rep to speak, huh? Sounds like you're crossing into full-on sexual harassment. Sexual? Harassment? What do those English words mean anyway? Why don't we just call it *sexual khorosho* and bridge the Cold War gap by combining English with Russian?"

"K-Kida, that's not funny!"

Nasujima hastily let go of Anri and turned around to scold the speaker. Anri turned as well to see one of those few friends of hers, Masaomi Kida from Class 1-B, standing in the hallway.

She hadn't sensed anyone around. Yet there was Masaomi right there.

Only the top half of him, though. His legs were still in the classroom as he leaned out into the corridor.

It was the carefree pose of a grade-schooler, which helped defuse the antagonism slightly, but things definitely felt weirder now. How much Masaomi had seen or heard would affect their reactions greatly.

Since there was no one in the hallway, he must have heard them from inside the classroom. In any case, he clearly saw that Nasujima had his hand on Anri's shoulder.

But even then, Nasujima had an excuse. He could just say he was being friendly, making human contact. Nasujima planned to go with that, but before he could speak, Masaomi's eyes narrowed and he chuckled.

"Whoa, whoa, whoa, not so fast, Mr. Nasujima. It's one thing to talk smack about Kitchy in Class A, but bringing our Master Satochy into this? Not cool."

"...!"

Realizing that the boy had overheard everything, Nasujima was left without an excuse, his mouth flapping soundlessly. He seemed to recognize that the conversation ought to end there, so he put on a broad, deliberate smile and turned back to Anri.

"Kidding...I'm just kidding, Sonohara. Don't get the wrong idea and spread any weird stories about me. Okay?"

In contrast to his forced laughter, the teacher's eyes were filled with twice the desperation as before. Anri wasn't sure how to respond to this, so Masaomi filled the gap, still leaning out of the doorway.

"Ha-ha-ha, c'mon, Teach! Does Anri really look like the shallow, gossiping type?"

"............."

"Exactly. So don't worry—I'll spread all the nasty rumors for her!"

"Wha—?"

It sounded like a joke, but the threat was no laughing matter to Nasujima. He tried to gather up a weak excuse for dignity and scolded the boy.

"Kida! Quit wasting your time with this nonsense and—"

"Study? Heh, it's true that studying is very important. But of course! We're right in the middle of the age where you want to say, 'I'll never use physics or algebra in my future!' But depending on your future, you probably *will* have to use physics and math, so it's best to learn as much as possible while our futures are still in flux... Isn't that right, sir? But the thing is, I've decided I'll be a pimp in the future, so I pray to some statue of a goddess from some religion or another, and I won't need to know anything about physics or algebra. If anything, I should study Japanese and English, so I can be a world-class gigolo!"

Masaomi's machine-gun jabbering was so fast that Nasujima couldn't form any thoughts about the boy's intentions other than the simplest of reactions.

"But...your Japanese grades must be terrible."

"Heh-heh...sorry to say, I've actually got full marks. But even a teacher should know that your scores on test questions and essays don't have much bearing on your normal conversations, do they?"

"What? Is that how you speak to a teacher?" Nasujima demanded, trying to derail the conversation, but Masaomi held out his hand, undeterred. There was a white cell phone in it, and he spoke in a low, threatening voice.

"Now, I've got all of what just happened captured, audio and video both."

"Wha...?"

"So," Masaomi began, strolling into the hallway with eyes narrowed like a reptile's, "can you show me how to pressure people into doing what you want, for the sake of my future career as a pimp? Well, Teach?"

"Heh-heh-heh. So now I have some of the questions on the final exam. I didn't think it would be that easy," Masaomi gloated with his usual breezy smile as they walked out to the front gate of the school.

After their confrontation, Masaomi went into the classroom to work out some kind of deal and had apparently gained some of the questions on Mr. Nasujima's final exam.

Anri looked at him sidelong, unsure whether she should thank him for saving her from trouble or berate him for blackmailing a teacher.

If it had been anyone else, Anri wouldn't have said a thing. She didn't want to criticize someone and wind up on their bad side.

But Masaomi was one of her few friends, someone whose bad behavior she could call out for what it was. And in part, she didn't *want* him to behave badly.

Still, she held back on saying so. It was quite likely that he'd inserted himself into the conversation not for the material gain of the blackmail, but to help Anri out of her pinch. If that was true, she didn't know how to respond.

He seemed to sense her hesitation and put on a childish grin.

"I got to help you out of trouble, and I got myself the exam questions. Two birds with one stone."

"Huh?"

"You weren't sure whether to thank me or not, right? I agree with both sides, so…it's even. They cancel each other out. How about that?" he suggested nonsensically.

Anri had no words.

He took that as affirmation and continued talking. "So let's say no words need to be traded. How about we start by holding hands instead?"

"Can I be angry with you?"

"Nope. But I am at that age where I want a girl to hold my hand, kiss me, or even more than that."

Masaomi had professed his love for Anri since the moment they met. But he did the same thing with 60 percent of the other girls he met, and hardly anyone took him seriously. And anyone who took that seriously would chew him out just as seriously.

"You say that to everyone. Who do you really like?"

"Me? I like all the girls I've asked out, of course. With all my heart! And I'm head over heels for you, Anri. And you can believe me."

"…Um, I don't know what to say…"

Though she was exasperated by his lack of shame, Anri couldn't help but allow a relieved look to cross her face. Oblivious, Masaomi brought up the other boy who was part of her life now.

"On the other hand, Mikado really doesn't have any game, does he? He still hasn't asked you out yet, has he?"

"Huh?"

"I mean, you do know that he's crazy about you, right? You have to."

Masaomi never pulled his punches when it came to sensitive topics. Because he felt no shame about his own romantic travails, he freely stomped all over the business of others in that regard.

"Ryuugamine is...a very good friend..."

"Heh-heh. Well, my best friend's totally in love with you, so I'll take the backseat and observe for now. That's my way of life. I've got to be free to get along with all the pretty girls in the world, so I can't let you steal my heart all to yourself," Masaomi babbled on, completely ignoring what Anri said. She realized that nothing else was going to get through to him when he was like this, so she gave up and let him continue.

"Ooh...did I sound cool just now? Or was that lame? Are you in love? Did you fall for me? Fall colors? Fallen off the wagon? Fall-falla-falla-falloo?" he jabbered on, engulfing Anri in nonsense syllables. But Anri was ignoring him and paid it no mind.

"By the way, Kida..."

"What? I'll answer anything you want. *Heh-heh!* By my visual gauge, your measurements are thirty-three, twenty-two, thirty-two...the type of girl who really slims down in her clothes. Or were you going to ask for heroic tales of my middle school exploits? Well, there was the time I had hundreds of henchmen..."

Anri ignored Masaomi's fond reflection and raised the question she'd been mulling over.

"What did you mean when you said you wanted to be a pimp?"

"Whuh?"

"What kind of job is a pimp?"

It wasn't sarcastic, but a straightforward question from an innocent girl who was ignorant of the seedier side of adult society. Faced with a curious gaze from behind her glasses, Masaomi had no answer for a moment.

As he grasped for words, Anri looked up at the evening sky and murmured quietly, "You're so lucky though, Kida. Already got your future and life planned out."

"Er, well, actually—"

"I don't even know what I'm doing with my life *right now*, much less my future…"

She turned to look at him with a note of sadness in her eyes, then noticed a figure standing at the front gate of the school. The boy had noticed them as well, and he waved to Anri and Masaomi with a big smile on his face.

Masaomi raised a hand back and muttered in a voice only loud enough for Anri to hear, "Speak of the devil, it's the wimp without the guts to ask a girl out."

Anri felt her cheeks blush just a little bit, but she didn't respond.

There was nothing else she could do at that moment.

♂♀

There were already stars sparkling in the sky, an all too faint layer of glitter next to the brightness of the city lights.

Under that winter sky, Anri walked alone through Ikebukuro.

After they met up with Mikado, the three went shopping at the Parco department store on the way back from school, and then she left the two boys to continue her trip home.

Anri looked around idly as she walked the street to Sunshine City. It was essentially the same Ikebukuro as ever, people passing wrapped up in their own thoughts, approaching and leaving.

But it was only "essentially" the same, because there was something just slightly off.

Yellow.

It seemed that many of the young people walking about the town were wearing yellow bandannas.

What could that be about?

she headed straight for home.

Off the main road, she headed into a narrow alley in the direction of her cheap apartment. Despite being barely half a mile from the shopping district, this might as well have been a different world altogether. There were no passing crowds. The streetlights cast lonely colors on the empty alleys.

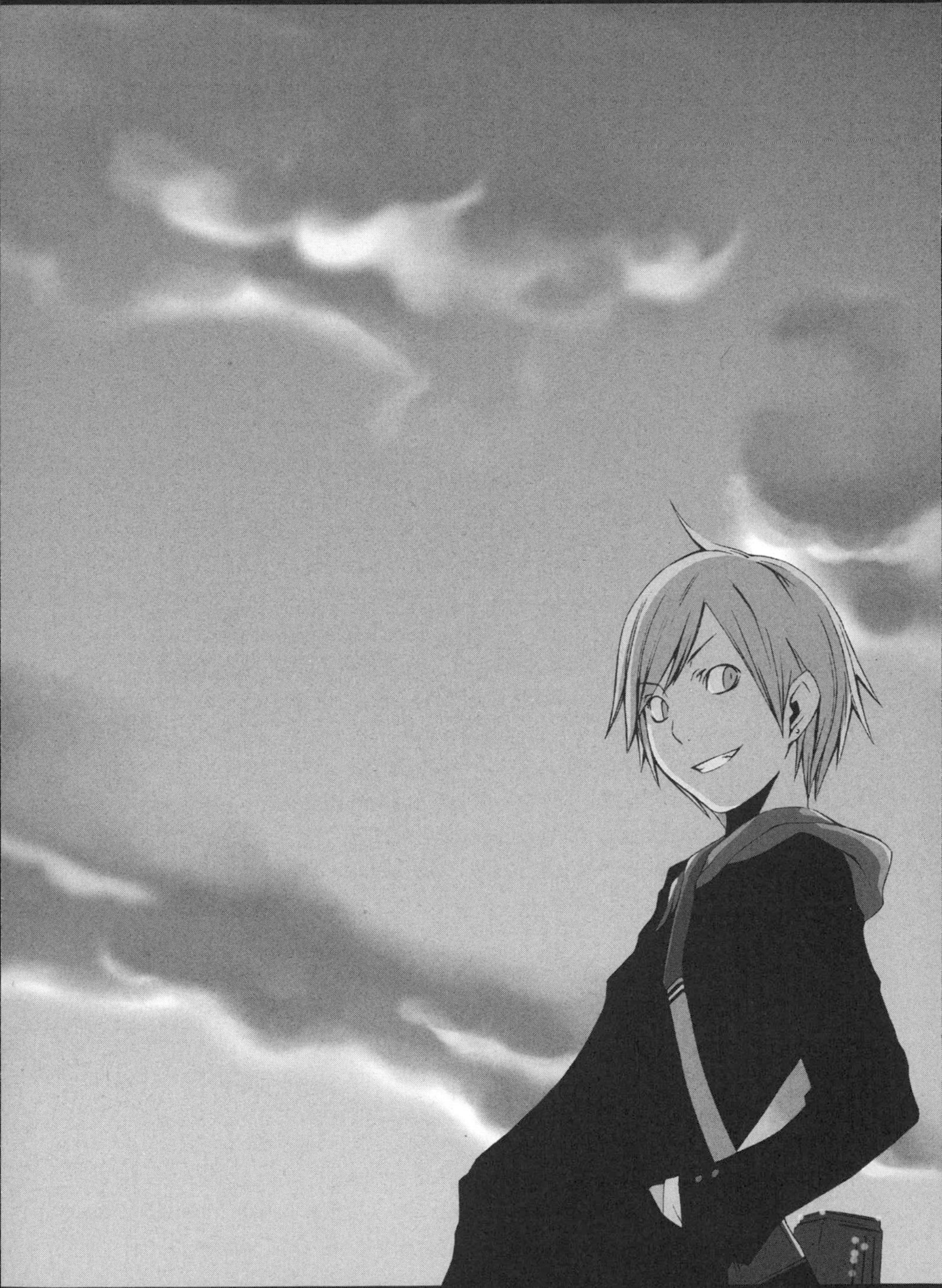

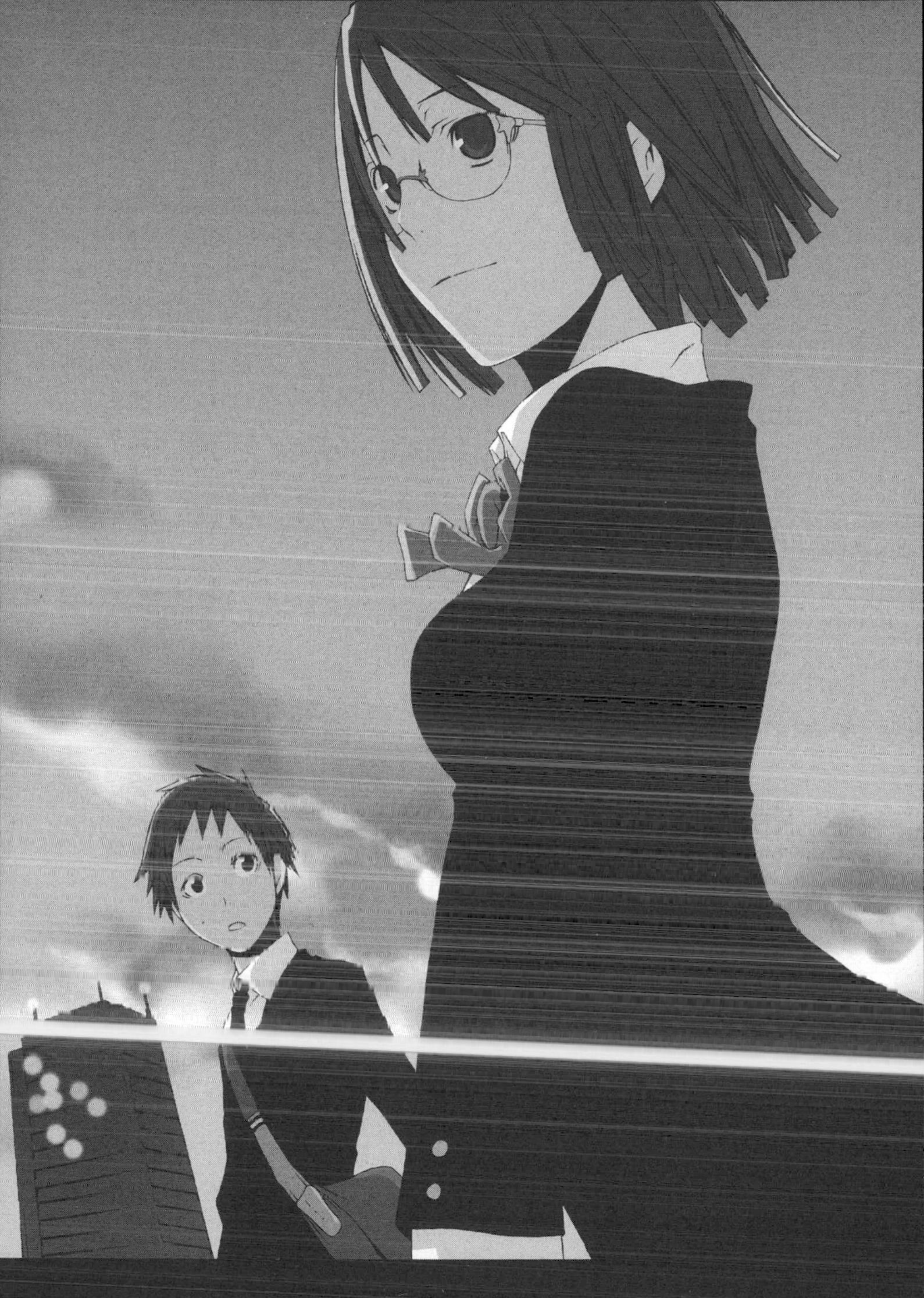

At first, the trip from the train station to this point was such a drastic shift that she felt like her heart was shriveling up, but after a year, the loneliness of the trip became familiar to her.

As she headed down the empty path, Anri thought about what Masaomi said as they split up.

"You know…you really should be careful, Anri."

"?"

"I'm talking about Nasujima. Most of the rumors are just that, but it's true that he's put the moves on his students."

"…!"

She held her breath in shock at this sudden pronouncement. Masaomi was not the type to lie or joke about this topic. She'd imagined the story might be true, but learning its veracity put a suffocating clamp over her mind.

"There was an older student, a second-year named Haruna Niekawa. She transferred out in the middle of the second semester, but it was apparently because her relationship with Nasujima was about to be exposed. Either the school didn't want the scandal and forced her to go, Nasujima threatened her himself, or Niekawa decided to transfer on her own accord."

"…"

If Niekawa transferred out in the middle of the second semester, then that was the same time Nasujima started putting the moves on Anri. That confluence of details gave Masaomi's statement weight in her mind.

"Just be careful. And if anything happens, Mikado and I will do something about it. Right, Mikado?"

Mikado hadn't been paying attention. He blinked in surprise as the conversation suddenly focused on him.

"Um…I don't know what you're talking about, but if it's within my ability, I'll be there."

"*Tsk-tsk-tsk.* Don't be an idiot, Mikado. In this situation, you're not a real man unless you say, 'Even if it's beyond my ability, I'll accomplish it with the power of love'!"

"That's a contradiction."

"Ha-ha-ha! Well, you don't know what you can or can't do until you observe it for yourself... I call this rule 'Schrödinger's Mikado.' What that means is that I'll lock you inside a box and pump poison gas into it, thus testing whether you can resist it or not with the power of love. But in fact, I'll just be doing that to get rid of you so Anri can be my girlfriend. Is that cool?"

Anri smiled and nodded, glad to see Masaomi back to his usual goofy self.

"Yes... Thanks, both of you."

Anri tried to get her emotions in order as she walked the lonely route home.

She liked Mikado Ryuugamine.

She understood this fact.

But she also liked Masaomi Kida, and she even still liked Mika Harima.

It's the same. My love for Ryuugamine is the same as for Kida and Mika.

Which told her that it probably wasn't a romantic feeling. It must be still in the realm of a love for a friend.

If Mikado told her that he loved her in a romantic way, she probably wouldn't be able to accept or reciprocate that. She could tell that somewhere in her heart, she would feel that she was cheating on him with Masaomi, and the guilt of that knowledge would be too much to bear.

It would be so much easier if she could just love either Mikado or Masaomi.

But she couldn't really tell the difference between friendship and romance, and even if she had the option of choosing to love them, that different from being able to *choose* one of them.

It felt like choosing one of them would what they had going now.

Even here, in this happy place, she was unable to find her proper standing.

As if to underscore this, she remembered the upperclassman Masaomi had mentioned just minutes earlier.

Haruna Niekawa.

While she knew the girl had ended up transferring, what was the truth behind that decision?

Was she able to find her place in the world?

Even if it ended up in disaster, had she felt true love for Nasujima at the time? Or had their entire relationship been the product of coercion?

No amount of imagination would provide an answer. Anri stopped at the side of the road and heaved a sigh.

The next instant, a light shock ran through her back, and Anri lost her balance, falling to the ground.

She turned around, baffled at what had happened to her, only to see a familiar face.

"*Haw-haw!* She fell on her face."

"It was just a little love tap, and she fell right on her face."

"You really are a sick little worm."

Three girls wearing the Raira Academy uniform stood in the glow of the streetlight. It was the trio that had it out for her, the ones Mikado called the "old-fashioned manga bullies."

"..."

Anri stared up at them, but there was no fear or anger in her eyes. She was simply watching them emotionlessly, waiting to see how they would act next.

The trio did not appreciate this. One of them put a foot on Anri's shoulder as she rose, knocking her over backward.

"First, you suck up to Mika, then Ryuugamine and Kida, and now you're cozying up to Nasujima?"

"When are you going to stop selling your body to get ahead, you dirty slut?"

"It's like you can't survive unless you're leeching off of someone else."

Despite the cascade of insults, it was all Anri could do just to stare back at the girls. She understood their meaning.

It was true that she'd been dependent on Mika Harima before this, and she had no means or intention of arguing that point. Perhaps it seemed like the same thing with Mikado and Masaomi, and even in that case she was still searching for where she belonged.

The case of Nasujima was where they were completely wrong, but nothing she could say to the girls in this situation would convince them. In fact, whether or not they were convinced by her answer was beside the point to them.

As they barraged her with jeers, Anri felt an illusion that she was actually something from another world, watching all of this happen to her from afar. Perhaps it was a kind of self-defense.

"What are you spacing out for?"

"You live around here, don't you? Show us the way."

"It's time for a little home inspection."

Anri viewed the world from her eyes as events happening within a picture frame. The girls' voices seemed to be coming from the painting within the frame.

Until middle school, Mika was in front of the frame, and she glared back at it to keep the painting from talking.

When the picture frame appeared this spring, Mikado came through the frame to stand on this side.

When Nasujima's attention started, it just meant that the picture of Nasujima slid in front of the picture of the bullies, nothing more.

But nobody was going to save her now.

It was better not to resist in this spot. Nothing good would come from fighting back with force.

Yes, nothing good at all...

Just when Anri gave in and decided to sit through the situation, the world within the picture frame went abnormal.

The girls in the painting were moving their mouths.

Behind them, a black shadow squirmed.

As Anri looked into the shadow's eyes, she absentmindedly held her breath.

Huh? What?

A human figure appeared beneath the streetlight. It was behind the girls, so the face and clothes were indistinct. But the general air it carried told her that this was a man. And most striking of all...

The man's eyes were red, so red.

*   *   *

"Why don't you say some..."

One of the girls stopped mid-sentence, and the black suddenly spread in Anri's picture frame.

The liquid that she'd assumed was black took on a reddish hue in the streetlight as it sprayed around the area.

The world was dyed red.

The sound of screaming.

The sound of screaming.

Blood on the gray asphalt still just looked black.

Only for the moment that it flew in the air did she remember the drops were blood.

The sound of screaming.

The sound of screaming.

The screaming eventually reached Anri's ears as an actual voice.

The figure disappeared at once, leaving one screaming and wailing girl and her two friends paralyzed with fright on the ground.

The scene was so unreal that it somehow brought Anri back to reality.

Why? Why is this happening?

Anri was surprised to find that she was quite calm as she sat on the asphalt, watching the scene impassively. Not because she was helpless to do anything, but because she didn't know what to do.

What—what do I do?

Should she cry?

Should she scream?

Should she rage?

Or should she laugh that they'd gotten what they deserved?

What was she to the girl who'd just been slashed?

An enemy or a friend?

A stranger or an acquaintance?

Even here in this situation, Anri couldn't tell exactly where she stood.

She got to her feet on the asphalt, the action devoid of meaning.

In the midst of blood and screams, the only thing Anri Sonohara could do was stand.

♂♀

Chat room

《Hey, did you hear? A student at Raira Academy finally got hit by the slasher!》
【What? Are you serious?】
[It's violent out there.]
《Deadly dead serious! A first-year girl!》
【Sorry, I've got to make a call. BRB.】
<Private Mode> 《Don't worry, it wasn't your girlfriend.》
<Private Mode> 【Oh...thanks. But I'm still worried about her, so...】
[Hmm. Do you know where it happened?]
《Well, it was a little ways away from Zoshigaya Station in south Ikebukuro.》
《I'm sure you can find it from all the cop cars still hanging around the area.》
[I see... Uh, sorry, I've got to drop out for a bit.]
《Eww! Setton, are you going to find the spot and gawk?】
[No, nothing like that.]
[See you later.]

—SETTON HAS LEFT THE CHAT—

《Argh, no fun!》
【Sorry, I've got to head out, too.】
《Oh? Were you able to reach her phone?》
【She's with the police now or something... Apparently she saw it happen...】
【So I'm going over there.】
《Really?!》

—TAROU TANAKA HAS LEFT THE CHAT—

《Then, I suppose we can't meet up today.》
《Oops, already gone.》
《Guess I'll pop out, too, then.》

*   *   *

—SAIKA HAS ENTERED THE CHAT—

|kut|
《Oh?》
|today|
|cutt|
《Ugh, it's that troll that was here yesterday! Don't you make trouble again! Harrumph!》
|cutted|
|cit|
|cut|
《How did you even find the address for this chat room anyway?》
|rong|
|wr|
|weak, wrong, cannot, rule|
|not, enough, love|
《You've been trolling other Ikebukuro-related chat boards, haven't you?》
|want, love, human|
|cut, but, wrong, not, enough|
《Take that!》
《There, I banned 'em. Tee-hee. ☆》
《Well, that's a relief. So long!》

—KANRA HAS LEFT THE CHAT—

—THE CHAT ROOM IS CURRENTLY EMPTY—
—THE CHAT ROOM IS CURRENTLY EMPTY—
—THE CHAT ROOM IS CURRENTLY EMPTY—
—THE CHAT ROOM IS CURRENTLY EMPTY—
—THE CHAT ROOM IS CURRENTLY EMPTY—
—THE CHAT ROOM IS CURRENTLY EMPTY—

—SAIKA HAS ENTERED THE CHAT—

|more|
|more, strong|

|strong, love, wish|
|wish, is, want|
|more, strong, love, want|
|want, love|
|want to, love|
|want to love, strong, human|
|human, strong, who, ask|
|ask, who, strong|
|ikebukuro|
|wish, me, mother, mother|
|mothermothermothermothermothermothermothermothermothermother
mothermothermothermothermothermothermothermothermothermother
mothermothermothermothermothermothermothermothermothermother
mothermothermothermothermothermothermothermothermothermother
mothermothermothermothermothermothermothermothermothermother
mothermothermothermothermothermothermothermothermothermother
mothermothermothermothermothermothermothermothermothermother
mothermothermothermothermothermothermothermothermothermother
mothermothermothermothermothermothermothermothermothermother
mothermothermothermothermothermothermothermothermothermother
mothermothermothermothermothermothermothermothermothermother
mothermothermothermothermothermothermothermothermothermother
mothermothermothermothermothermothermothermothermothermother
mothermothermothermothermothermothermothermothermothermother
mothermothermothermothermothermothermothermothermothermother
mothermothermothermothermothermothermothermothermothermother|

—SAIKA HAS LEFT THE CHAT—

—THE CHAT ROOM IS CURRENTLY EMPTY—
—THE CHAT ROOM IS CURRENTLY EMPTY—
—THE CHAT ROOM IS CURRENTLY EMPTY—

.
.
.
.
.

CHAPTER 3 IKEBUKURO'S MOST DANGEROUS

I just wanted to know.

Not as a writer for a third-rate gossip-slinging tabloid, but purely out of personal curiosity.

Curiosity.

Funny to think that a man in his thirties still possessed that artifact of boyhood. Even the panic over the Headless Rider incident back in the spring didn't inspire this kind of fervor in me. I figured that story was best left to the occult rags or the motorcycle gang specialists, not me. My paper handled that sort of stuff, too, of course, but we couldn't match the experts at their game.

I just wrote up whatever happened here in this place called Tokyo and made it sound interesting. That's all I wanted to write, and the readers seemed to be happy enough with it.

It was the key word the editor in chief gave me as the theme for this in-depth Ikebukuro scoop that inspired this youthful energy in me.

Strongest.

That's right...strongest.

Nothing more than that one word.

Taken literally, I had to assume he wanted to know who was the strongest in the city.

A stale, clichéd, but powerful word.

But as a matter of fact, maybe it was the fact that it was such a cliché that made it resonate with me. Just like *love* and *freedom*.

So who's the strongest in Ikebukuro?

When I asked the citizens of Ikebukuro this question, I got a lot of answers.

"Oh, I know! It's the guy on that black motorcycle!"

"Dunno…probably some local yakuza."

"No way, it's gotta be Simon."

"Hmm… An amateur wouldn't know about him, but there's a guy named Izaya Orihara who left for Shinjuku…"

"Nope, the strongest now is whoever started the Dollars."

"You seen the guys wearing these yellow bandannas, right?"

"Has to be an official. The cops, I mean. There's this officer at the station on the corner named Kuzuhara. He's unbelievable—whole family's police. Even his three sons all say they want to be cops when they grow up."

The most fascinating part was that essentially no one said they didn't know.

All of the local citizens and self-proclaimed "well-informed" folks I asked this question, whether their answer was vague or specific, all had their own predecided mental image of who the "strongest" in Ikebukuro was.

That's what made it so fascinating.

In that case, what would all of these people already identified by someone or other as the strongest in town think? I approached these folks as best I could manage in order to find out the answer.

♂♀

Testimony of Mr. Shiki, Awakusu-kai lieutenant, Medei-gumi Syndicate

"The strongest in a fight… Hmm. You know it's not really like that anymore, right? On the other hand, sure, you can't let anyone disrespect you, so when it comes time to kill, we'll still go at it until we win. If you come after us, we don't care if you're an amateur. We'll bring the numbers, the knives, the guns, we'll go after your family…anything to crush our opponent. But that hardly ever happens nowadays. Leaves a bad aftertaste for us, too.

"...So who's the strongest? Well...like I said, in our line of work, it's not really about who's the toughest in a fight anymore. Huh? Including amateurs, you said?

"...

"...Hmm.

"Don't put what I'm about to say in your article.

"I'm just saying, officially, we don't mess with civilians. But like I just told you, all bets are off if they're attacking *us*. But...I will say, there's an amateur out there I wouldn't want to mess with, personally.

"Yeah, if we get a bunch of men and weapons together, we'd win. But in a brawl, like one-on-one, I don't know if I could beat this guy even if I had a machine gun.

"Huh? Simon? Oh, the sushi guy. He's easy to get along with, so I can't imagine fighting with him. I bet he would be real tough though. They say he can pick up a motorcycle like he's lifting barbells. But I don't see myself losing to him.

"Your guess isn't far off though. It's a guy who associates with Simon a lot...

"Shizuo Heiwajima.

"We tell the new kids, don't mess with him.

"I mean, if you've seen Shizuo fight at all, you'd understand... He just exudes cool. It's not elegant in the least. He's a real wild man... like Godzilla... When you watch him fight, he looks cool the way that Godzilla looks cool to the kid watching it. I guess that sums it up. At any rate, he's one crazy bastard.

"The thing about these cool guys is, you can't really pick a fight with 'em. It's a lot more fun to stand aside and watch 'em work from a distance. That way, they're not in your business, either.

"Gotta admit, I've got some admiration for him. Wish I could tear things up the way he does...

"But I need you to keep that part close to your chest.

"...

"So, Mr. Reporter, I hear your daughter's in high school. Raira Academy, was it?

"When you called about setting up this interview, we did some background checks on you.

"Now, now, no need to stare holes through me. We have our own source of information.

"Don't worry, we're not low enough that we'd threaten an amateur.

"But...only if you don't pick a fight with us first.

"So please keep that information out of your article, pal."

♂♀

Ultimately, most of what I had on that tape was unusable.

He said that I could go with what was in the first half...but in any case, the stuff about Shizuo Heiwajima was off the table for me. I didn't hear anything concrete about the guy, for one thing.

But if anyone else brought up his name, then I'd be onto something.

At this point, I decided to get in touch with the black man named Simon who people in town mentioned.

"Hey, you. Sushi, good for you."

"Uh, er, actually, I was hoping to speak with you personally..."

"One for dinner, boss."

I tried to decline his offer, but I eventually gave in to his force and found myself seated at the sushi counter.

The interior was made out to look like that of the Russian Winter Palace, with a traditional sushi counter slapped right in the middle. The seats there were fine, but the booth seating was tatami under marble walls, an extreme imbalance of design if I'd ever seen it. It was impossible to guess at the price of the sushi based on this, but there was a hanging curtain on the ceiling that promised "Hassle-Free Pricing! All Items Market Value!"

Despite the simplicity of that promise, it left me feeling more uncertain than ever.

It was already a low-expense project, and I had a feeling I'd need to pay for this one out of pocket.

True to expectations, the Russian who ran Russia Sushi recommended all of the most expensive items. I tried to maintain a pleasant face to keep him in a talking mood. I soon found out that the manager and Simon knew each other from the same city in Russia.

I didn't know why a black man like Simon would have been in Russia, but it had nothing to do with my research, so I left that detail for another time.

After sampling a few sushi (it wasn't bad at all), Simon had come back inside from his duties advertising to pedestrians outside, and I asked him about the man named Shizuo Heiwajima.

"Oh, Shizuo. My best pal."

So they did know each other. After what the yakuza had said, I half assumed he would be a legendary figure, a tall tale I'd been fed, but this looked to be solid info.

I put aside the topic of Heiwajima and asked Simon about fighting in town, but I didn't get far.

"Oh, fighting, very bad. Get very hungry, need food coupons. You eat sushi, good for you," Simon told me and started ordering me fresh urchin and salmon roe sushi.

That was the last straw. Before long I'd have no choice but to run before the bill arrived.

As I checked the contents of my wallet, the Russian chef took note of what I was after and spoke to me in fluent Japanese.

"Sir...Simon's a pacifist, so you won't get anything worthwhile about fighting out of him."

"N-no, I'm just asking who's the strongest fighter around here..."

"You talking about Master Heiwajima? You just brought him up yourself."

"Uh—"

It all snapped into place. The chef gave me an extra piece of info on the house.

"You won't get anything out of Simon about Heiwajima. He'll just tell you he's a good guy. If you truly wanna know about the real Heiwajima..."

♂♀

"Who told you about me?" the man demanded with expressionless eyes, rolling a shogi piece in his fingers. "If they even knew my address, it must be a pretty close client of mine..."

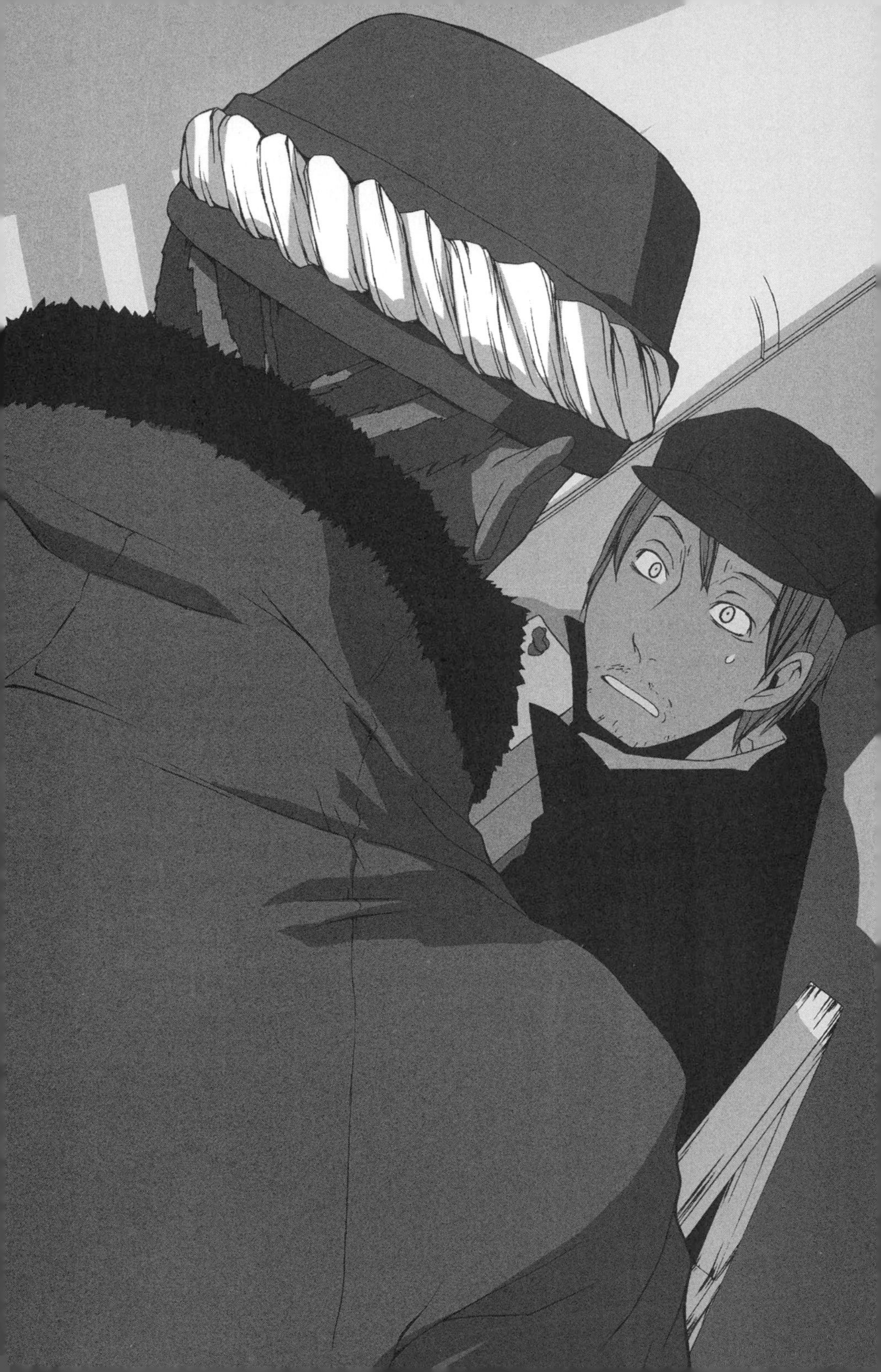

He was much younger than I expected. Very young to have a suite in a high-class apartment building in Shinjuku and unnaturally young to be such a well-connected information dealer. He didn't look much older than twenty.

His name was Izaya Orihara. I heard about him from the chef at the sushi place, but his name also turned up several times during my first round of surveys on the street from the more knowledgeable types.

"My source is confidential," I said, covering for the sushi chef. The slender young man put on an inscrutable smile, leaning back against the sofa.

There was a shogi board on the table between the two of us. Interestingly enough, there were three kings on the board.

"Claiming confidentiality to an information dealer... Fine, that's your prerogative."

I began to describe the course my research had taken me, leaving out the sushi place. But to my surprise, he had apparently been reading my articles.

"You write 'Tokyo Disaster,' don't you? The column about odd events and the various groups active around Tokyo... If I recall correctly, the next issue will be having a big Ikebukuro special."

"Oh, you read us? That should make this easy," I said, somewhat relieved that things would proceed smoothly.

I was wrong.

"Is your high schooler well?"

"Wha...?"

"Wasn't Mr. Shiki from the Awakusu-kai considerate?"

"..."

Then I understood everything.

The *source of information* the yakuza lieutenant had mentioned was none other than Izaya Orihara. And like a poor ignorant sap, I'd come right to the guy who sold them their information.

Anger, frustration, and a hint of fear.

The three emotions interlocked within me. I wasn't sure what kind of expression to wear anymore. But the information agent across from me continued talking, completely unconcerned with my struggle.

"But...enough about that. The strongest in Ikebukuro, huh? Well, there are plenty of tough people around this neighborhood...but if I had to narrow it down to one... In a fistfight, it's Simon. But if anything goes...that's probably going to be Shizu."

"Shizu...?"

"Shizuo Heiwajima. I don't know what kind of job he has now. I don't even want to know."

There was that name again.

I never brought him up, but even Izaya Orihara was giving me the name Shizuo Heiwajima. And yet again, I still hadn't the least idea what kind of person he was.

"Um...so who is this Shizuo guy?"

"I don't even want to talk about him. I know him, and that's enough. No one else should."

"You can't toss me a bone?"

"I try to find out more about him because he gives me so much trouble, but even that's unpleasant enough..."

It didn't seem like I was going to get anywhere with him, but after pushing a little bit more, Orihara put on a creepy smile.

"All right. I'm a busy guy, so I can tell you about someone who knows him well. If you want more, this is your source."

Good grief. Once again, I might as well have learned nothing. The trip to Shinjuku, all for nothing. Perhaps I should have bugged him a bit longer, but he knew my address and about my daughter. No use making enemies with someone like that.

At this point, my only hope was placed in this acquaintance of the young man's.

...I just had to hope it wasn't going to end up being Simon again.

♂♀

"Hello, I'm Celty the courier."

...

No idea how to respond to this one.

The being in front of me was showing off a PDA with a message typed out on the screen.

When I showed up at the park at our meeting time, I was met by a very strange person wearing an all-black riding suit and an oddly shaped helmet.

The courier showed up on a motorcycle without a headlight, with everything from engine to driveshaft to tire rims in pitch-black. There was no way to see inside the helmet, and to be honest, I couldn't tell if it was a man or a woman. The moment I saw it, I thought it was a man, but the slender form told me that it might be a woman.

But this couldn't be right...

I never counted on meeting the Black Rider urban legend in a place like this.

I was more curious about what I was seeing here than in the topic of Ikebukuro's strongest. No, I didn't believe in occult rumors of ghosts or spirits. And it was still the middle of the day. But from the moment I saw him (her?) I could tell that he was something different.

I'd assumed that whoever was riding the black bike had to be doing a street performance or making some kind of antisocial statement. But the person I was seeing here was far too natural and comfortable in this setting, as if to say that *he* was the one who truly belonged here in this world. And the name Celty—that wasn't Japanese, was it? I had more questions than answers now, but I suppose that was what made it a "real urban legend."

I knew more journalists and writers than I could count who would leap at the chance to talk with the mysterious rider. Was it right for me to make contact regarding something completely unrelated?

It only took moments for me to get over my doubt. Nothing good happened in this business if one got too curious.

"Umm...it's nice to meet you. Mr. Orihara told me that you knew Shizuo," I said for starters.

Celty hammered away at the PDA keyboard with frightful speed. For an instant, it looked like a shadowy digit was extending from those fingers and tapping along on the keys next to them—but that had to be my imagination. *Don't get curious. Focus on today's job, me.*

"Shizuo Heiwajima, right? Yes, he's a very close friend. To me, at least."

"I see."

"He can be scary when he's mad though."

There we go. Now we're talking—er, typing.

I tried to keep my excitement to a minimum, calmly getting to the point of my questioning. "Interesting... Well, as a matter of fact, I'm taking statements for an article where I'll be figuring out who the number-one fighter in the neighborhood is."

"Ahh, your magazine likes topics like that, doesn't it? You did that motorcycle gang ranking, and the ones who got left off the list tossed Molotov cocktails at the company office, didn't they?"

"Well, that wasn't my article… But from what I've heard so far, some people claim *you* might be the strongest in town…"

For a moment, Celty went quiet, shoulders trembling. Based on the way the helmet was shaking, I judged this to be laughter.

"Me? No way! They're just afraid of the way I look."

After another moment, Celty typed away at the PDA with great confidence.

"Shizuo's much stronger than me. I doubt there's another person in this town who can beat him in a pure fight."

"He's that tough?"

"Oh yeah, real tough. He's so dangerous, it's almost moving. It's not just a brawling or martial arts thing—it's like he lives in a different world from the rest of us. If you told me he was a werewolf or a lizard-man, I'd believe you. Oh, but I hope he's not an alien. Those grays are traumatic to me."

Celty's typing was even faster than a spoken conversation. The text almost struck me as…excited? As though Celty was bragging about this friend, Shizuo Heiwajima.

"It's not that he does some MMA thing or anything. It's like, you know how even the toughest combatant will go down if they get shot? How to explain this…?"

After a moment's hesitation, Celty increased the font size on the PDA.

"That's it—his strength is like the power of a gun. Even comparing him to others makes no sense."

After discussing a few other topics, I finally learned where Heiwajima worked. Once I was certain that my article research was done, my discipline finally cracked.

I got curious.

"Um…"

"What is it?"

"I don't need this for a story, it's more of a personal curiosity thing, but…do you mind if I ask what you are? Um…might I see under your helmet?"

It wasn't so I could expose the rider's identity or report it to the authorities. It was just simple curiosity, a desire to know the gender and age of the person I was talking with. I certainly didn't think there would be no head underneath, like the silly paranormal shows suggested.

"Er, sorry, didn't mean any offense. I'm just curious," I stammered.

Celty began typing on the PDA without any hesitation. *"Sure thing. If I take this helmet off, you'll see exactly what I am. Plus, you still won't be able to write an article about my true identity… You won't even be able to tell anyone about it."*

"Huh?"

I was about to ask what that meant when the rider put a hand to the helmet…

———

I was sitting on the ground, completely paralyzed, as the shadow walked away.

Celty must be an illusionist, I thought. I figured that wasn't actually true, but I was desperate to convince myself.

This was what happened when you let your personal interest get the best of you.

It's why you can't let your curiosity take control in this line of work…

♂♀

Satisfied that I'd bought my ~~~~ lie, I continued with my interviews.

Next was the color gang wearing yellow bandannas. They took the name Yellow Scarves and had been consolidating power within the city since last year. They appeared just at the moment that it seemed the color gang fad was going out of style, and now they wielded a quiet presence throughout Tokyo. They weren't suffering any crackdowns, as they hadn't shown any propensity for criminal activity or turf warfare, but the simple fact that they were a color gang was enough to intimidate plenty of folks.

Even the people inclined to scoff at the idea of color gangs still existing would be overwhelmed by the sight of several dozen clad in the same colors walking the streets—not that anyone who talked trash was dumb enough to pick an actual fight with them.

According to Mr. Shiki from the Awakusu-kai, the Yellow Scarves didn't seem to have a working relationship with any of the criminal syndicates. They weren't interfering with the business or causing trouble with the motorcycle gangs under the syndicate's umbrella, so the Awakusu-kai had little reason to care about the group.

I made contact with one of them and succeeded in getting introduced to one of the group's officers. What I heard from him, put simply, was the same thing I'd been getting all along.

"We're not beefing with anyone. We just exist... A big group of friends getting along. Oh, but the Shogun gave us the name Yellow Scarves—we gotta call the boss 'Shogun,' that's the rule. All the guys at the top love manga about the *Romance of the Three Kingdoms*, see... Oh, sorry, got distracted. Anyway, I'm pretty sure we're more than a match for the Dollars when it comes to numbers, but the Yellow Scarves' Shogun always says there are two guys never to mess with. One of them is a guy you should never let talk you into anything, and that's Izaya Orihara..."

I was a bit surprised to hear Orihara's name, but I'd been doing this long enough to predict the other name he mentioned.

"The other one is this guy named Shizuo Heiwajima, who wears a bartender's outfit and sunglasses. We're not supposed to go near him... I've seen that guy in a fight once, and he was a freakin' monster."

Finally, I got a statement from someone in the mysterious Dollars organization.

"We're not trying to pass ourselves off as big shots in Ikebukuro... And even if we wanted to, we don't have a team color, so there's no way to rep ourselves."

The Dollars seemed to have zero interest in or connection to the "strongest" qualifier. Once I'd figured this out, I was ready to wrap it up early, except he dropped a bombshell right at the very end.

"Oh, but there is one thing we can brag about! The Dollars have this guy named Shizuo who's a real monster! And Simon, and Izaya, and even the Black Rider are in the Dollars! I'm serious! Isn't that nuts?!"

No way.

I was going to laugh it off, but—Simon, Izaya, Black Rider, Shizuo. I already knew for a fact that these four were connected personally, so I couldn't just shrug it away, but I didn't feel like presenting it as fact, either. I ended the interview early.

Through the magazine's connections, I was also able to speak with someone connected to the police.

It wasn't an actual officer, which made me wonder how exactly they were connected. When I asked about this, the only answer I received was that the nature of the connection was confidential. Probably just someone involved with stocking equipment for them, I guessed.

"The kids in Ikebukuro these days are all up to no good, between the Dollars and the Yellow Scarves... It's all trouble, if you ask me. On top of that, you've got this serial slasher and the Black Rider. Well, at least it's still better than when Izaya was in Ikebukuro... Sorry, just talking to myself. At any rate, you gotta keep an eye out for the yakuza and foreign mafia while handling the weirdos and the kids. It's hard to be an active officer on the force these days."

I wanted to get back to the topic of my article, not that I wasn't interested in what this so-called police-related figure had to say.

"What's that? The biggest problem child out there? Excluding the _____? Hmm...well, in terms of crime, that's Izaya Orihara, not even close. But the biggest p___ in the ass would have to be Shizuo Heiwajima, I'd say."

The man started describing Orihara, but when informed that I'd already met him, he launched straight into Shizuo's exploits instead.

"Once there was a time when the cops were closing in on Izaya Orihara...and they got Shizuo's name as an accomplice. Shameful as it is to say, the guy in charge of that case got fooled on that one. It was a frame job. Anyway, they were bringing him in as a minor, and he ended up proving the charges were false, but he got locked up anyway for obstruction of justice and property damage in the process."

"Property damage?"

"I actually thought it sounded far-fetched, but I'll tell ya... As he kept resisting arrest, what do you suppose he destroyed?"

"I don't know... A bicycle? Windshield on a patrol car?"

"A vending machine."

???

That one baffled me. Didn't your average middle school delinquent trash a vending machine with a baseball bat? All these stories built the guy up to be a monster, but it sounded like your run-of-the-mill street vandalism.

But what he said next had me at a complete loss for words.

"He threw it."

"Huh?"

"He *threw the vending machine*—at a cop car!"

♂♀

Interesting.

Very, very interesting.

When I asked people around town who the strongest person in Ikebukuro was, I got a whole variety of answers. But when I asked the same question to the various "strong" people mentioned, they all spoke of the same man.

Shizuo Heiwajima.

If everything they said was true, I'd never heard of a guy who lived up to his name less. There was no hint of the "peace" and "tranquillity" from the kanji characters in his name.

But how was it possible that the random people I met who claimed to be in the know didn't actually hear about these Shizuo rumors? I began to wonder about that and turned back to contact some of the first people I asked.

Every single one of these well-connected people, when asked about Shizuo, had the same answer.

"I didn't want to get involved with him."
Simple as that.

And now I was attempting to meet with that very monster.

I could tell that my inner boy was knock-kneed with excitement at seeing this guy in the flesh. But the adult me was trembling with nothing but fear.

It was a strange sensation that filled me as I stood before the small building. It was the kind of place that had a vibrant, constant flow of tenants in and out. There was no sign outside.

"You the dude who wants to see Shizuo?"

A man came out of the building. His tanned skin and dreadlocked hair suited him well, and his face made him look like a host in a nightclub. He wore typical street fashion clothes, which made it hard to gauge what he did for a living.

"He's upstairs, so he'll come down if you want...but don't you dare piss him off."

"Okay..."

Despite his obviously Japanese heritage, the man introduced himself as Tom Tanaka. I found out that he was Shizuo's supervisor at his current job, where they went around collecting fees from members of a dating/hookup website.

I didn't bother asking if the site was legal or not. Usually my interest would run straight to that topic, but Shizuo Heiwajima was a far more pressing matter at this point.

Now I wasn't just exuding curiosity, I was gushing it.

"Seriously, don't piss him off. It's a huge pain in the ass," Tom repeated.

I'd heard about Heiwajima's dangerous nature from many different people at this point. But the more times the same thing got repeated, the more I felt like I was being treated like an idiot.

"Here's my advice: Don't talk. Ask what you want to ask, then shut up and look like an idiot while Shizuo talks. Wrap it up with a simple 'thank you very much,' and even Shizuo shouldn't be too angry with you."

What was that supposed to mean? If I didn't talk, I couldn't ask what I needed to ask. It was the role of an interviewer to take the subject's statements and expose their contradictions. Also, I wasn't stupid enough to tick off a person I'd never spoken with before. When Izaya Orihara got angry, that was because of his antagonism toward Shizuo Heiwajima. It wasn't my fault.

But I chose to be patient and not raise any of these issues to Tom. Speaking of which, he looked like a pretty decent fighter himself. I definitely didn't want to cause any trouble here…

Tom disappeared back into the building as I mulled it over.

It was showtime.

The man I was about to meet was the toughest fighter in Ikebukuro. That was the only title he had to his name. There was no public record for this, and he wasn't making any money off of it.

In modern Japan, there was nothing to gain from a full-grown man boasting about his fighting skills. If he really felt confident in his ability, he could go into professional fighting—if his skills matched his boasts, he could find money and fame that way. But Shizuo Heiwajima was just a collector for a pay website. In society's view, it was hardly a position that anyone cared about or lauded.

But the curious boy inside of me had been up late with excitement for three straight nights. I could tell that my instincts had my heart hammering away in my chest.

The real question: Was it excitement or fear?

"Um."

It would all be clear once I met him.

"Hi…I'm Heiwajima."

Hmm?

I was so busy trying to calm my own excitement that I completely failed to realize that someone was already standing in front of me.

The young man wore luxury-brand sunglasses on his slender, gentle-looking face. And as I stood there dumbfounded, he had introduced himself as Heiwajima—

Hmm?

Heiwajima?

"Shizuo…Heiwajima?" I asked, confused. He nodded flatly.

Uh…

For an instant, I was unable to believe the situation.

*   *   *

That's him?

That's the…strongest man in Ikebukuro? The most fearful man in town?

Shameful as it is to admit, I had built up my own mental image of the monster named Shizuo Heiwajima. His body was covered in steel muscles as thick and huge as tires, with the icy expression of a movie assassin, not to mention scars. On top of that, a full-body tattoo of a dragon…

About the only part of my image that matched was the height. The sunglasses that hid his gentle eyes didn't match the man's atmosphere at all. They looked like a sad attempt to add cool character to his look.

I was prepared for something a bit different than I imagined, but this was such a huge shift that it suddenly cast all of the stories I'd heard into doubt.

This was not the kind of man that yakuza would avoid, and he certainly couldn't pick up and throw a vending machine.

I knew that appearances could be deceiving, but there had to be a limit to that cliché.

Had I been set up? Did that yakuza Shiki or someone else get the sushi place and the information agent and the police connection all to match their stories and fool me…?

No. The color gangsters I had chosen at random. They couldn't possibly have coordinated to arrange that somehow.

So was this a different man with the exact same name?

No, this office was the very place the Black Rider told me.

So what was different, then?

What was it…? Where did I go wrong?

Is this guy just hiding his true nature at the moment?

…No, that wasn't it, I'd seen a lot of people in my life, and I could tell right away when someone was lying or hiding his true ability from me. But the man here seemed to be gentle and well-behaved to his core. He wasn't lying or on guard around me in the least.

What did it mean?

What was this all about?

Was it some kind of martial arts? Did he have really good special attacks?

What if that slender build disguised the fact that he was actually an aikido master... *Nahh.*

A person might be able to throw another using the target's own strength, but that wouldn't be enough to throw a vending machine.

This was a troubling development. If I wrote up an article proclaiming this fellow as the strongest man in Ikebukuro and anyone saw him in real life, I would look like a flat-out liar.

At this point, there was only one choice left to me: I had to assume that he possessed some hidden power that he was sealing away from me at the moment. It seemed too silly to be true, but I couldn't possibly get into the mind-set of the interview unless I told myself that.

Hey, maybe I should find some way to work that hidden power out of him.

Half-desperate now, I held my external agitation in check to speak to the man. At first I'd been planning to move over to a café for the interview, but I no longer had the patience or consideration.

"Well...there are two or three things I'd like to ask you, Shizuo..."

"'Kay," he grunted.

Was he really that tough at fighting? I felt I could probably take him myself. I'd put myself in danger a number of times on assignment. I'd investigated shady bars, been threatened by street thugs, and even been surrounded by foreign mobsters.

I'd made my way around some dangerous fights, even if it hadn't been through actual fighting prowess. I had courage to spare.

"I've heard lots of stories about you, Shizuo... Are you often involved in fights and confrontations?"

"Um...no?"

He had a look on his face that said, *Why would you even ask that?*

"Really?"

"Actually, I detest violence."

Oh, brother, are you kidding me? The guy's a dud.

My inner boy went right to sleep. The human instincts within me no longer felt any kind of fear or expectation toward the man.

I was ready to wrap this interview up, so I finished as quickly as I could.

"What do you think of the town these days?"

"Not much… It's a nice place."

"I hear you know the famous Headless Rider."

"Celty? Yeah, Celty's great."

Fine…so he *was* the man the Black Rider mentioned after all. But the problem was that the rider had stated that this was the strongest man in Ikebukuro…

Just as I was about to ask about that, the man spun around on his heel and started walking back into the building.

"H-huh? Where are you…?"

"…That's it, right?"

"Huh?"

"You said you had 'two or three questions,' didn't you? Well, I answered three, and I have nothing more to say."

…*Are you kidding me? What is he talking about?*

Did he take that literally? Must be a by-the-book type of guy.

At any rate, I needed more than this.

I decided my best chance at drawing out the conversation was to challenge him a little.

"Okay, just one more. They say you fought with the police and threw a vending machine…but that's not true, is it?"

"…"

"Izaya just tricked you into—"

Flew.

Flew?

…*What flew?*

At first, I couldn't tell what flew.

Shizuo Heiwajima turned around and flew with terrific force.

Where? Above? In front?

No. Behind.

Everything in my field of vision was happening in slow motion.

Oh, wait. It wasn't just Shizuo Heiwajima that went flying.

So was the building he came out of, and the asphalt base, and all the air surrounding it—

I get it.

I understood at once—I just didn't want to admit it.

I was the one flying.

He sent not just my body, but my wits flying as well.

A shock ran through my back, telling me that I'd fallen back onto the ground.

"...! Uh—! Aghk...gah..."

I gurgled weakly as both intense pain and numbness fought over my body. My brain scrambled to process what had happened.

The moment Shizuo Heiwajima turned back, I felt a tremendous impact on my throat, and the next instant I was in the air.

It was like being on a launcher-style roller coaster that shot me backward. The only thing I felt in that brief instant was...what I assumed was Shizuo Heiwajima's arm muscle.

But—was that truly muscle?

It was more like the tire of a dump truck, shrunk down to a small enough size that it could catch me around the neck. A thick, strong bundle of fibers, still smooth and supple. Upon calm recollection, that seemed like an apt description. But the moment that it hit me, I was unprepared to analyze the sensation—the only thing that filled me was instantaneous terror.

My head's going to be torn off.

That was actually what I felt. At that very moment, I felt sure my head would tear off—the same way you might feel that having the Grim Reaper's scythe pressed to your neck means your head would be cut off. It was due to the powerful shock and the centrifugal force of being pushed backward.

A lariat.

He hit me with one of the most basic pro wrestling moves in the book.

Some people watching it on TV might think that the lariat does less damage than a good punch or a German suplex. Some might even claim that anyone suffering heavy damage from a lariat had to be throwing the match.

But that would be a mistake. I once accompanied a writer from the sports page on his beat and got to try out being hit by a wrestling move. I chose the lariat, hoping for the least painful move possible.

The wrestler couldn't have been using even half of his full strength. But I fell hard onto the ring and passed out. It was less the damage of the fall than the powerful impact of that arm.

That prior experience was possibly the only reason I could even identify that it was a lariat I'd just suffered.

But there was one thing I couldn't quite buy yet. How did the skinny man I was seeing have the strength to lariat me straight up into the air? A man who clearly didn't have half the body mass of a pro wrestler!

I got my nearly convulsing lungs under control and took focus on the approaching shadow.

Damn, eyes foggy. My vision was unclear.

The shadow of Shizuo Heiwajima stood over me, speaking softly.

"The reason I was turning around to leave…"

His voice was indeed quiet—and chilling. Some people had voices of ice. The man named Izaya that I met a day before had one of those. But the chilling edge to Shizuo Heiwajima's voice was something else entirely.

If Izaya had the kind of chill that froze his listener, this one was enough to cause frostbite. No, frostbite was too gentle to describe it. It was like liquid nitrogen boiling, a bubbling something enveloped in pure chill.

"…was because you were asking stupid questions, and I was about to snap."

The voice was the same one that belonged to the man just moments ago. But the temperature of the voice was completely different. Before now, they'd been just words—there was no inflection to them in any way…

"See, I was leaving to make sure that I didn't end up killing you."

Now there was strength in his words.

It wasn't like he was speaking words of power. There was no real meaning to what he said. But was it possible to strike fear in another person just with a tone of voice? Even that fact alone terrified me.

Finally, my vision was recovering from the shock of the blow.

My eyes found the man standing in front of me. It was undoubtedly the same man I had been standing with just moments before.

It was the same man…

…but…strange…why did his sunglasses seem to suit him now?

Those odd, out-of-place shades were now a perfectly natural feature of his face.

The shape and bridge of his nose hadn't changed; neither had his hair. He wasn't wearing a particularly different expression. The only thing that seemed to have changed from moments ago was the slight smile playing on his lips. But that smile itself had no effect on the look of the glasses.

It was the air.

The air around him seemed to have changed. There was no other wa-wa-wa-wa-wa-wa-wa-wa-wa-way-wa-wa-way-wa-wa-wa-wa-way-way-way-way-way-way-wa-wa-wa-wa-wa-wa-wa-way-way-way-way-wa-wa-way-way-wa-way-wa-way-way-way-way-way-way-way-way—

"Who said you could go to sleep?"

He grabbed my collar, and for an instant I couldn't breathe. When he lifted me off of the ground, all I could feel was his incredible, monstrous strength.

I was scared.

At this point, I was jealous of scared the disappointed scared me from scared a minute ago. If the scared man scared here scared was scared truly scared that scared weak, scared scared scared how lucky scared scared I scared scared scared would scared scared scared be scared scaredscaredscaredscaredscaredhelpscaredscaredhelpscared scaredhelpscaredhelphelphelphelphelpohshitshitshithelpshitshithelp scaredI'msorryI'msorryI'msorryI'msorryI'msorry—

Every part of my body screamed in terror.

"Were you actually trying to piss me off? Huh? I'm not an idiot, you know. I can tell that much. But just because I understand it doesn't mean I won't get pissed off..."

There was no time for my boyish curiosity to open his eyes or my instincts to scream.

"So I give in to the provocation and get mad, I lose? Fine, I lose then. That's all right. Because I don't stand to suffer for losing this one, do I? Besides, you won, and your reward is that I kill you..."

That was the moment.

"Aaaaaa*aaaaaaaaaaaaaaaaa*!"

The scream sounded.

Not from me.

I was unable to speak, paralyzed with fear.

The howl that echoed off the alleyway was from Shizuo Heiwajima himself.

The liquid nitrogen suddenly transformed into boiling oil, spitting all of the rage stored inside his body outward.

"Raaaah! *I told you, I hate violence!* Didn't I?! *And now you forced me to get violent!* Who do you think you are? God? You think you're God?! Huh?!"

That's not fair, I started to think, before I was flying again.

It was not a proper judo throw. That would involve some element of technique. There was none here.

He just picked me up and threw me forward, the same way one would throw a baseball.

I'd never done it, of course, but I could imagine a strong person being able to throw a toddler this way. But I weighed many, many times more than that—possibly more than Shizuo Heiwajima himself, in fact.

So how was I flying virtually horizontal?

If this were an American cartoon, I'd crash into the wall of the building across the way and leave a human-shaped hole behind. It certainly felt like there was enough force for that, but in reality, after just a few yards of flight, I crashed to the ground and rolled across the asphalt.

Is he going to kill me? I wondered, my mind suddenly calm now that the fear had been eradicated by the force of his throw.

I didn't want to die.

But he was going to kill me.

Once that logical calculation was finished, the fear began creeping back into my heart.

But at that moment, a voice of salvation came down from above.

"Hey, Shizuo."

I recognized that voice. It belonged to Tom Tanaka, the man who showed me here.

"...What is it, Tom?"

"Remember that cup of instant ramen you opened? It's been three minutes."

"...Seriously?"

And just like that, Shizuo Heiwajima was shockingly uninterested in me. He reentered the building as if nothing had just happened.

So he never meant to speak to me for more than three minutes to begin with.

But that didn't matter now.

All I wanted to do was savor the joy of being alive.

A little while later, Tanaka emerged from the building and came over to where I was lying.

"Well, there you go. Warned you not to piss him off, didn't I? Lucky for you, while his boiling point is low, he's also quick to cool off. I hope you learned your lesson and aren't stupid enough to go to the cops about this."

Though it didn't make perfect sense, I decided to nod my understanding. Satisfied, Tom turned back and went into the building.

All alone now, I rolled over to face the sky, limbs outstretched. It wasn't that I wanted to savor the sensation of stretching out in the middle of the street—I was just in too much pain to stand yet.

Even as I gave thanks for my safety, I was stunned to realize just how powerful that instantaneous fear had been.

When I was surrounded by the foreign mafia, the fear was more of a creeping sensation, the feeling of my body rotting from the inside out. Yet I'd managed to avoid my death by shooting or stabbing in that case.

But what I'd just experienced was instantaneous fear. An explosion of fear—the feeling one must feel when stabbed out of nowhere by a man passing in the street.

In fact, a knife wasn't adequate to describe this. A katana...yes, the victims of the katana slasher running wild in Ikebukuro right now might have felt this same fear.

And now that the fear had passed...

...I remembered why I wanted to be a journalist.

I wanted control, to monopolize.

I wanted to gain the best, most shocking information on my own and tell the world about it myself. By doing so, that "truth" became mine.

It was the search of that pleasure that drove me to become a journalist, but after getting married and raising a daughter, my bubbling passion had cooled off.

And now it was back.

It had all come back just now.
Brought back by the fear I'd just tasted.

Incredible.
It's incredible.
How stupid I must have been to doubt this.
But it was that very stupidity that led me here.
Here to my article!
The boy screaming about curiosity in my heart was dead. He had just died.
And now, the adult me was screaming it for him.
"Write!
"Seize it!
"Seize all of the truth, even if you have to fabricate it!
"Turn the fear that man put in you into your own strength!
"That's right, I'm coming out ahead.
"I found this through the experience of fear and pain!"
No matter how much I screamed them out, my heart kept overflowing with new words.

I want to tell the world about that fear.
I want to write an article about Shizuo Heiwajima.
With my hands, my own hands!
I want Shizuo Heiwajima and everything abnormal about him to belong to me, without exception.
That's right.
I'll get over this.
I'll get over my fear, research everything about him, and announce his exalted strength to the entire world. That's my duty as a journalist. In fact, when you _____ for what had to happen for me to come across him, you could say that it's my *fate.*
I don't care if all the rumors swirling around him are lies.
The instant of terror that I felt is an eternal truth! I don't even care if you tell me he's not the strongest. My article will *make* him the strongest!
That's right! I've got better things to do than lie on the ground here.
I stood up at once and took a step forward to conquer my moment of fear—no, to make that fear my own weapon.

That's right. I'm a journalist.

I'll uncover everything about him—starting with his tastes, his personal ties...and how he can wield such incredible strength in such a thin body! Everything: past, present, and future!

If I can write this article, my life will get back on track. I'll patch things up with my daughter. I can rekindle the old flame with my wife. It'll be just like it was before...

I clenched my fist with absolute determination, ready to write the greatest article ever about Shizuo Heiwajima. Clenched it hard, so hard...

♂♀

That night—chat room

《Did you hear? Today's slasher victim was the guy who wrote the "Tokyo Disaster" articles for *Tokyo Warrior.*》

【Oh, a magazine writer?】

[...Uh, is that true?]

《When have I ever lied to you?》

[Is he all right?]

《Well, apparently he's in a coma, critical condition! For some reason, he had bruises all over his body in addition to the slash wound. But the cut's already scabbing over, so they're saying that he probably got it earlier in the day!》

[Is that so...?]

【? Do you know him?】

[Er, no... But I'm a fan of those articles.]

【Oh. Maybe I should start reading them...】

【Anyway, these slashings are getting scary, aren't they?】

《Really! I can't even set foot outside!》

[Hmm. I wish the police would get a handle on this.]

—SAIKA HAS ENTERED THE CHAT—

《Here we goooo!》

[Ah.]

【Huh?】

|cut|

|cut, today|

《Well, I wish you would cut it out instead!》

【What's going on with this person? I saw the logs earlier...】

《It's a troll who keeps messing up all the Ikebukuro boards and chat rooms!》

[Evening, Saika.]

|cut, person, but, still, bad|

《There's no point, Setton. It won't respond to our messages.》

[I'm guessing it's a bot of some kind.]

|must, love, more|

《Maybe you're right.》

|love, strong person. so. want love, strong person|

【Kinda creepy, isn't it?】

《But it seems like it's very slowly typing better sentences...》

【Can't you just ban it from the chat?】

《I keep doing it...but it doesn't work.》

|must, cut, more|

[Wow, really?]

《I keep banning the individual remote host, but it just pops in with a different host.》

【Is it using a proxy?】

|must, get, closer|

《Hmm, doesn't seem to be the case.》

《The one common thread is that all the hosts are located around Ikebukuro.》

《So I think there's a high probability it's someone living around here.》

《Could be just jumping from manga café to manga café, for example.》

|to, strong person|

[It seems like the other message boards don't know how to deal with it, either.]

【You know, the way it keeps talking about cutting people...】

《Are you thinking what I'm thinking, Tarou?》

【What if it's the slasher?】

《Ha-ha-ha-ha! Nice.》

[...I can see why you would think that. This is clearly irrational activity.]

|keeping cutting|

【Keeping cutting?】
|get, stronger|
[...It really does seem to be connected to the slasher.]
《As a matter of fact...it always shows up on the days when I announce there's been a new victim.》
【"Always"? You've only said it twice.】
《Then it *is* the demon blade! A big ol' sword tapping away on a keyboard!》
[Monsters don't use the Internet.]
《Come on, Setton! Haven't you ever heard about cursed e-mails?》
[Um, no. Why would I have heard of that...?]
|moremoremoremoremoremoremoremoremore|
【I think we should just leave the chat room until it calms down.】
《Oh, don't worry. It usually leaves pretty soon.》
|in the end, approach, cut, I, love|
|found, goal, found, love|
[Well, let's hope so.]
|Shizuo|
|Heiwajima|
|Shizuo, Heiwajima|
|Heiwajima Heiwajima Heiwajima Heiwajima Heiwajima Heiwajima Heiwajima|
|Shizuo Shizuo Shizuo Heiwajima Heiwajima Heiwajima Shizuo Shizuo Shizuo Shizuo|
|love Shizuo cut Heiwajima I Heiwajima cut Shizuo love|
|for love for love for love for love for love for love for love|
【Huh? Is this someone Shizuo knows?!】
|Shizuo, Shizuo, Shizuo|
<Private Mode> [...Izaya?]
<Private Mode> 《I get what you're saying, but I don't know, either.》
|mother|
|mother's wish, is, same as, my wish|
|mother loves people, so do I|
|born born born to to to love love love I I I|
<Private Mode> 《Damn, is this someone Shizu knows...?》
<Private Mode> 《No... No way he would let someone this annoying live.》

<Private Mode> 【Anyway, we should probably clear out for a bit.】
【Well, I'm logging off now.】
[Oh, me too…]

—SAIKA HAS LEFT THE CHAT—

—TAROU TANAKA HAS LEFT THE CHAT—

[Huh? It just left…]
《Either way, we're done for today.》
[Good point.]
[So long.]
《Good night!》

—SETTON HAS LEFT THE CHAT—

—KANRA HAS LEFT THE CHAT—

—THE CHAT ROOM IS CURRENTLY EMPTY—
—THE CHAT ROOM IS CURRENTLY EMPTY—
—THE CHAT ROOM IS CURRENTLY EMPTY—

.
.
.

CHAPTER 4 THE IKEBUKURO CALAMITY

Noon, early March, Ikebukuro

The neighborhood began to bustle when March started.

The school exams were wrapping up, putting expressions of joy and mourning on the students' faces.

The office workers looked frazzled from the pressure of the fiscal year's approaching end.

The young adults without jobs or school loitered around the same way they always did.

People of every kind filled the city as the chill of winter began to wear off.

But the bustling of Ikebukuro these days was not due to the season.

Everyone who breathed in the air of the city could feel the abnormality hanging in the atmosphere.

♂♀

"...Yikes," muttered a young man with sharp eyes in the backseat of a van driving along the main street. The other two people in the backseat looked up from their books, distracted by the serious tone in his voice.

"What's up, Dotachin?"

"What happened, Kadota?"

One of them was a woman wearing black as her base color, and the other was a baby-faced boy who looked to be half-Caucasian.

The man named Kadota (or Dotachin) looked out the window and muttered darkly, "After the attack last night, the victim count is up to fifty. Fifty slashing victims."

"No way, up to fifty?! Wow, it's like a manga! Are you getting heart palpitations, too?"

"That's incredible. It'll *be* a manga before long. Oh, but none of them are fatalities, so it makes for kind of a weak villain."

"What's the slasher like? Katana? With a katana? Think it might be like Shizu? With a dog and everything? *Lone Wolf and Dog*?"

"No, this one's an original *Lone Wolf and Cub*, I'd say. So would that mean the Headless Rider is Kino?"

The two readers, Karisawa and Yumasaki, were off in their own world, making comparisons to characters from novels they'd read. Kadota sighed in exasperation. "I was an idiot for assuming you two had any sense of morality."

While the pair chattered away as though none of this had anything to do with them, Kadota thought over the state of the neighborhood.

The first incident had happened more than a year ago. A tough guy walking the streets at night was attacked, but it didn't make the news under the assumption that it was just a fight of some kind. The victim claimed he was attacked with a katana, but he eventually gave up on that, and it was classified as a street squabble.

But two months after that, an average salaryman with no history of violence got hit, which drew the media's attention and served as fuel for the daytime variety shows.

While there was no difference in human value between the thug and the salaryman, the media found the topic of an indiscriminate attacker to be much more salacious than an underworld squabble.

More time passed, and on Christmas night, a couple was attacked. Authorities announced it to be likely the work of the same attacker. The fuel for the variety shows went from a wooden log to a tank of gasoline.

The fact that the victims never saw the face of their attacker, combined with the location of Ikebukuro—smack in the middle of the capital—added a touch of mystery to the incidents. It posed a riddle to the world but didn't quite capture all of society, because as luck would have it, there were no fatalities.

But at this point, it was far more than gasoline.

The slasher was nitro fuel, blasting through the variety shows, prime-time news, and the front page of weekly tabloids and national newspapers alike.

After all, the number of victims only rose after the New Year, and by the end of February, the pitch rose to a victim every day.

And while the media wasn't reporting it, the yellow bandannas were also on the rise. They were members of the Yellow Scarves, a color gang. Many of them were young, with about half of the members in middle school. There had always been kids that young in color gangs, and the Yellow Scarves were founded a few years back by middle schoolers, which meant most of them were now in their first or second year of high school.

But just because they were made of students didn't mean they posed no threat. For one thing, there were several hundred of them. But even worse, kids didn't know when to hold back. And on top of that, they had the worst kind of knowledge on their side.

They knew what ages were too young to be prosecuted for crimes, and when they got into trouble, they made sure to have the youngest members do it. The Yellow Scarves themselves hadn't gotten involved in crime yet, but they were growing in number. No doubt those kids on the fringes would utilize the team name to get up to no good.

The street slasher and the Yellow Scarves.

To Kadota and the other Dollars members, these two things were cause for concern.

"So you haven't heard anything about the slasher or the victims?" Kadota asked, turning to Karisawa and Yumasaki, but they were already in a far-off world.

"I'm telling you, Riselina has to be the heroine. I mean, she got the bridal carry!"

"No way, it's obviously Urc! I mean, she's the protagonist's child-hood friend!"

"Ha-ha-ha, oh, you are so naive, Karisawa! Knowing that author, Riselina's gonna turn out to be a childhood friend, too."

"Even though she's from another world?! Well, either way, I don't care, 'cause I've got the hots for Bradeau."

They seemed to be deep in a heated debate involving a whole lot of unfamiliar names. Kadota couldn't imagine a more confusing and obnoxious development.

"People are mourning here, and you're blabbering on about some stupid video game!"

"Don't be silly, it's not a game. We're debating who the main heroine is in the Dengeki Bunko novel series *On a Planet Where the Skybells Ring*. Really, Kadota, you need to stop distancing yourself from fantasy and give it a shot!"

"Good grief... If either of you ever commit a crime, the media will never let it go. 'The uber-nerds who could no longer tell the difference between manga and reality,' they'll gasp."

Shocked, Yumasaki shouted, "What do you mean, Kadota?!"

"?!"

Startled by the sudden outburst, Kadota stared right at his compan-ion. He had never seen Yumasaki angry like this.

"You think we've lost touch with the distinction between 2-D and 3-D? Don't be ridiculous! A true nerd knows the difference between 2-D and 3-D and chooses 2-D every freakin' time! Toss the 3-D life in the garbage, man! Anyone who gets tired of 2-D and turns to crime in the real world isn't a true nerd at all. Don't compare us to those losers who give up on the 2-D life! I wish the variety shows and newspapers would figure that out already!"

"Uh...okay, man...," Kadota murmured, leaning backward with the force of Yumasaki's speech. He looked over to Karisawa for help, who didn't exactly oblige.

"Don't be dumb, Yumacchi. The media is totally aware of what they're doing. It's an easier message to sell. Plus, whether they're committing crimes or not, anyone who sits around for days at a time fangasming over anime without bathing might as well be a criminal anyway. That's creepy."

"Ugh. This is exactly why we put so much effort into our fashion—to help update that old image of us."

"If that's what you're hoping to do, stop shouting about otaku crap in the middle of the train. And stop using manga and novels for torture ideas," Kadota snapped. The other two ignored him and continued their conversation.

"Goddammit… What if the slasher was a crazy fan of period pieces? Would the TV stations ban all of their boring samurai specials?!"

"I hope not, I like those shows," Kadota muttered.

Yumasaki turned to him with a clenched fist. "Listen! The only 3-D objects I'll acknowledge the existence of are figures and plastic models."

"But not *us*? Screw you…"

"Hmm…oh, and maybe that dream demon who visited me in the summer. At least she was a maid. Maybe if she tries hard enough, she'll be able to morph into a 2-D girl."

"Yumacchi, what's this about a dream demon?"

"See? This is what I keep saying—you can't tell the difference between manga and reality!"

The chaos inside the van was interrupted by the sudden ringing of a phone.

It wasn't just Kadota's. Karisawa's and Yumasaki's phones were playing anime theme songs, and even the driver Togusa's phone was going off in the front seat.

All the cell phones in the car were active at once.

It might have seemed like an effect from a horror movie, but all of them knew what it meant: They'd all received the same message.

It wasn't just the people in the car, either. Certain people all around Ikebukuro would be receiving this together.

Kadota was the first to check the text. He ground his teeth and nearly cracked the flip phone shut.

"Okay, you guys. This is officially now our business. Get your heads back in reality."

"?"

The others noticed the look of foreboding in Kadota's eyes and checked for themselves.

The message itself was quite simple.

Dollars member has been attacked by the slasher. Need info, need info, need info.

There was that short "need info" repeated at the end.

Kadota took a number of emotions from that simple message and muttered.

"The town is starting to fall apart."

♂♀

Near Kawagoe Highway, top floor of apartment building

About the same time that people around the neighborhood were checking their cell phones, Celty was reading the same message on hers.

Celty lived in the spacious apartment, which was larger than some stand-alone houses, with her partner, a black-market doctor. Earlier she had been nothing but a freeloading guest, but after a time last year, she was now happily (?) his lover in a cohabitation arrangement.

But this was not a time for reflecting on her love life. She checked her phone and put her elbows on the desk in a pose of heavy thought.

Black shadows squirmed in the face of the bright light flooding through the windows. Amid that unbelievably eerie sight, she thought to herself, *I wonder if Mikado's starting to lose his grip.*

She thought of the childish face of the Dollars founder when she met him around a year ago and folded her phone shut.

Without a mouth to speak, Celty might appear not to need a cell phone. But as a courier, being able to send texts to clients or Shinra while on the move was extremely convenient, and it was also quicker to operate than the e-mail client on the PDA.

Even the camera function, which she'd thought was totally useless before she bought it, was finding plenty of use. It all came down to conveying information quickly. It wasn't great for clandestine activity, given the loud shutter noise, but in Celty's case, she almost never ever *needed* to be that stealthy.

And now, more than anything, Celty wanted a cell phone photo.

If just one person could capture an image of the slasher who was terrorizing the town...

No one had died yet from the attacks, but Celty couldn't bring herself to believe that fact.

When it attacked her, that red-eyed shadow had chopped her head off. She'd considered the possibility that the slasher knew she was headless already, but that only made the act of knocking her helmet off even more pointless and baffling.

The most reasonable explanation Celty could think of was that the attacker was only trying to wound her, and when she didn't bleed at all, it knocked her head off instead.

But wait, what if I was just a normal human being with a prosthetic arm?

In either case, this could not be allowed to stand. Celty clenched her fist in determination. She wouldn't let this wanton behavior continue in her home of Ikebukuro.

In a sense, though, before the slasher happened along, the most wanton behavior of all had come from Celty herself—but perhaps that just meant she couldn't forgive the idea of anyone *else* committing crimes around here.

"Now, now, Celty. No need to get so tense," said a bespectacled young man in a white doctor's coat. He had noticed the headless knight's sighing motions in front of the computer.

"*Oh, you're back*," Celty typed lifelessly into the computer screen without turning around.

"It's always darkest before the dawn. Just do what you can—put your human, so...put your dullahan affairs in order and let fate do the rest? Hmm. Given that a dullahan's fate is to tell others of their death, it sounds like a pretty dark story in the making."

"*Yeah, yeah, I get it.*"

Shinra had no hesitations about treating Celty as something inhuman, but this actually made her happy. Nothing was more reassuring than knowing that someone accepted and loved her for what she really was.

If Shinra had originally professed his love for Celty by offering to think of a way to make her human or claiming that his love would make her human, she'd probably have left him behind.

Instead, Shinra Kishitani loved Celty just as she was, without her head. That might have been the only way that she could face her own feelings for him.

"So anyway, do you have a plan? You can't just go out patrolling the town every night, can you?"

"Maybe not. At the very least, I'm suspected of having a connection to the slasher. If I wander around too much at night, I might as well be claiming that I'm the attacker myself."

"The slasher? Reminds me of that killer from five years ago," Shinra murmured ominously. Celty thought back to the incident that had unsettled the neighborhood several years earlier.

The Ikebukuro tsujigiri *incident*

It was named after the old practice of "testing out" a new katana by attacking random passersby, because as with this ongoing incident, the victims claimed they'd been attacked with a traditional Japanese katana. But a clear portrait of the attacker was never established, and the book on the case stayed open.

Centuries in the past, Ikebukuro had been a place of many *tsujigiri* incidents, so some caused a stir by suggesting a curse was in effect. But once the attacks suddenly stopped, it passed completely out of the public interest in just the span of a year.

"Wasn't that only two or three attacks though?"

"The main difference is that five years ago, people actually died. In the last incident, the killer barged into a house and cut down two people. The other victims got away with minor injuries, fortunately..."

"But they never caught whoever was responsible."

Celty shrugged in resignation.

Suddenly, Shinra muttered to himself. "...Saika."

"Psyche?"

"No, Saika. Written with the characters for 'song of sin,' pronounced Saika."

Song of sin.

Celty typed the characters into the computer, then turned to Shinra in shock.

Saika. The mysterious troll who'd been messing up all the Ikebukuro-related chat rooms and message boards, including the one she'd been frequenting lately.

"Do you know this person? It hasn't been you this whole time, has it?"

"No, no, I wouldn't do that. If I wanted to troll people, I'd just get my super-hacker friend to take the boards down entirely."

"Does this super hacker really exist? And what makes him super? Is that a joke? ...Whatever. What about Saika?" Celty prompted, not in the mood to play along with Shinra's jokes at the moment.

"Well, there's been all that trolling about cutting stuff."

"Yeah, the weird lists of words. But it also talks a lot about loving, so I'm not sure if there's a connection or not..."

"Hmm... You've always been in Ikebukuro, so maybe you don't know about it..."

"?"

Shinra looked at the question mark she typed onto the screen, then waited a long dramatic moment to build the tension.

"Saika *seems to have happened* a long time ago in Shinjuku."

"???"

She added a few more question marks to show that she wasn't following his meaning. Shinra found that to be unbearably adorable, and his face crinkled into a childlike grin.

"Well, the confusing part is that you could say Saika 'happened' or that Saika 'was around'..."

"Stop beating around the bush and explain."

~~Fine, fine.~~ ...and fidgety at the same time," he said, accurately reading her emotions despite the lack of a face to scrutinize.

"Saika was a real, actual, authentic demon blade that existed in Shinjuku years ago."

"..."

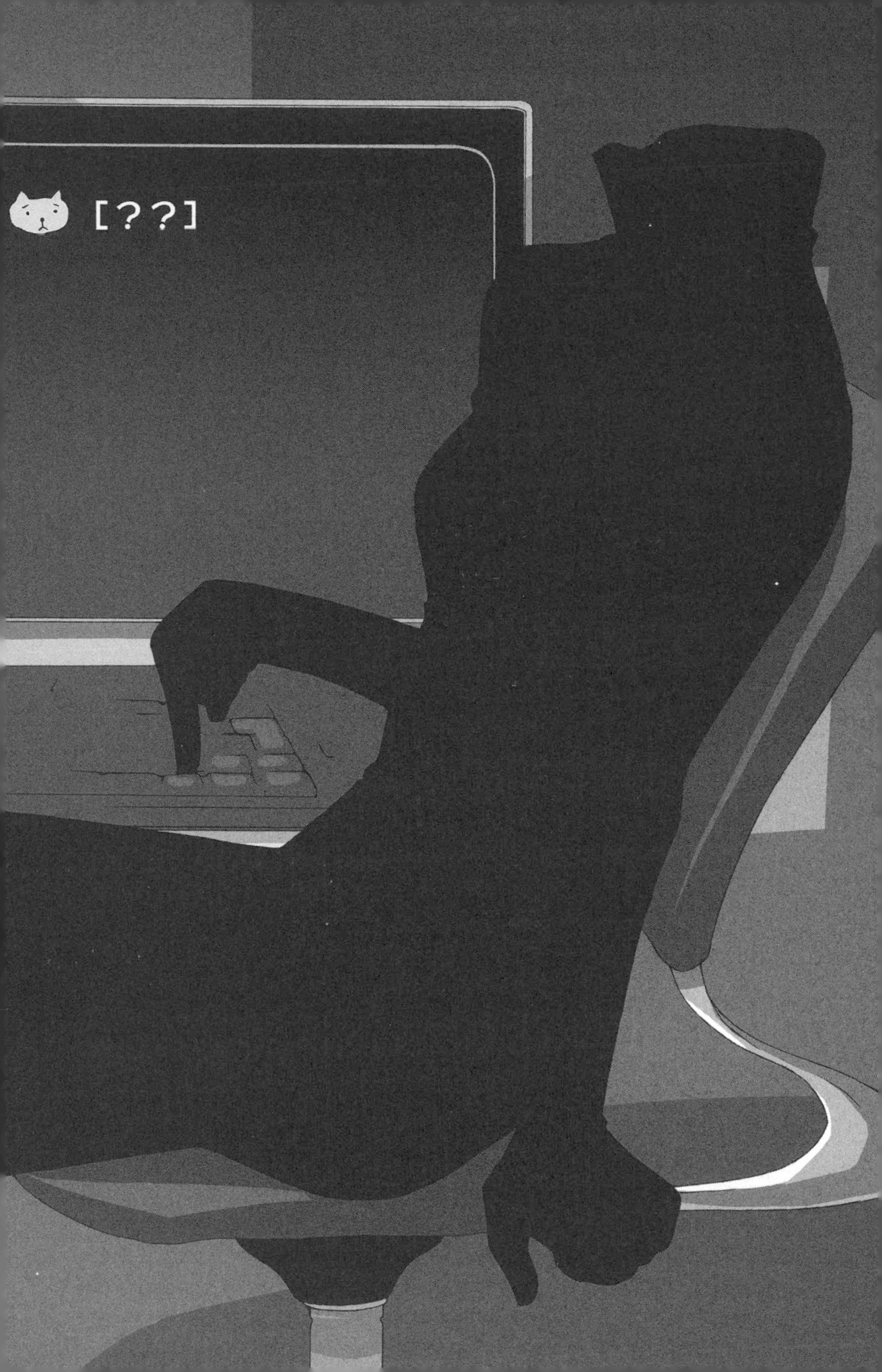
[??]

Celty actually went to the trouble of typing in her silence.

"......"

The silence continued. She was apparently waiting for Shinra's reaction.

"..."

But Shinra was waiting for Celty's reaction as well. An awkward silence fell upon the room.

Celty lost her patience first. She typed her honest emotions into the keyboard.

"...*Ohh?*"

"What does 'ohh' mean?"

"..."

"..."

The silence was back. Celty hurried to fill it with a question.

"*Demon blade... You mean like a Muramasa Blade?*"

"You really do like those *Wizardry* games, don't you?"

"*Stop spying on my chat logs.*"

"I apologize for that—sorry. Matter settled! Now...don't you remember that Kanra person in the chat talking about a demon blade? Anyway, that jogged my memory about some old books I read once, so I looked them up again, and...surprise! There was a demon blade named Saika in Shinjuku once!" he announced proudly. Annoyed, Celty typed in her response.

"*Setting aside that the matter is most certainly not settled...I don't know. I thought you were more of a realist, Shinra. There's no such thing as a cursed demon blade. Look at reality.*"

As she typed, Celty was keenly aware that she might as well be denying her own existence. She made a show of a laughing motion to get her point across. Shinra only shook his head—he knew Celty better than anyone else, including how to get under her skin.

"...Remind me who was it that was trembling in fear at the image of grays that they showed in that UFO special? Who was it that saw the video of the cow being sucked up by the UFO and couldn't stop talking about how scary it would be if that happened to her?"

"*Sh—*"

"Who got suckered in by that April Fool's show and came to tell me all about the revelation that 'the Apollo mission never actually landed on the moon'?"

"*Shut up, shut up, shut uuup! It...it's obvious! Aliens are much more likely to exist than cursed swords!*" she snapped back lamely.

Shinra just shook his head, the picture of smugness. "What if the aliens made the cursed sword?"

"*Wha—?*"

"A katana created with secret space technology. Seems like it would have a mind of its own, right?"

"*W-well, in that case...*"

The conversation was clearly going in the wrong direction, but Celty couldn't think of a good rebuttal. Or a reason for one, for that matter.

"*...It seems...plausible...*"

Begrudgingly convinced, Celty decided she ought to ask about the sword.

I have to admit, I'm curious about the fact that it's using the same name, she told herself and listened closely to what Shinra had to say.

"Now, just after the war ended, this demon blade Saika rampaged through Shinjuku for blood."

"*I see.*"

"And then, after an incredible, thrilling battle with a magical sword from the West..."

"*Now wait a minute!*" Celty grabbed Shinra by his lapel, feeling that she'd been tricked into buying his story. "*What boys' manga did you rip this story out of?*"

"Settle down, Celty! Adolescents aren't going to take to a manga without human characters. It would get canceled! In fact, it wouldn't even make it through the editors' meetings! Just hear me out until the end!"

"*...I'm listening,*" she prompted, her hand still clutching his collar.

"Their battle was brought to an end by the bamboo spear of intelligence, which was carved from a magic stalk of bamboo. After that, Saika was forced to flee Shinjuku for—"

"*Forget I asked.*"

She let go of Shinra's coat and started walking for the front entrance of the apartment.

"But I was just getting to the good part."

"I've heard enough. I'm going out for a bit. I'm not taking any jobs tonight," she typed into her PDA and held backward for Shinra to read. He didn't make any attempts to stop her and switched topics on a dime. This was virtually a daily occurrence in their lives.

"Where are you going?"

"To see Shizuo."

"Wha...? A-are you cheating on me, Celty?! If you're unhappy with me, can you say why?! No, wait, not directly; that'll just crush my spirit. Say what's wrong with me with three different kinds of misdirection! Seventy percent praise and thirty percent insults, if you can!"

"Don't worry. I've got no complaints," she replied innocently and stepped into the entryway. *"It's just that this Saika character's been repeating Shizuo's name over and over. If you've read my logs, you should know. If he's really got something to do with the slasher, it's worth finding him and hearing him out."*

krch
  ripcrik
  snp krack
Sound.
The sound of joints and muscles breaking down.
rip snap rip snap crakk
With every unpleasant crackle, terrible pain ran through this body.
The boy had no choice but to endure this endless hell.
He knew that it was nothing but a manifestation of his own rage.

Shizuo Heiwajima came to understand that he was different in third grade.

He had a fight with his little brother over something pointless. And when he snapped, he tried to throw the refrigerator, which was easily taller than he was.

At the time, he didn't have the strength to lift it, of course—but as a result, he pulled muscles all over his body and dislocated numerous joints.

That was just the start of the abnormalities.

When he got into a fight with his friend in the classroom, the boy threw a pointed compass at Shizuo. That was bad enough, but what Shizuo did in response was far worse. It was enough to make the phrase *self-defense* pick up and scamper away.

He lifted an entire desk packed with textbooks with his skinny nine-year-old arms, did a half rotation, and hurled it with all of his strength.

The target of his anger was nothing short of dead lucky.

All of that weight passed to his side, just barely brushing his arm. The next instant, the wall behind him sounded like it was falling apart.

With trembling legs, the boy turned around to see the desk stuck halfway into the classroom wall.

There's a phrase: *brute strength.*

When humans think they're exhibiting all of their strength, they're really not.

The muscles naturally limit themselves so that what we think of as "full strength" is actually far weaker than their maximum capability.

But when placed in a situation of extreme danger, such as a house fire, the brain unlocks that potential. Suddenly the body is strong enough to lift heavy furniture or other people from the site of a disaster or to leap over obstacles that should be too tall to scale.

Shizuo Heiwajima possessed one unique feature. He could call upon that brute strength at any moment, not just in emergencies.

This might have appeared to be a great benefit—but it wasn't anything of the sort.

The reason the brain prevents the use of full strength is to protect the body's joints and muscles. The body's limits are limits for a reason; putting it under that much stress will only cause it to break down.

In exchange for the gift of incredible power, Shizuo lost the ability to control his strength.

In other words, if he attempted to put all of his strength into something, his muscles would faithfully tear themselves to shreds in the attempt.

That overflowing physical strength soon became an extension of his own rage.

Whenever he got angry, that uncontrollable muscular strength would jump into action on its own. When his brain was wielded by great strength, it demanded the body make use of it: *Pick up the heaviest object here, destroy everything, destroy everyone.*

As a result, young Shizuo heeded his instincts.

Destruction. He sought absolute destruction, and it was always his own body that collapsed first.

A collapsing body and uncontrollable strength.

Trapped between these two things, the boy's mind began to fall apart bit by bit. At some point, he forgot the concept of controlling his anger.

If I can't hold back and I'm going to fall apart first anyway, I'll feel so much better by just allowing my mind to be free!

He gave up on self-control.

He unleashed all of his instincts, ready to give up his own life.

As a result of that choice, he destroyed even more.

He wreaked an untold amount of violence...on his own body.

Day after day, he broke down.

When his body broke down, he flew into a rage and destroyed himself even more.

It was an unmanageable juggling act.

He gained nothing. Only the scars of destruction piled up behind him.

His muscles destroyed themselves repeatedly—and before they could rebuild stronger than before, they broke down again.

The boy was drowning in a hell of his own creation.

He struggled and strained and strove but could not escape himself...

And time passed.

"My dad and mom were always super nice about it," Shizuo muttered, his eyes narrowed behind the sunglasses. "Even my little brother, whom I always fought with, screamed for an ambulance after I tried to lift the fridge and collapsed. He waited there with me until the paramedics arrived... I had a really nice family. They didn't spoil me or anything, but I think I was raised in a happy home."

Celty listened in silence as Shizuo spoke about his upbringing. The bartender's outfit and riding suit were shoulder to shoulder on a bench as evening descended on South Ikebukuro Park. There were other people in the park, but the eeriness of the sight kept them all away.

"So...how did it turn out this way?" he muttered sadly into the air, a self-deprecating smile on his lips. "What was the catalyst for my change? I didn't have any trouble at home. There was no childhood trauma, and I wasn't obsessed with hyper-violent anime or manga. I barely even watched any movies. So was it me? Did the cause come from nothing but me myself?"

Celty maintained her silence. She wasn't ignoring him but was attempting to absorb all of Shizuo's confessions within her own shadow.

"I just want to be strong," he admitted, but his voice *was* strong. "If I'm the cause of all this, then I hate myself most of all. I don't care about the fighting. I just want the strength to control myself."

It was an utterly honest confession. The only reason he could speak like this was because Celty didn't waste his time with pointless rebuttals or jokes. Of course, it wasn't only that—he'd been around her for a long time and had grown to trust her implicitly.

Shizuo knew that everyone in the neighborhood was afraid of him. Because of that, the fact that Celty would listen without fear made her a very precious thing to him.

If he was talking to someone who had no idea who he was, they would probably manage to drive him into a rage somehow, and just like all the others, they would find themselves terrified of him. Shizuo understood how the process happened.

But understanding its ways did not give him any better control over it.

After a long, long time, the number of people in his vicinity shrank down naturally.

There was his boss at work, who knew how to handle Shizuo. There was Simon, who was capable of defending himself against Shizuo's extreme violence. There was Izaya Orihara, who stayed close because of his utter loathing. And there was the silent Headless Rider, who never made him mad.

He already knew that Celty was the Headless Rider. But he wasn't particularly concerned with that. She'd always interacted with him while wearing the helmet, and knowing that she couldn't actually speak meant that it made no difference to him.

Shizuo's thought process was very simple, though it wasn't the result of some kind of strong belief or ideal. He put everything in the world into two categories.

People who pissed him off and people who didn't piss him off. Those were the only two choices.

"Sorry for griping at ya again," he said with a slight smile. At this point, he didn't look like anything but a mild-mannered young man. "So what do you want today? You came out here because you wanted me for something, right?"

"..."

Celty took out her PDA and conveyed the information in the fewest words possible.

The slashings taking place in town.

The person on the Net named Saika who was using his name.

That Saika might be connected to the attacks somehow.

That the journalist who'd been asking about Shizuo was one of the slasher's victims.

And that Shizuo's name had popped up in chat the night the writer was attacked.

Once he'd read all of this information, Shizuo raised an eyebrow.

"What the hell? Are you saying you suspect me?" he asked directly.

Celty shook her helmet side to side.

If Shizuo were responsible and swinging a katana around, there was no way the victims wouldn't have died. There was no obvious reason for Shizuo to conduct the random attacks, and even if anyone made him mad enough to want to ambush someone under cover of night, he'd just twist the poor sap's head around 180 degrees.

Shizuo claimed that he had no control over himself, but the fact that he wielded such strength and hadn't committed homicide yet spoke to a nearly miraculous level of personal restraint.

Of course, it had occurred to Celty that he might have sent a number of people to an early grave after all, and she just didn't know about it.

"A Dollars member has been attacked."

"Yeah, I know. I got the message," he replied shortly, pulling out his cell phone. "Honestly, I'd love to help out, but I only joined up because Simon asked me to. I'm not really that close to the Dollars to begin with... Of course, that shallow connection is what allows me to be a part of their group."

He snorted wryly and looked up at the sunset. The sky was redder and more beautiful than it had any business being.

"*Tsk*. What the hell is the city sky doing looking like the country-side? What does it think it is?" he growled nonsensically as he got to his feet and started to leave. "Look, I'm sorry. I don't have any clues for ya. Besides…why are you so intent on making the Dollars your business? Just don't get yourself hurt."

It was rare for Shizuo to show consideration for anyone else. Celty quietly typed away.

"*It's not just for the Dollars. I'm also getting revenge for myself.*"

"*?*"

"*I was recently attacked by the slasher, too. Cut straight across the throat. If I wasn't headless, I'd be dead.*"

She typed this message in with a wry intention of her own, but the confession had huge, fateful consequences.

Not for Celty's fate. For Shizuo's and all of Ikebukuro.

"You asshole…"

"*Huh?*"

"Why didn't you say that first?! You idiot! They say whoever calls someone an idiot is the real idiot, but I already know I am, so I'll say it anyway! Say that first, you idiot! Why are we standing around with our thumbs up our asses?!"

It was exceedingly rare for Shizuo Heiwajima to be angry for the sake of another person.

He was angry about one of his companions being hurt, so in a broader sense he *was* angry for his own sake, but logical quibbling aside, Shizuo was full of pure rage.

"Someone's gonna die. I'll kill 'em. Butcher 'em. Murder 'em."

"*Hang on. Look, I'm the Headless Rider. I'm perfectly fine.*"

"No, no, no. That's not the point. Swinging a sword at you equals death. That's all there is to it."

But this was not his usual explosive rage, as the target of his anger was not present. Shizuo's rage today was the kind that bubbled away and stored its energy up in his stomach.

"Celty, did you know there is power in words? So I'm trying to stifle my overwhelming urge to destroy everything by putting it into a single word."

That was exactly what Celty was afraid of.

"Kill, kill, kill, kill, kill, kill, kill, kill, kill, kill, kill, kill, kill, kill, kill…"

If this situation continued and the slasher happened by, she knew who was going to die.

The slasher.

He wouldn't leave them a moment for repentance. If Shizuo punched a person with all of his force, they'd be lucky with just the skull caved in. If worst came to worst, he would snap the neck and tear all of that flesh so that the target of his rage was just as headless as she was.

The only difference was that humans died when they lost their heads.

Celty allowed herself a moment of sympathy for the attacker as she watched Shizuo hop onto the back of her motorcycle.

"What about work? Aren't you on break?"

"Who cares anymore?"

"Hey! You'd better not get yourself fired on account of me. Plus, we still need time to collect information on the slasher. Just wait until your shift is over. I'll go make preparations."

"…"

Shizuo thought it over for a few moments, then grumbled, "All right…but make it quick," squeezing the words out in between his chants of "kill, kill, kill…"

It made him look like an exorcist attempting to resist the control of the devil.

"All the emotion that's building up inside of me is screaming to be unleashed…and if I don't take care of it…"

"…It's pretty likely that I'll end up destroying myself."

♂♀

Thirty minutes later, Shinjuku

There was a very good reason that Celty decided to split off from Shizuo momentarily.

Naturally, she was concerned with the state of his employment, but there was a much bigger rationale behind her choice.

*   *   *

If she was with Shizuo, there was one person she could never meet, and she had to make contact with him for information now.

"Hey... I'm delighted you decided to come visit me."

"I just met you last month for the job you had me do."

"Oh, what's the harm? We didn't get to chat last time. So how are things? It's been a year now since the Yagiri Pharmaceuticals incident. Have you found your head yet?"

Izaya Orihara offered Celty a cup of tea with a sardonic smile. His nasty personality hadn't changed over time—he knew full well he was offering tea to someone without a mouth to drink it.

"My issues aren't important... I'll be direct. Any suspicions as to the slasher?"

"It'll cost you three bills," he stated.

Celty pulled a wallet made of solid shadow from her riding suit of the same material. The bills inside were real, of course. She removed three ten thousand–yen bills and handed them to Izaya.

"So not only is your scythe made of shadow, so are your wallet and clothes. If I shined a bright enough light on you, would the shadow dissipate and show me your naked body?"

"You want to see?"

Izaya responded to Celty's challenge by squirming backward and smirking.

"Not really. I'm not a pervert like that student or that unlicensed doctor. I don't get all hot and heavy over a severed head or its headless body."

The moment he tossed that insult back to her, a black scythe entwined its way around Izaya's neck.

The end of the scythe was curled up like a spring, forming a twisted circle around Izaya's neck, with the tip at the center. She had thrust the weapon up against his neck and morphed it into that bizarre shape in the blink of an eye.

Izaya's smile faded just the tiniest bit, and he raised his hands in a sign of surrender.

"Insulting me is one thing. But if you slander Shinra again, you will pay dearly. Let's say...with injuries that will take three days to recover from."

"...Thanks for the detail. You're calm enough to tell me that this isn't a bluff."

"Yes, Shinra might be abnormal. But if he's weird, then he's only weird to me and no one else. You have no right to judge him."

"You sound like quite the couple," Izaya noted coolly. Celty retracted her scythe in resignation.

Unsatisfied with just being released, the information agent had more sarcasm for the headless woman. "But what if your biggest fan just happens to have a thing for headless women? What if another dullahan comes along and seduces him? He might just fall head over heels for her instead."

"Somehow I doubt that...but I wouldn't mind. All I'd do—"

"Is kill Shinra and commit suicide?"

"No, I'd just make certain that no other headless women get near him. It's not just that he loves me. Now I love him, too..."

The first instant that Izaya saw the confident text on the PDA, the smile vanished—only to be replaced by a great guffaw.

"...Kah-ha! Ah-ha-ha-ha-ha-ha-ha-ha! I didn't expect this! Since that last incident, you're more human than ever! But be careful. The closer you get to being human, the larger the gap might be when you finally do get your head and memories back!"

"I can worry about that once I have my head. Actually, to be honest, I'm starting to think I don't really need my head after all... But enough about that. Give me information on the slasher. You're not going to take my money and tell me nothing, are you?"

With the topic back on business, Izaya shook his head and began to tell her the "product" she'd bought.

"Don't worry, I've got some juicy intel I haven't sold to the police or media or put on the Internet. I won't lie—I was waiting for you to come to me."

"What do you mean?"

"...it's straight out of the world of ghosts and goblins," he teased. When he spoke next, it was in the hushed tones of one beginning a scary story.

"...Have you ever heard of the sword called Saika?"

"Huh?"

"You might not believe me, but once, here in Shinjuku, there was a *demon blade...*"

♂♀

Thirty minutes later, near Kawagoe Highway, top floor of apartment building

"Shinra! Shinra, Shinra, Shinraaa!"

"Whoaaa, don't just barge in here with your PDA thrust out like that! I'd like it more if you showed this kind of initiative in bed—*ghrf!*"

Celty gave Shinra a light knee in the stomach and rapidly typed out her next message.

"Hey! That demon blade story! Was that all true?!"

"Nngh… I have gone on a journey of despair now that I know you doubted my ironclad word. I'm done for—the only thing that can save me is your love. I need about level thirty-seven love. In the ABCs of love, a B should do…"

"Stop joking around! Listen!"

She yanked Shinra up to his feet and began to type out what she'd just heard from Izaya.

—That Izaya was also concerned with the connection between the online troll Saika and the slasher and was investigating on his own.

—That there was a legend of a demon blade named Saika with a mind of its own that could possess other people.

—That when the victims' testimony was combined, no one had seen the attacker directly, but as they all passed out, they remembered red eyes.

—That each day the Saika username appeared online was the same day in which a new slashing victim appeared later that night.

Once she finished showing him these details, Shinra sadly rolled around on the carpet in his white coat.

"Ahh, how can this be? When I said it, you chuckled through the nose—no, wait, you don't have a nose. You chuckled through your breast at me, but sure, you'll take *Izaya's* word for it! …Aaah!"

"What is it?!"

"I like that phrase, 'chuckled through your breast.' Sounds kinda sexy, if you ask—*gffh!*"

She caught him in the temple with a low kick, sprawling him out on the floor. Somehow, Shinra kept his wits about him and turned back to Celty with a deadly serious look on his face.

"So what's the plan?"

"Well...if it was a spirit or fairy of some kind, I would have sensed its presence...but I didn't feel a thing when I was attacked."

"Well, of course. A katana might have a mind, but it doesn't have a presence. As far as I know, the demon blade Saika possessed the mind of its wielder and controlled his body. If that was a strictly human body, then there would be no otherworldly presence or aura for you to sense. Plus, we don't know that all spirits or fairies possess this 'presence' you're talking about."

"So there's no way I can search for it, then."

Celty clenched her fist in frustration at Shinra's calm conjecture. But he only grinned at her and extended one last lottery ticket to his lover.

"Actually, there is, my dear."

"Huh?"

"Let me start off by apologizing: sorry. I took another look at the chat room you hang out in... Have you seen this? It's quite interesting. I've heard that Saika was a female blade, and based on this, it seems to be true."

"What...?"

"Check out the past logs. Good thing this chat is the kind that saves a long backlog."

Celty booted up her computer as he suggested.

And then she saw it.

She saw how much the thing named Saika had evolved in the time she'd been away from the chat...

Chat room

—THE CHAT ROOM IS CURRENTLY EMPTY—
—THE CHAT ROOM IS CURRENTLY EMPTY—

—THE CHAT ROOM IS CURRENTLY EMPTY—
—THE CHAT ROOM IS CURRENTLY EMPTY—
—THE CHAT ROOM IS CURRENTLY EMPTY—
—THE CHAT ROOM IS CURRENTLY EMPTY—

—SAIKA HAS ENTERED THE CHAT—

*   *   *

|I cut one person today. But one is enough. It's not good to be greedy.|
|But I'll cut again tomorrow. The more lovers, the better.|
|My strength has reached its peak.|
|I'm looking for a person.|
|Shizuo Heiwajima.|
|The man I must love.|
|Tomorrow night, I'll cut again.|
|I know where Shizuo is. But there are too many people to be safe.|
|I want to know where Shizuo Heiwajima lives.|
|Does he live alone? Is it in Ikebukuro, too?|
|I want to know more about Shizuo.|
|About the strongest man in this town...|
|I want to love him, I want to know him.|
|I'll cut someone again tomorrow. Every day, until I meet Shizuo.|
|I want to see Shizuo, soon, soon, soon...|

—SAIKA HAS LEFT THE CHAT—

—THE CHAT ROOM IS CURRENTLY EMPTY—
—THE CHAT ROOM IS CURRENTLY EMPTY—
—THE CHAT ROOM IS CURRENTLY EMPTY—
—THE CHAT ROOM IS CURRENTLY EMPTY—
—THE CHAT ROOM IS CURRENTLY EMPTY—

—KANRA HAS ENTERED THE CHAT—

《...Well, it seems like this person is only posting here now.》
《I was trying to figure out why.》
《When the name Shizuo popped up here earlier, Tarou clearly reacted to it.》
《So it seems like they think this Shizuo person might be reading these messages.》
《Now, I'm only guessing, but...》
《This is advance warning for the crime, right? If something happens tomorrow night, should we report it?》

《As the moderator, I'll need to do something as soon as possible.》
《Well, so long.》

—KANRA HAS LEFT THE CHAT—

—THE CHAT ROOM IS CURRENTLY EMPTY—
—THE CHAT ROOM IS CURRENTLY EMPTY—
—THE CHAT ROOM IS CURRENTLY EMPTY—
—THE CHAT ROOM IS CURRENTLY EMPTY—
—THE CHAT ROOM IS CURRENTLY EMPTY—
—THE CHAT ROOM IS CURRENTLY EMPTY—
—THE CHAT ROOM IS CURRENTLY EMPTY—
—THE CHAT ROOM IS CURRENTLY EMPTY—

—SETTON HAS ENTERED THE CHAT—

[When did all of this happen...?]
[Tarou, are you still seeing all of this?]
[I'd really appreciate it if you responded.]
[On the other hand...]
[The log's from last night...so "tomorrow" would mean tonight, yes?]
[Oh, I need to go out and do something, so I'm taking off...]
[I know it's hard, Kanra, but please hang in there.]
[So long.]

—SETTON HAS LEFT THE CHAT—

—THE CHAT ROOM IS CURRENTLY EMPTY—
—THE CHAT ROOM IS CURRENTLY EMPTY—
—THE CHAT ROOM IS CURRENTLY EMPTY—

.
.
.
.

CHAPTER 5 RIGHT TO THE POINTS

In her dream, the girl met her dead parents.

At a theme park, surrounded by the smiles of her family.
On a mountaintop covered with flowers.
At a riverside blanketed with warm sunlight and the smell of barbecue.
In her own kitchen with a birthday cake in the center of the table.
"You're going to be just as pretty as your mother someday, Anri."
"No, I think she gets it from you."
Her mother and father were smiling.
There were no mirrors in her dream, but she was probably smiling, too.
Mom, Dad.
We'll be together forever and ever, right?
Anri Sonohara always repeated the same phrase in her dreams.
A happy home.
Her family's smiles.
So small and insignificant, but the greatest joy of all to a young girl.

The more she had those dreams, the more she recognized they were
dreams as they happened.
But within her waking dream, she would smile.
She indulged in the happiness of her dreams, knowing they repre-
sented times that would never return.

*   *   *

Food was set on the table.

It was a meal she cooked with her mother.

Her father ate it and smiled, said it was delicious.

She would smile again.

That symbolic process repeated over and over.

Just a repetition of the most orthodox, simplistic series of events, so standard that if *happy home* appeared in a dictionary, this would be the definition. She'd seen the dreams so often that she knew exactly what would produce smiles in each and every one. There was no need for any other action. She just repeated the process.

That was enough for Anri.

She was fine with the happiness in her dream being a simple, predictable, repetitive process. That was what it took to get her to smile. She could relive the same dream over and over without growing tired of it.

She convinced herself that this was true happiness. And she *was* truly happy.

Perhaps it didn't look like happiness to someone else, but this was the world of her dreams. No one else could see it for themselves.

In her dreams, she was in early elementary school. She would talk to her dream parents with a face full of innocence.

"Mom, Dad, we'll be together forever and ever."

Her parents grinned and nodded, and the dream ended there.

It was the same dream every single time, and it ended at the same point every single time.

Together forever and ever. It was like a magical mantra that ensured she would have the same dream the next night.

The same process. The same happiness.

She felt that happiness over and over and over, as regular and predictable as breathing.

And on this particular day, just like any other day, she would wake from that dream.

Anri's eyes opened to take in the morning sunlight filtering through her curtains.

The sleepiness was gone. The last words she spoke to her parents in the dream were always the alarm that snapped her out of the final REM sleep of the night.

Anri stretched and hopped off the bed to trot to the bathroom in her pajamas.

Before she washed her face, she looked at her reflection in the mirror—blurred without the help of her glasses—and smiled.

But when the reality of her parents' death set in, the smile faded a bit, turned cynical and self-deprecating.

Anri's parents were dead.

It had happened five years earlier. So she would never again taste the happiness that she found in her dreams.

It was in her dreams that she sought what was impossible in reality.

It wasn't that she could have whatever dream she wanted. In fact, the first time she had the dream, she hadn't been hoping for it.

In the dream, she just lived with her parents, with no upheaval or excitement. But after they died, she began having the dream more and more often. Now she experienced it every single night.

A popular theory said that dreams were the brain subconsciously processing memories, but that would mean that her brain cells were processing the same things over and over. Taking out something that was already neat and ordered, then rearranging it into the exact same pattern. If that process was completely pointless, Anri certainly didn't let it bother her.

At first, it felt completely empty.

Dreams were hollow things, producing nothing, providing no solace.

But as the dream came to her again and again, Anri changed her mind very quickly.

Was it really just a hollow fiction?

Yes, the table and the meal sitting atop it were false. No amount of eating would provide her real body with any nutrition.

But what about the emotion?

In her dreams, Anri felt happiness. She felt her heart being at ease.

Was an emotion produced by a fiction really false? Did that mean the emotions she felt when watching a movie were utter lies as well?

No. That wasn't true.

Anri denied the fiction. Movies weren't fiction. Whatever happened on the screen was *real*. And if that was true, then the events in her dream that moved her heart were just as real.

Since then, Anri had the same dream every night.

She indulged in a happiness of her own creation, over and over and over...

But in the real world, she was just a bit—just a *bit* further away from happiness.

The horrible incident that had taken her parents' lives was five years in the past.

And Anri Sonohara still couldn't find where her life belonged.

♂♀

At the same time that Celty bolted out of her apartment, Anri Sonohara was wandering.

All through Ikebukuro without a destination.

The end-of-term exams were over, and only graduation and the end of the school year ceremonies were left. So she walked about the town with a goal in mind.

A goal, but not a destination.

She didn't know where she should go, but she wasn't in a mood to hang around her house. So she wandered the neighborhood.

The night was cold despite the imminent arrival of spring, and its chill winds tore mercilessly through Anri. She took in the sights of the town through her glasses as she walked and suffered the cold.

The usual waves of humanity. It seemed like the ratio of yellow bandannas was higher than before, but she didn't give it any more thought than that.

As the various people walked past her with their own various troubles in mind, Anri sought out just one of them.

Haruna Niekawa.

Anri was wandering the night in search of the girl one year her senior. She hadn't been back home. Once school had wrapped up, she came out here still dressed in her uniform. Raira Academy allowed for students to wear private clothes, but the uniform looked good and was suitably warm in the winter, so plenty of people wore it.

But when it came to the city at night, that number dropped precipitously. If you were out at night, chances were high that you'd still be out very late, and wearing a uniform just meant it was easier to be singled out by the police.

Anri wasn't planning to be wandering the streets that late, but she didn't know what the most effective time to return home was, either.

"...What should I do?"

It was an honest lament of her present situation.

So why was Anri searching for Haruna Niekawa?

The answer to that question came earlier in the afternoon.

And the cause was nothing other than Nasujima's fixation on her.

"Hey, Anri... Have you finished all your preparations for the Raikou Festival?"

The Raikou Festival was an event held the day after graduation along with the remaining students of the school, a type of thank-you party. Participation was optional, but because the class representatives of the underclassmen were central to the planning, Anri and Mikado were enrolled by default, and the preparations for the event were ongoing.

It was after school, and Anri was walking the empty halls on her way to get ready to leave, when Nasujima's imposing face loomed up, as though he'd been waiting to ambush her.

"Well, Anri? You're here awfully late again... Is everything all right?"

"Um, yes..."

She felt a small measure of unease and fear at the fact that he was calling her Anri now. If he'd started off calling her that, she would have told herself he was just one of those teachers who used first names...but until recently, he was calling her Sonohara. Now she was Anri to him.

It made her feel like the distance had suddenly shrunk between them. Perhaps that was exactly Nasujima's intent.

After she saw her personal bullies attacked by the slasher and had to undergo police questioning, Anri was nearly caught by a TV

interviewer for a segment. She barely managed to escape, thanks to
the arrival of Mikado, who had come out of concern for her. But given
the stress of the encounter, she took several days off of school to let
things calm down.

The final exams were starting just as she came back, and thanks to
her diligent studying, she did just fine on the tests. Things were slowly
getting back to normal, until…

"I thought you'd still be taking a break from school. Why didn't you
just tell me you were feeling better, Anri?"

She had no reason to report something like that to an instructor
who wasn't even her homeroom teacher. She didn't tell him anything
specific at all, but Nasujima kept badgering her.

"Don't you know how worried I was? They say that Nomura was
the one who got attacked, and she was apparently one of those bullies
harassing you… Why were you together? Were they picking on you
again? I'm worried for you…so, so worried. But more importantly, I'm
worried about that street slasher. I know you said you didn't see a face
on TV, but the slasher might think you *did* see him!"

He had found his perfect excuse—feigned concern over the incident.
The other teachers simply avoided the topic out of consideration for
Anri, or ignored her to sidestep the trouble entirely, or showed obvious and honest concern—but Nasujima was the first to reference the
attack directly to her face.

Today was the first time she'd seen Nasujima since coming back
to school. It was almost as though he'd been waiting to catch her in
another lonely situation with no one around.

"Are you sure you want to be waiting around here this late? Don't
you think it would be safer to have someone escort you home?"

He wasn't even bothering to hide it. Anri's willpower helped her
resist the urge to turn her face away in disgust.

She just wanted to live in peace and quiet.

Her dreams every night gave her the happiness she needed. So she
didn't expect much from reality. She just wanted to avoid trouble.

That was exactly why she wasn't sure if she should reject the teacher's advances explicitly. She was already garnering enough attention
because of the slasher attack. If she raised a fuss about sexual harassment from a teacher next, that attention might turn against her.

Besides, even if she complained to someone about Nasujima's actions, what he was actually *doing* wasn't against any rules. The best she could do was raise a new rumor among the girls, and that was altogether too risky. If Nasujima claimed that she was the one who tried to seduce *him*, she might be forced to transfer schools.

She was fine with being shunned. She felt that no matter what happened to her, Mikado and Masaomi would take her side and believe her. That showed how much she trusted them, but it also caused her to realize something else.

I really am just leeching off of Ryuugamine and Kida after all.

But she didn't feel much regret about this. That was just the way she lived.

The problem was that the teachers and the school system were not that simple to deal with. If she caused a stir and caught the wrong kind of attention, the school might grow concerned with outward appearances. In that case, Anri would be forced to transfer whether she liked it or not.

On the other hand, she couldn't just let Nasujima continue to have the wrong idea about her. If she didn't stand up to him at some point, her peace of mind would be threatened in a different way. In fact, it already was.

In normal circumstances, she could just come out and say it plainly. But now, when Nasujima was in what Masaomi might call his "blown-fuse" mode, there was no telling how he might react. On the other hand, if she tried to be subtle about it, he wouldn't pay any attention.

Anri was so troubled about this turn of events that she started treading down the path toward the worst possible conclusion: that transferring schools was her best option.

Transfer... Yes, that's an option...

As she weighed the idea, Anri recalled a piece of information that Masaomi had taught her—and decided to try to *rattle* the teacher a bit.

"...Then, do you think I should hide myself by transferring schools...?"

"N-no! You shouldn't worry about that. The security here is absolute. You know that, right?"

Anri recalled an event a few days after the start of school, when a man in black and a mysterious motorcyclist went on a violent rampage, but she chose not to bring that up. It occurred to her now that it was the Black Rider that the whole city was talking about, but that didn't matter now. She ignored it.

"But…I was seen wearing my school uniform…and there are plenty of other schools in the area that I can attend… And, um…Miss Niekawa transferred to a local school, didn't she?"

Nasujima's expression shifted dramatically within an instant.

His reddish, tanned face rapidly went pale blue, and though his eyes were still pointed in Anri's direction, they were losing focus and looking through her to a point far in the distance.

His eyeballs rattled and shook as he regained his focus, and he put on a smile that didn't extend beyond his mouth. He spoke hesitantly, trying to ascertain where she was coming from.

"Wh-what's this, Sonohara? You know Niekawa?"

"No, not directly… I just remember when people were saying she transferred, since she had an uncommon name," Anri replied, looking away slightly.

Nasujima's eyes were still shaking. "Ah, I…I see. Y-yeah, Niekawa was my student last year. I think she moved to a school in west Ikebukuro. But hey, that doesn't really matter, does it?"

He was trying to force the conversation to a different subject, and it showed. Anri was now certain that something had happened between Nasujima and this Niekawa girl, and it was the cause for her transfer.

But why was he so panicked now? Anri couldn't help but wonder, but no matter what it was, it had nothing to do with her.

"Well, sir, I should be going."

She bowed politely so as not to sound nasty and turned to leave. What she didn't see when she turned her back was that Nasujima's hand reached out to grab her shoulder, only to swing through empty air.

Rather than following or trying to pull her back, Nasujima stayed put, his menacing face looking even darker and uglier as he watched her go.

The expression contained elements of anger, of longing, and terror that she might be onto something about him…

Only Nasujima knew exactly what that was, and when the school bell rang emptily down the hallway, it wiped the look off of his face.

I'm such a horrible person.

Anri was calmly analyzing her own actions as she watched the night streets in search of Haruna Niekawa. Technically, it wasn't correct to say that she was "searching" for Niekawa. She had no trail, no clues to follow, so it was less a search than a chance to sort out her own thoughts under the guise of searching for the girl.

If she somehow managed to find Niekawa, what would she even ask? How would she approach her? There was no way she could walk up out of the blue and ask, "Were you in a relationship with Mr. Nasujima?"

Even if I don't ask directly, I might be able to figure out that there was something between them...and that could be the leg up I need to "convince" Mr. Nasujima to leave me alone.

It didn't need to be anything major. She just needed material that she could use to keep him away from her.

I really am horrible.

She was using Haruna Niekawa's past as a tool to put distance between herself and Nasujima, knowing full well that the girl probably bore emotional scars from that past.

Anri knew that she was a shallow, self-interested person, but she had no intention of changing her plan.

In the end, I value my own peace of mind most of all. That's why I'm going to use Miss Niekawa as a stepping-stone. I'm an awful human being. But maybe I actually enjoy this way of life.

Right after school started and Mikado helped her out of trouble, he'd seen right through that aspect of her and pointed it out.

But...he decided to be my friend anyway.

After the loss of Mika Harima, her previous host, this was a pure joy to Anri, and it was why she was determined not to let Nasujima ruin it for her.

She wandered the town.

Searching for the shadow of Haruna Niekawa.

I wonder if she truly loved him. Or if she regretted the way she lived her life. How did she feel about Mr. Nasujima?

It was a matter of personal curiosity. While the information wasn't necessary to Anri, she found herself more and more intrigued by those details in the hours since she'd escaped from Nasujima.

There was a reason for that curiosity. Something had been wrong with Nasujima earlier.

The reaction he had when she mentioned Niekawa's name wasn't just panic at the thought of his relationship to her being revealed— there was actual fear mixed in.

Not the kind of fear of losing his job if those salacious details were made public. Those things were already the subject of Masaomi's rumor mills, and if he was afraid of being fired, he wouldn't be messing with a student.

What had happened between Nasujima and Niekawa?

While the mystery was alluring, Anri forced herself to suppress the curiosity.

It was an emotion she didn't need in the life she'd chosen for herself.

"Excuse me, miss."

Anri looked up with a start when she realized the voice was directed at her. There were two policemen standing dead ahead.

"Y-yes...?"

Anri was confused, thinking that they were going to take her in for more questioning. She'd told them everything she knew about the attack. What more could there be?

But the policemen didn't know that she was a witness in the recent attack. One of them pointed to his watch and warned her with concern in his voice, "It's almost eleven o'clock. You should be home by now."

"Oh..."

Anri was surprised to learn that she'd been walking the town for so long. Thanks to the frequency of the slasher attacks, the number of police patrols was through the roof now.

As a result, the number of minors out enjoying Ikebukuro late at night was vastly decreased. Of course, most people who stayed out late had moved on to other night districts like Shibuya to continue their business.

"Oh, already? S-sorry, I'll go home right away!"

"Take care, miss."

Her straitlaced appearance apparently helped her escape any further questioning, but if she didn't go right home, she'd only end up in actual trouble before long.

Anri bowed several times to the officers and started on her way home.

"Hang on. If your home is nearby, shall we escort you there?" he asked in a voice devoid of Nasujima's ulterior motive.

If they were offering, perhaps she ought to take them up on it. In all honesty, though, Anri felt more worried about an ambush from Nasujima than from the slasher.

She didn't think he would stoop to that, but there was no eliminating that nagging possibility in the back of her mind.

I might as well...

But just as Anri opened her mouth to respond, both officers suddenly raised a hand to one ear, their faces serious. She realized that they must be wearing earpieces and receiving some kind of message.

"...Roger that. We're on our way. C'mon, Mr. Kuzuhara."

"Sorry, young lady. We've got something to respond to. Take care on your way home. If you want, you can also stop by the police box next to the Parco and wait for an escort."

The officer named Kuzuhara and his younger partner melted into the night crowd.

"Ah..."

Anri tried to stop them for just a moment, then sighed and turned back on her way. She didn't desire an escort enough to wait around at the police box for one, and if they were going to break up a fight, there was no telling when they'd be back.

Anri turned her back on the bright town and headed down a silent, empty side street. If she went straight down this way, her apartment would be just ahead, she told herself to calm her nerves.

But she didn't realize that she was being followed.

The eyes watching Anri's back were red, so red.
Redder than anything...

"Demon blade?" Shizuo read off of Celty's screen, raising an eyebrow.

When she tore out of the mansion and headed back to pick up Shizuo as she'd promised, Celty knew she owed him a proper explanation. She couldn't help but worry, though, that he'd punch her when he read the term *demon blade*.

"Yes, I know it sounds unbelievable...but it's a sword with a mind of its own that possesses people."

Even as Celty typed it out in all seriousness, she realized how stupid it all sounded.

Who's going to believe in this nonsense?

"All right, gotcha. Let's go."

—?!

"You believe me? I mean, I'm not sure if I believe it myself yet," Celty said incredulously. Shizuo looked directly at her, wonder in his eyes.

"Is this demon blade weirder than a motorcycle steered by a Headless Rider driving sideways along the wall of the Tokyu Hands building?"

"...Good point. My bad."

She didn't bear any fault, but Celty couldn't help herself from apologizing. Shizuo was already on the rear of the bike, though, balancing himself expertly as he waited for the driver.

"A blade dies if you snap it in half, right? And hell, I'll still kill it, whether it can die or not," Shizuo muttered, quiet rage smoldering in his eyes. It was as though the murderous rage that had built up within him during work was boiling itself into a caramelized state.

Celty found that both reassuring and terrifying. She straddled the motorcycle, feeling the same nerves she felt that one time she transported nitroglycerin.

The dullahan's familiar, that pitch-black bike, took its terrible, ferocious engine whinnying into the night.

Thus the accumulation of power focused into a single point known as Shizuo Heiwajima joined the speedy engine known as Celty Sturluson in prowling Ikebukuro without a clear destination, exuding a different kind of fear from that which the stalker spread...

♂♀

Meanwhile, a strangled yelp sounded inside a van crawling around Ikebukuro.

"You have to stop... You have to stop replacing the word *brief* with *ephemeral* and thinking that makes your sentences sound cooler!"

"Is this that age where you like taking contrary opinions on everything, Yumacchi?"

"Denying all the common sense of ordinary adult opinions might make you more popular with antisocial teenagers…but stop thinking that way, too! Stop saying that all power is evil, when you don't have the knowledge or determination to back that up! If you got wrapped up in some violent nonsense, you'd be begging the power of the police for help, and you know it!"

"You're at that age where you think bashing ideology and society makes you look cool, but all it does is make you shallow. The thing is, actual adults are smart enough to take that social criticism and write cool stuff about it."

Yumasaki was bellowing as he read passages from a book in his hands, while Karisawa inserted her own barbed reactions. Their back-and-forth woke up Kadota, who stretched in the backseat.

"You idiots. Whether a book is shallow or deep, as long as it *suits your taste*, who cares… And I don't think I've ever heard Yumasaki making fun of a book before. What's he reading?"

"Oh, um…well…"

Yumasaki was at a loss for words. Karisawa cackled at her partner's consternation and answered for him.

"Oh, it's this novel he self-published a while back."

"…Okay, I have a whole lot of comments about that, but I'll save them. More importantly, I know that it's rich of me to say this when I was just taking a nap, but can you seriously get to collecting intel? One of our group was attacked, remember? Put the same effort into it as when Kaztano was kidnapped."

Kaztano was a foreign guy in their group. Rumors said he was an illegal immigrant, but they didn't care about that. When Yagiri Pharmaceuticals' henchmen abducted Kaztano a while back, Yumasaki and Karisawa developed a number of horrendous torture methods on the men responsible.

"Okay, but Dotachin, Kaztano is our friend, so that's one thing. But we don't actually know the person who got hit. I mean, just because they're in the Dollars doesn't mean…"

"Seriously? You can't even have the courtesy to shed a tear for someone else?"

One of the Dollars had been hit by the street slasher, and yet Yumasaki and Karisawa were carrying on like any other day. Kadota knew that was both their weakness and their strength, but he felt it was worth the warning anyway.

"I think it's sad, but I choose to feel nothing."

"I cannot forgive the slasher, but I choose to feel nothing."

Kadota raised an eyebrow at the phrase they repeated.

"...What do you mean?"

"In my heart."

"...Is this another stupid manga or novel phrase?"

"Yes, it's from *Lunatic Moon*. Heh-heh, whenever something bad happens, you just shut your heart and feel nothing. Life's a breeze if you never let your emotions get heightened."

Kadota cut Yumasaki off before he could explain more of his twisted views on life.

"I told you, stop assuming that everyone in the world has read the same books as you have! Anyway...is it true that you actually want a breezy life?"

"My desire for a tumultuous life of excitement is powerful, but I choose to feel nothing. But enough about that. Recently I realized something. For one, there *aren't* seven mystical balls that once gathered will grant any wish. Also, there isn't a shrine near my house that houses a magical fox spirit named Kugen that transforms into a beautiful girl. Also, there's some road construction happening at night out in front of my place, but there aren't even any vampires working there! Plus the Black Rider won't grant my wishes, and the dream demon babe hasn't shown up since then!"

Wait, you seriously didn't know all of those things until now? Also, what the hell is this dream demon he keeps bringing up?

Kadota had no end of questions to ask, but he couldn't bring himself to overcome the sad, fiery look in Yumasaki's eyes.

"So you see, I've learned patience and self-control! I don't ask for much; I just want a simple, peaceful life! Basically, I just want to visit abroad and adopt an adorable little girl with green hair, then move back to Japan right next door to three beautiful sisters and have a heartwarming life, that's all! Is that too much to ask?!"

"Is that *Yotsuba&!*? That's *Yotsuba&!*, isn't it?" Karisawa interjected, grinning madly. Kadota finally came to his senses and shut down the fun.

"First of all, yes, it's too much to ask, and second of all, shut up about manga already!"

"*Eeep!*" Yumasaki shrieked, shrinking into a ball.

Kadota turned away with a huff and looked out the window. "This is about the spot where the girl from Raira got slashed last month," he muttered.

They were crawling along a road a short way away from the business center. Kadota was irritated that one of their group had been attacked, yet they still had no information about it. So they rotated around to the various attack locations. He was hoping to discover some kind of common link between them, but so far they'd had no luck.

Behind him, Yumasaki was already babbling on about if they drew a diagram that connected all the attack locations, a demon would be summoned at the center. At this point, Kadota realized it would be pointless to tell him off.

As he grumpily stared out the window, his eyes eventually settled on a single teenage girl walking on her own.

She had glasses and plain, undyed hair, which suggested that she wasn't looking for trouble. It was almost unnatural to see someone like her, wearing her school uniform and everything, out this late.

"Ah, geez, how careless can you get? This is exactly what gets you targeted. Doesn't even have to be by the slasher—she could easily get abducted by folks like us driving a creepy-lookin' van around," he grumbled. After they passed the girl, he turned his eyes back to the road ahead... until he noticed the presence of a suspicious man.

His age was uncertain. There was nothing particularly noteworthy about his outfit, except that he was wearing a rather thick coat, given that the weather was warming up lately.

But far more notable than that—

"Were that guy's eyes...red?"

♂♀

Was Officer Kuzuhara back there...the father of that Kuzuhara boy from the Discipline Committee at school? Anri wondered, noting the similarities in the faces of the policeman she'd just encountered and the boy from her class. Her apartment was just about to come into view.

She suddenly stopped in the middle of the street, which was neither wide nor narrow.

It was the very spot where Anri's bully had been attacked.

She dropped her eyes to the asphalt. There were no bloodstains anymore.

Why did that happen?

Anri shook her head, feeling miserable. Was it just simple coincidence that the girl was cut down right before her eyes? Or was there some kind of fate at work?

Maybe...in fact, it must have been...

Just as she was searching for an answer within her memory...

A man stood right behind her.

He pulled a blade out of his coat and took a silent step forward.

The blade swung high up into the night air.

♂♀

"Oh, shit! He's got a weapon!"

Togusa's shout from the driver's seat shot through the van. Kadota and the others looked forward through the windshield from the backseat to see a tense scene playing out.

At the side of the road was the uniformed girl, face down and back turned—and a man in the middle of the road raising a blade and slowly approaching her from behind.

Kadota had noticed the man's odd behavior and told Togusa to turn the van around after they'd passed originally, and they were finally at the same street heading the other way—and sure enough, they were witnessing the slasher at work at this very moment.

But he already had his weapon in the air. He didn't seem to notice the lights or engine noise of the van, as he didn't turn toward them in the least.

Yet they were still too far away to reach him if they got out of the car and ran. Kadota thought for a second and called out to the driver, "Togusa, can you do something crazy?"

"What's that?"

The sharp-eyed driver jammed down on the gas pedal, clearly anticipating what Kadota was about to say. He delivered the expected order.

"Run him over."

♂♀

A car horn blared, jolting Anri back to reality.

She quickly pressed her back to the wall and looked toward the headlights to see a large van barreling down.

And just in front of her, there was a man with full red eyes, holding a blade pointed at her.

"Red" eyes could certainly be explained as so bloodshot that the whites appeared red. But there was too much blood involved here, if that was the case.

There was no white left in his eyeballs. They were simply points of glinting black pupil in the midst of red spheres.

"…!"

Anri grasped the situation and was turning to run—

—when the van slammed into the slasher with merciless force.

♂♀

Celty and Shizuo patrolled the streets of Ikebukuro without a clear destination. Shizuo was wearing a pitch-black helmet, hastily fashioned out of shadow by Celty.

It wasn't for the sake of avoiding trouble with the vastly increased number of police officers out. After all, Celty's motorcycle didn't have a license plate or even a headlight and chases with traffic cops were a regular occurrence for her.

But if that happened tonight, Shizuo stood to wind up in trouble if his face was spotted. So she made him a full-faced helmet to hide his identity. Of course, he was still in his distinct bartender's outfit, so anyone who knew him would recognize him anyway.

Still, I can't aimlessly wander around without any leads.

Barely any of the attacks had occurred in the bustling shopping

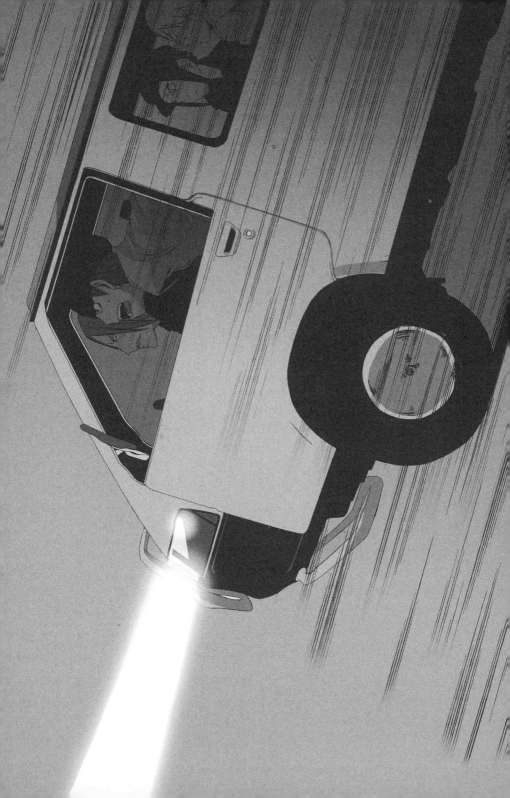

district, and there were too many cops. But even the full police force didn't have enough men to stake out every single street, so Celty was able to travel around using back alleys.

If the Saika in the chat is the actual slasher, today's attack was already announced in advance.

If she wandered around too much on her own, people might assume that the Black Rider had to be the street slasher, but the danger of that was lessened if she had a passenger with her, Celty assumed. That made Shizuo's presence a bonus, it seemed, but...

I was naive.

While they were waiting at a light, some people with yellow bandannas decided to stare them down. Celty was used to this and perfectly content to ignore it—but today she had Shizuo with her.

He stepped down off the idling bike and walked over to the youngsters before Celty could stop him.

"When you point a knife at someone, you lose the right to complain if they kill you in self-defense," he started to lecture, his helmet still in place. The young men, who weren't carrying any knives, were completely baffled.

He continued to deliver his sermon to the Yellow Scarves, who were looking more irritated by the moment.

"Listen, stares can kill. Whether it's a curse or a magical death stare, the possibility of it killing a person is at least as high as 0.0000000000 00000000000000000000000675 percent."

The boys' misfortune was that Shizuo's helmet covered his face and that they didn't notice the significance of his bartender's outfit. The Yellow Scarves hadn't realized that they'd picked a fight with none other than Shizuo Heiwajima.

"Huh? Dude, what the hell are you talking ab—?"

"I'm saying, if you stare down a man, *you aren't gonna complain if he l-ill*—"

What followed was ten seconds of absolute hell.

Shizuo clobbered the three men in an instant. He didn't just accept their challenge; he welcomed it.

Celty pulled him away and drove off, but there was no doubt that multiple police officers would be converging on the scene in no time.

Even as they rode away, they passed two officers rushing in the other direction. She recognized one of them, a pushy senior patrol officer at the local police box named Kuzuhara.

Crap, crap, crap.

She wheeled the bike around to avoid attention and sent it racing in the opposite direction of where the officers had come from. She didn't want any police attention right now.

Once they were safely free, they resumed their steady patrol of the local streets. Suddenly, the part of Celty's shadow that acted as her sense of hearing picked up the honk of a car horn, followed by a hard collision.

♂♀

As Anri pressed herself against the wall, wide-eyed, a number of people got down out of the van.

"Is he dead?"

"That was really messed up, Kadota! How can you act like this, just after I was telling you about my desire for a life of tranquillity?!"

Karisawa and Yumasaki didn't seem to be fazed in the least by the events. Only Kadota looked nervous as he stared down the street.

A few yards away from the van, a man lay sprawled out on the pavement. There were no major external wounds to be seen, and there didn't appear to be a pool of blood on the asphalt, either. There was a kitchen knife at least a foot long in his right hand.

Kadota eyed the knife and muttered, "Ahh, I see... It's a little too short, but someone in a panic who didn't know any better might confuse it for a katana."

After he was struck by the van, the man flew through the air and sprawled out magnificently upon impact with the ground. He hadn't budged since then.

Suddenly, the figure rose.

"!"

The silhouette got to its feet. His left arm was twisted at an unnatural angle. With the knife still gripped in his other hand, the bloodshot eyes glared *straight at Anri.*

"?!"

He looked to be in his late thirties or early forties. The middle-age man awkwardly began to stumble in Anri's direction.

"Hey! What the hell?!"

Kadota's group, assuming he was coming after them, were taken flat-footed for an instant—then snapped into action to stop the man. But he only paid them an instant's notice, swiping the knife sideways with incredible force.

"Whoa!"

The tip passed just in front of Kadota's nose with tremendous speed. Yumasaki and Karisawa behind him actually felt the breeze from the swing.

The slasher kept swinging with the same force, bouncing back and forth like a spring-loaded toy. Like a fan whose blades were all knives. The group couldn't very well do the child's game of stopping *this* fan with a finger—they were completely taken aback.

But the man wasn't even looking at them anymore.

He created an entire impassable sphere of spinning knife, gradually bringing the sphere closer and closer to Anri.

"Stop, you idiot!"

It was too late to hit him with the car again. Kadota recognized the gravity of the situation and was prepared to charge in at the risk of personal injury...

But the moment he began to step forward, a shadow passed by Kadota's side.

Celty's motorcycle, engine on silent, plunged right into the slasher while doing a wheelie.

The underside of the tire tore right through the knife's sphere of range, flattening the man beneath it.

Stunned by the series of action-movie scenes unfolding before her eyes, Anri didn't even conceive of running away.

"Ah..."

Then she realized that it was none other than the infamous Black Rider who had saved her and gasped with surprise.

The bike rode straight over the man and came to a stop a short distance away. There were two people on it—behind the monstrous black-suited rider was a man in a bartender's outfit who slowly stepped off. The rider followed him and turned to face the group.

"The Headless Rider...and...Shizuo?!" Kadota blurted out, recognizing the helmeted man in the bartender's outfit. But the instant he said the name Shizuo, the slasher on the ground suddenly sprang to his feet again.

"?!"

As Kadota and the others looked on in shock, the man finally spoke.

"Shizuo... So you're...Shizuo Heiwajima? Is that so? Are you Shizuo...*sweetie?*"

Kadota murmured, "Huh? Is he...a queen?"

"No, Dotachin, you're not actually a drag queen unless you're dressed as a woman," Karisawa explained patiently, but no one cared.

"Oh, I've been dying to meet you... I've been waiting and waiting and waiting and waiting and waiting and waiting...tee-hee!"

While his appearance was male, his speaking style was unmistakably feminine.

But even more alienating than that was the fact that there was no hint of damage from the way he was speaking, despite separate collisions with both a van and a motorcycle.

Shizuo took a quiet, menacing step forward and said, "Okay, I'm killing you."

"I'm so happy... Finally, finally, we meet. *My beloved.*"

"You're happy, huh? Then I'll kill you."

This conversation makes no sense, Celty and Kadota thought simultaneously, but neither wanted to set Shizuo off, so they kept that to themselves.

"I love you, Shizuo Heiwajima."

The middle-age man spoke words of love in a feminine tone to a person he'd never met before. Add to that the redness of his eyes, and it was clear he was not sane.

I see. He must be under the demon blade's spell. I just didn't expect it to be a kitchen knife...

Celty reached out a hand to Anri, who was slumped on her behind against the wall.

"Eeek!" she shrieked, but when she realized the Headless Rider meant her no harm, she timidly grasped the hand and used it to get to her feet.

"Are you okay? Not hurt?"

When Anri saw the message on the PDA screen, she looked with surprise at Celty's helmet. The only thing visible in the black visor was the reflection of the streetlights, and nothing beyond.

"Oh…yes. I'm…fine."

"Well, that's good. You might want to keep your distance," Celty typed for Anri, who was barely able to respond.

The dullahan turned to Shizuo and produced a shadow scythe within her hand, brandished it behind her, and advanced on the slasher.

So after knocking my helmet off last time, now it wants to ignore me entirely…

Irritated by this change in attitude for some reason, she wondered how to deal with both Shizuo and the slasher now.

Meanwhile, the slasher had stopped talking and was now slowly approaching Shizuo. He had the knife in his right hand held over at his left hip, an odd stance that resembled an *iai* quick-draw position.

But there's no point to doing an iai if it's not in a sheath to begin with. That's the whole point…

Yet the slasher's eyes were filled with mad confidence.

Based on the speed with which he swung the knife moments earlier, something was clearly wrong with him. But the veins still pulsed in Shizuo's temples, and he smiled quietly.

"I can't catch a blade with my bare hands."

Anyone who knew Shizuo well would understand just how dangerous that subdued, suppressed smile was. The instant Celty saw it, her goal shifted from how to crush the slasher to how to keep the slasher from dying.

She'd seen the man's hardiness for herself when he stood up after she ran him over with the bike. Even then, she couldn't possibly envision the man in the trench coat beating Shizuo.

"So if you wanna wave a knife at me…you can't complain when I murder you…"

Shizuo reached out toward the van stopped next to him. The slasher didn't know what Shizuo was doing, but the look in his twisted, supremely confident eyes said that he didn't care.

"There is nothing you can do to me. You really think you can avoid my sword? Let me tell you: one millimeter. That's all it takes—one tiny little scratch—for you and me to share our love."

Celty and Kadota were confused by this statement, but Yumasaki and Karisawa both reacted with surprise and excitement.

"Oh, there must be poison spread on the tip! Poison so powerful just a drop of it could knock out a dragon!"

"Or how about this? The kind that slowly eats away the victim from the inside, like with parasites or flower seeds or something!"

Nobody reacted to their nerdy brainstorming. Only the slasher himself put on a knowing smile. It seemed they might not be that far off.

If that was the case, it meant that Shizuo's personal fighting style, self-sacrificial "losing the battle to win the war," wasn't an option. Celty suddenly didn't feel so confident.

But she needn't have worried.

Shizuo, still wearing Celty's shadow helmet, turned to his conveniently present acquaintance and made a bizarre request.

"Hey, Kadota…I'll give your door right back."

"?"

Before Kadota could respond, Shizuo put a hand on the van's open rear side door and tore it off the hinges as easily as pulling a ticket apart.

——*Huh?*——

It was the opinion of every other person present.

Kadota, Yumasaki, and Karisawa.

Anri.

Celty.

Even the slasher.

He did it one-handed and didn't show any sign of effort in the process. He didn't put all of his weight into it, he just used his arm strength alone to pull the car door off.

As they all watched him in silence, Shizuo put his fingers through the inside handle and held the door aloft with his grip alone…pointing it toward the slasher.

"Uh…"

The slasher seemed to grasp Shizuo's intention, and unease colored his features for the first time. His *iai* stance and his secret wild card that required only a scratch were rendered meaningless.

Shizuo Heiwajima was using the van door like a giant shield, protecting his front side from the slasher.

"I live a messed-up life. I ain't nice enough to fight a man…with my bare hands!"

The instant he finished speaking, the asphalt at Shizuo's feet seemed to explode. The asphalt itself was perfectly fine, but his speed was so great that it tricked all of the witnesses' brains into viewing it that way.

The man with the door for a shield hurled himself at the enemy like a cannonball. Directly in a straight line. Simpleminded in its directness.

But the cannonball was too fast to be dodged. That's all it came down to. All of the slasher's tricks were nullified by sheer speed and strength. No one would ever know what those tricks were because he hadn't been given the time to deploy them.

"No…wait…"

Collision.

First, a *whud* sound.

Just the sound alone was enough to cause serious damage to the slasher's brain, but next came the actual vibration.

He might as well have been hit by an enormous hunk of metal. A vortex of strength thrust him upward. That hardy body, which had bounced right back from a collision with a van…

It's an even stronger impact…than the car?!

But by the time he realized that fact, his body was already afloat on the current of force transmitted via the slightly upturned shield.

The slasher had no time to think of resisting or breaking free before he was crushed between the shield and the wall at the side of the street.

The deadly battle against the slasher ended far too quickly, and suddenly the street was as silent as if nothing had ever happened.

No one spoke for several moments, until Togusa stepped out of the driver's seat and asked, "So who do I bill for the door repairs?"

Only then did they regain their senses.

*   *   *

"What do we do with him?" Shizuo asked, gently pulling the door away from the wall. Behind it was a man whose body was half-embedded in the crumbled concrete. He peeled off of the wall and crumpled to the ground.

Celty took out her PDA and showed Shizuo her opinion.

"Well, first we have to figure out if he's being possessed by the blade or just an actual street slasher doing this under his own discretion. We should take the weapon away and tie him up until he wakes. If he's only a puppet, it doesn't seem fair to put him at the mercy of the police."

Assuming he wakes up at all, she thought, examining the man's face. *Huh?*

Suddenly, Celty felt as though she recognized that face. She beckoned Shizuo over.

"What?"

Shizuo was already cooling off from his fury. His face was calm as he looked down at the man.

The man's eyes flew open, exposing the bloodred eyeballs.

"!"

Celty and Shizuo both leaped back. The slasher looked at them and groaned, "I suppose...I can't handle you. I always knew you were abnormal..."

He seemed to have given up on beating Shizuo. Celty started to type a question into her PDA, keeping her guard up, but she barely had time to start.

"But if I can't have you...I'll settle for *her!*" the slasher cried, leaping to his feet.

Right for Anri Sonohara, who was timidly watching events unfold at a slight distance.

"...Uh," she stammered, unsure of what was happening.

The man everyone assumed was in critical condition leaped for her, knife in the air.

Shudd.

A dull sound rang out, and the slasher's knife plunged deep into her breast.

The breast of Celty Sturluson covered in black shadows.

"—!"

Anri shrieked soundlessly, her entire body tense.

But not a single drop of blood dripped from Celty's chest. She clamped down on the wrist holding the knife and extracted it from her chest through arm strength alone.

Next, she flipped the slasher's feet out from under him, pulled his hand with the knife around behind his back, and shoved him into the ground.

His joints locked, the slasher was completely immobilized. Once he realized that no amount of strength would allow him to move, the man spat with loathing.

"You...you're not human, are you? Filthy! Abhorrent! How can my pure love be defiled by such a *stupid-looking* monster?!"

Well, excuse me, you —— —— piece of —.

Celty tried out one of the insults she'd liked from the last Tarantino film she saw and increased her pressure on the arm held behind his back.

There was an odd *grunch* sound, and the slasher's arm was suddenly not where it had been before. The knife fell out of his hand and clattered onto the asphalt. He had finally gone entirely silent, apparently unconscious at last.

Celty suddenly realized how angry she'd gotten and shook her head to clear it.

If Shinra found out I'd called this guy a —— —— piece of ——, he'd be so disgusted. I have to watch myself, she reflected idly.

Celty left the man sprawled out on the ground and looked up at the knife ahead.

Who would have guessed that Saika was just a kitchen knife?

She assumed that it would be dangerous to touch it herself, so she increased the shadow density around her hands to twice the normal level before pinching the handle delicately.

She still didn't sense anything special from it. Either Shinra was right and the demon blade didn't have a presence of its own, or there was no cursed sword to begin with...

I really should have just asked him if he was Saika.

But in any case, the slasher was dispatched. The only thing left was to wait for the man to regain consciousness. She could explain the situation to Kadota and Yumasaki and have them handle the rest.

But for now, the knife needed to be disposed of. If she used Shinra's connections, she could probably find a blast furnace to toss it into. She fashioned a net of shadow to hang from the underside of the motorcycle and stashed the knife inside of it.

With that out of the way, she pulled out her PDA and started to explain the situation to Kadota, but Shizuo's quiet monologue interrupted her.

"What the hell...? I just don't feel satisfied... Why is that?" he wondered, his face growing more and more upset by the moment. "Ahh, dammit, I just don't feel right... I'm gonna head to Shinjuku and kill Izaya."

He tossed the shadow helmet back to Celty. It dissipated like mist in her hands, reabsorbing itself into her body.

Shizuo left the scene with no apparent concern for that otherworldly effect. No one made a move to stop him, despite his announced intent to commit murder. They knew that Izaya wasn't the kind of man who would go down easily, of course, but first and foremost, none of them felt like they would be capable of stopping Shizuo.

Karisawa watched him walk away, her cheeks rosy red.

"I just knew Shizu was in love with Iza-Iza all along. I've always had the feeling that behind closed doors, they were actually—"

"That's not true."

The answer came from Celty's PDA, Kadota, and Yumasaki all at once. Yumasaki covered her mouth with his hands, his heart quaking in his chest.

"If you ever say that within earshot, they'll pound you into mincemeat!"

Celty tried to imagine the sight of Shizuo and Izaya making love. A feeling of nausea rushed up from deep within her. Then again, she couldn't expel anything from her severed neck but shadows anyway.

It was surprisingly easy to explain matters to Kadota's group.

She was expecting them to doubt her story, but the mention of a cursed demon blade got Yumasaki and Karisawa on board immediately with sparkles in their eyes.

On top of that, when she said that Saika was a demon blade with a female personality, Yumasaki shrieked something about "moe personification of inanimate objects" and tried to grab the knife from its storage space under her bike. The rest of the group battered him to a pulp and tossed him into the van along with the slasher.

They would be capable of handling the rest. She instructed them to call Shinra if they needed help, but otherwise everything should resolve itself. If he was being controlled, he was just another unfortunate victim of the incident—but given that he attacked Shizuo and still survived, perhaps he should actually consider himself to be fortunate, Celty tried to tell herself.

If we find out he did nothing wrong, I'll have to send him some support money or something...

When she turned around, the girl with the glasses was timidly staring at her.

Oh, I forgot.

Celty stared at the victim and wondered what to do. How much should she explain? If she chased the girl away, she might call the police. Then again, the local residents might have heard the uproar and called them already. Celty just wanted to extract herself from the scene as quietly as possible.

But when she got a better look at the girl's face, Celty realized something.

She's the girl I always see with Mikado Ryuugamine...

Mikado Ryuugamine.

The founder of the Dollars was one of the few people who was aware of Celty's nature, one of the most secretly influential people in the neighborhood. And yet, hardly anyone actually knew that Mikado had created the Dollars.

She spotted him in town every now and then, and he was usually in a group of three.

There was the girl with the glasses right here and another boy with dyed brown hair and earrings. They were almost always together, so she didn't know the full nature of their connection.

The girl looked up at Celty and said sadly, "Umm...thank you for saving me..."

Despite the timid look on her face, the girl took a major step forward into the incident that had just engulfed her.

"Um, can you tell me…what's happening in this neighborhood?"

Ack.

Celty wasn't hoping for thanks to begin with, but she'd have much preferred if the girl had just thanked her and run off. But she did have one question of her own.

Why had the slasher under Saika's control decided to go after *her* at the very end?

Perhaps it was just a desperation move, or maybe he had some other reason. If that was the case, she couldn't just ignore the girl.

After a long time to think, Celty shook her helmet in resignation and began typing away on her PDA, explaining all about the serial slashings happening in Ikebukuro and even the demon blade Saika…

But once she had finished typing out the whole story, the girl named Anri asked her something completely unrelated to the incident.

"So, um…about your…"

That question again. Celty inwardly snorted at her own luck. Recently, every single person who would talk to her asked the same thing. The TVs were obsessed with the topic of the Headless Rider, so when people found out that she was actually quite easy to talk to, they all got curious. They couldn't help themselves.

She wants to know if I really don't have a head.

Celty typed out, "*Don't be scared,*" imagining the timid girl screaming in terror, then yanked the helmet off without any fanfare.

Well? Your move.

But Anri was completely silent. As though she were waiting for Celty's next comment.

"*…You aren't startled?*"

"Uh, well, I know that you didn't have a head because they said so on TV…so I wanted to ask *why* you didn't have a head…and then I realized what a rude question that is! I'm sorry, I hope I didn't anger you!"

The girl bowed in apology, tears in her eyes. Now it was Celty's turn to be taken aback.

Shinra, Mikado, the kids in the van, Shizuo…

Are all young people like this now? Celty wondered. She leisurely typed into her PDA.

"It's a very long story... If you give me your e-mail address, I can tell you in detail later."

She meant it to be considerate to the girl, but Anri replied, "Oh, um...I don't have an Internet connection..."

"Oh...too bad. Well, we can't just stand around here all night..."

Celty was beginning to wonder if she should just go home and leave this all behind, when Anri lifted her head and spoke with determination.

"Actually...my place is just up ahead. Would you like to come in and have a cup of tea?"

♂♀

Late night, near Kawagoe Highway, apartment building

"Welcome home, Celty."

"*I'm back.*"

She walked inside to find Shinra waiting for her. It looked like he had nodded off on his desk while looking something up.

"Man, the researching I did! I was looking up all this different stuff on Saika. It was really complicated. Very hard to put all the text together into a coherent picture."

"*I see... Thank you, Shinra.*"

"But of course, I'd do a millennium of work in a day for your sake, Celty. After that, they'll have to change the definition of the word *millennium!*"

He laughed excitedly while Celty regretfully typed, "*But it's all over already. I'm sorry.*"

"Huh?"

... thing that had happened in the day and carefully placed the shadow-wrapped knife on the table.

"*Don't touch it, you might get possessed.*"

Shinra stared at the object on the table with fascination in his eyes. Ten seconds later he turned to Celty, a question mark floating over his head.

"This…is Saika? It's just a knife," he muttered, wide-eyed.

"I know, I was taken aback, too…but the man who was holding it had bloodred eyes, and he was going on about love and other nonsense and speaking like a woman," Celty typed regretfully.

"Ahh… I guess this must be it, then."

"But what's the connection between attacking people on the street and love? That's the thing I don't get. Is Saika just a sadist or what?" she asked. It had been on her mind before, but she didn't expect to bring it back up, given that the incident was over now.

"Oh…I guess I didn't go over that part, did I?" Shinra said, as though it were obvious or trivial. He made a show of clearing his throat, then leaned back in his desk chair and began to describe Saika's desires.

"What Saika wants…is to love a human being."

♂♀

The same time, Anri's apartment

My heart is still racing.

She'd hardly ever had people over at her home. The only ones in the year that she'd been living here were Mikado and Masaomi.

And today, she had granted entrance to someone she had barely shared introductions with—and not human, to boot.

This was quite an adventurous move for Anri, but she couldn't resist her curiosity about the otherworldly being. Her debt at being saved added to her momentum, a few other emotions rolled into the mix, and before she knew it, the Headless Rider was inside her home.

The rider explained many things.

The reason for coming here, what a dullahan was, various experiences in Ikebukuro, and what little of the homeland remained within the corners of those memories.

All of these things were vivid and fresh, and Anri noticed that they made her excited.

They talked about many things, up to the moment the rider left. Anri told her a bit about herself, but it probably wasn't very interesting. She didn't even remember the things she had said.

I wonder what she thinks about most days. I wonder what she thinks about human beings.

Even after the excitement faded, Anri thought back on all the things Celty said.

She said a dullahan knows when a person's death is approaching...but does that include unexpected accidents?

She thought back on the incident that changed her life five years ago and looked down.

If I'd known about it ahead of time...could I have stopped it from happening?

She could wish, but there was nothing she could do about it now. And she could see her parents every night in her dreams. There was nothing to agonize over now.

But there was one thing that made her sad in what they talked about. She thought of bringing it up on numerous occasions, but ultimately, Anri was never able to bring herself to tell Celty. Once the dullahan left, she felt a terrible regret.

Why couldn't I bring it up? The topic...of...

Suddenly, her doorbell rang.

Huh? It's so late!

For a moment, the image of Nasujima's face floated into her mind, and she twitched with fear. But then it occurred to her that Celty might have come back, so she looked through the peephole, careful not to make any sound.

Huh? A...woman?

It was a young woman wearing a uniform.

Anri didn't recognize her, but she checked to make sure there was no one else with her, then unlocked the door. She opened it up to reveal an incredibly beautiful girl with long hair.

~~She had~~ ~~a~~ ~~figure~~ but a face with a hint of innocence left. Her black, lustrous hair went halfway down her back. In all, ~~she created a~~ tiny little space of fantastical beauty in the middle of the plain apartment hallway.

"Um...can I help you?"

"It's nice to meet you, Miss Sonohara."

The long-haired girl smiled gently in replying to Anri's hesitant question.

But then she introduced herself.

"My name is Haruna Niekawa."

♂♀

Near Kawagoe Highway, apartment building

"Saika loves by cutting? So she is a sadist, after all."

"No, it's not quite the same thing. To put it simply, she's a cursed blade. Her voice can only reach her master, the one wielding her."

"Right. So why doesn't she just love her master?"

"The thing is, Saika wants to love all of humanity."

"...?"

"Not a specific human. She fell in love with all of humanity as a species. For us, it would be like a dog lover. A dog person doesn't just love one specific dog, they love all dogs. But that hardly ever advances to feelings of romance. No matter how much you love dogs, hardly anyone wishes to get married to their dog, and anyone who gets sexually turned on by a dog is a pervert. Then again, some people *are* like that..."

"Don't get distracted."

"Sorry, sorry! But don't you see how crucial this is? Anyway, Saika fell in love with people. At first, it was just something she kept to herself. But after loving and loving and loving and loving and loving and loving and loving and loving and loving...thinking of just one human no longer satisfied her. So she began loving all of humanity, but that sentiment eventually came to a standstill... She wanted to express her love through action."

"Action?"

"Yes, action. Humans express love in various ways, right? Through words, actions for the sake of the other, risking one's life, offering protection, luring with money, giving in to lust, doing nothing, picking on or teasing, even killing them to ensure that they're yours forever."

"...And the latter is supposed to be 'love'?"

"Twisted or not, as long as someone considers it a form of love, then it is. But Saika is a demonic blade. It has no body with which to love."

"..."

"All she wanted was to touch someone. She wanted to unite herself with the flesh of the humans she loved. She wanted to sink into them. She wanted to insert herself into them."

"This is starting to get vulgar. But...wait, doesn't this mean...?"

"Yes."

"In order to express her love, Saika chose to simply slash all of humanity. That moment of dissection is the only moment in which she is able to touch humankind. From flesh to blood to heart to life. See?"

♂♀

Anri's place

"Miss Sonohara...do you know why I came...to meet you?"

Anri and Haruna were sitting across from each other at the cheap little table. Haruna wore a fantastical, confident smile, while Anri's face was plain with troubled concern.

Haruna Niekawa. It was the very person whom Anri had wandered the streets hoping to find earlier that night, but she had no idea why the girl was here. How had she even found her address?

Haruna was rumored to be Nasujima's lover but had transferred to another school, those same rumors said. Anri didn't know any details beyond that. She wanted to make contact with Haruna to learn what those details were—but now that they were face-to-face, she found it hard to ask.

But now there was nothing. Haruna herself had just asked the question: Why did she come to visit Anri? There was only one obvious commonality they shared.

"Is it about...Mr. Nasujima?" Anri summoned up her courage to ask. Haruna gifted her with an angelic smile. Anri took that as an affirmative and hastily clarified, "Oh, um, but you know I don't like him at all, right? It's just dumb rumors..."

"Yes, I'm sure," Haruna answered swiftly.

Anri felt relief spread throughout her body. However…

"But I still love Takashi."

"Huh…?"

Takashi was Nasujima's first name. It was very strange to hear a girl just one year older than Anri, still wearing her school uniform, refer to him in such an informal way.

Feeling that this conversation might be going in an uncomfortable direction, Anri prompted the older girl.

"Um…were you in a relationship?"

"It was more than just a 'relationship.' We were madly in love. We were happy just confirming that fact, day after day. Forever. Forever and ever…"

Haruna's eyes stared at nothing as she spoke, positively glowing. She must have been reliving past memories in her mind.

But just as quickly, her expression clouded over into sadness, and there was almost mourning in her voice as she looked straight into Anri's eyes. Her eyes were beautiful and clear. But there was something eerie about them, an unfocused nature that made it hard to tell what she was actually looking at.

"But then one day, he rejected me… I was just trying to confirm my love for Takashi, like always. All I did was try to help our love take shape…"

♂♀

Near Kawagoe Highway, apartment building

"Saika manipulates her wielder into attacking over and over. Over and over, she tries to confirm her love. In order for her love to take shape. In order to make sure her lover never forgets her…she pierces and wounds her victim's body and mind at the same time."

"As proof of love…?"

"Exactly. That's how she's loved. But those incidents only spanned a period of ten years or so. As the years went on, Saika vanished entirely. It would be one thing if she'd grown tired of loving and had simply lost interest in humans…but based on the posts on the Net, I'd say she's still overflowing with love."

"Wait, that doesn't make sense. If she's been around humans for years and years, then why were her first messages in the chat room so primitive? That was Saika possessing a human body and making them type, right?"

"That's the thing. Could she have forgotten Japanese in the time that she was gone from human society? This knife is…*hmm?*"

"What's up?"

"Huh? Wait…"

Shinra looked back at the knife on the table, exclaiming with curiosity. Suddenly he reached out and grabbed the handle.

What?!

Celty hurriedly tried to snatch it away from him, but Shinra held tight.

He asked, "Celty…you didn't examine this in the light, did you?"

"Um, no, I picked it up outdoors. Are you sure you're all right? You don't feel like it's tightening its grip on your heart or anything?!"

"Not in the least," he laughed, then dropped a bombshell. "This isn't Saika."

"*What?!*"

"Here, look at this."

He pointed at a spot on the handle of the knife. There was a small piece of text carved into the grip.

MADE IN JAPAN 2002

♂♀

Anri's place

"Um…what do you mean by…tried to make your love take shape…?"

A cold sweat began to break out on Anri's palms. The other girl's abnormal nature was becoming apparent.

Haruna never let her beautiful smile fade as she spoke. It was as though she didn't even hear Anri's question.

"But then Takashi rejected me. But I don't hate him for that. After all, I'm in love with him. I forgive him for everything, including his rejection of me. I love him so much, I can accept everything he does."

"Uh, I was asking…"

"But I cannot forgive anyone *other* than Takashi."

The smile remained, but her words filled with madness. Anri could sense this shift, and the sweat began to trickle down her back as well.

"I can forgive Takashi for falling in love with something other than me. But…I cannot forgive the thing he falls in love with."

"Uh…"

"Miss Sonohara, you might love Takashi, or hate him, or not care about him at all—but none of that matters."

Anri got to her feet as the words of madness reached her ears. Her instincts were screaming at her that remaining sitting was a dangerous course of action.

"I'm not going to apologize to you, Miss Sonohara. I mean…everything I do is for the right reasons, for the sake of my love. Why should anyone apologize for doing the right thing? Why should anyone feel wrong for that?"

She wanted to flee the scene and leave it all behind. But Haruna was not likely to allow her to do that.

"…"

Anri had already given up on reasoning with Haruna. She knew it wouldn't work.

Haruna watched her closely and said, "But you know…it's not right to use people. If I want love, I need to take action myself. This is good proof of that…"

♂♀

Near Kawagoe Highway, top floor of apartment building

"Why would a demon blade that's been around for decades be made in 2002?"

"No, wait. You have to believe me. I know what I saw."

"I believe you, Celty. I would never doubt your word. This means the slasher was always crazy. It had nothing to do with the weapon. He probably just heard about the legend of Saika from somewhere."

"I don't know if I buy that... The man himself was also a victim of the attacks. Either he was possessed at that time or the demon blade ordered him to cut himself and thus remove himself from police suspicion..."

"Was it someone you knew?"

"Well, not exactly... It was the magazine writer who came to ask me about Shizuo at the end of last month. I heard he was attacked later that night, according to the chat room... When I looked further into it, the attack occurred right outside his own house."

"His name was...oh yeah, Niekawa. His name was Shuuji Niekawa."

♂♀

Anri's place

"I thought my dad could do the job better than anyone else...but it didn't quite work out."

What is she talking about?

Anri had no idea what Haruna was saying at first. But what came next, combined with the look on her face, told Anri exactly what she meant.

Exactly.

"So now...I'm forced to handle my own business. To get rid of my rival in love."

Haruna reached behind her back and pulled out a knife.

"Using the power of my very special partner."

The blade wasn't even eight inches long. Compared to what the slasher had earlier, it was much less imposing.

But Anri understood. The girl with her inside the apartment was actually far more menacing than the slasher. After all...

"I might not love you. But Saika, on the other hand, has all the love in the world for you..."

After all, when she pulled out the knife, her eyes went a shade of red much, much, much, much, much deeper and more crimson than the slasher's had ever been.

♂♀

Near Kawagoe Highway, top floor of apartment building

"I know, the chat! What is the chat saying?"
   Talking about the writer had reminded Celty of the chat room, so she loaded the page right away to see if anything had changed.
   And change it had.
   "What...the heck?"

What she found was not terror. Or unease.
It was simply chilling. A chill that ran straight through her back.
Deep, deep darkness that shunned all.
Something that froze Celty to her core.

♂♀

Chat room

—SAIKA HAS ENTERED THE CHAT—
—SAIKA HAS ENTERED THE CHAT—
—SAIKA HAS ENTERED THE CHAT—
—SAIKA HAS ENTERED THE CHAT—
—SAIKA HAS ENTERED THE CHAT—
—SAIKA HAS ENTERED THE CHAT—
—SAIKA HAS ENTERED THE CHAT—
—SAIKA HAS ENTERED THE CHAT—
—SAIKA HAS ENTERED THE CHAT—
—SAIKA HAS ENTERED THE CHAT—
—SAIKA HAS ENTERED THE CHAT—
|I screwed up. I screwed up.|
—SAIKA HAS ENTERED THE CHAT—
—SAIKA HAS ENTERED THE CHAT—

—SAIKA HAS ENTERED THE CHAT—
—SAIKA HAS ENTERED THE CHAT—
—SAIKA HAS ENTERED THE CHAT—
—SAIKA HAS ENTERED THE CHAT—
|The timing was all wrong.|
—SAIKA HAS ENTERED THE CHAT—
—SAIKA HAS ENTERED THE CHAT—
|How dare you break my sister.|
—SAIKA HAS ENTERED THE CHAT—
—SAIKA HAS ENTERED THE CHAT—
|Mother's orders are absolute.|
—SAIKA HAS ENTERED THE CHAT—
|The reasons I've stayed hidden are all gone now.|
—SAIKA HAS ENTERED THE CHAT—
—SAIKA HAS ENTERED THE CHAT—
—SAIKA HAS ENTERED THE CHAT—
|Now I can use forceful means.|
|I finally met Shizuo.|
—SAIKA HAS ENTERED THE CHAT—
|But the connection was lost.|
|I can't feel her presence anymore.|
|I can't feel her presence.|
|The timing was all wrong.|
—SAIKA HAS ENTERED THE CHAT—
|I screwed up, I screwed up, I screwed up.|
|But I won't fail this time.|
|I will give my love to Shizuo Heiwajima.|
|If I can love Shizuo, then I'm sure I can love every human in this town.|
—SAIKA HAS ENTERED THE CHAT—
|I can love this place humans created called Ikebukuro.|
|Come to me again, Shizuo.|
|Come to me and my sisters.|
|We will love you so much more this time.|
|My sisters are the same being as I.|
|This time we will love you all at once.|

|Come to me.|
|Shizuo Heiwajima.|
—SAIKA HAS ENTERED THE CHAT—
|Shizuo|
|Shizuo|
|Shizuo|
|If you don't show|
|I'll love someone else.|
|I'll love anyone, anyone, anyone.|
|Everyone, all at once.|
|I'll love the people of Ikebukuro, love, love, lovelovelovelo|
|velovelovelov|
|elovelovelovelovelovelovelovelove|
|love|
|lovelovelove|
—SAIKA HAS ENTERED THE CHAT—
|I'm waiting.|
|I'm waiting.|
|wait|
|I'm waiting.|
|At South Ikebukuro Park|
|At South Ikebukuro Park|
|I'll be waiting all night at South Ikebukuro Park.|
|Waiting for you, Shizuo.|
|I won't let the police or ordinary civilians come near the park.|
|There will be plenty of distractions.|
|So don't worry, Shizuo.|
|Ikebukuro will roil with chaos tonight.|
|But don't worry, Shizuo.|
|I will be there to love you.|
|I'll love you, too.|
|I'll love you, too.|
|And me.|
|And me.|
—SAIKA HAS ENTERED THE CHAT—
|I'll love you, too.|
—SAIKA HAS ENTERED THE CHAT—

—SAIKA HAS ENTERED THE CHAT—
—SAIKA HAS ENTERED THE CHAT—

.

.

.

.

.

And just after Celty checked on the chat room...

Ikebukuro suffered one of the worst cases of assault in its history, as fifty-four people were attacked randomly on the street at a variety of locations.

CHAPTER 6 SWORD AND STRESS

It drifted.

And drifted.

Everything drifted away from the boy.

He only wanted to be loved by someone.

He only wanted to love someone.

The shy boy didn't even have the bravery to control himself.

He was afraid of hurting the one he loved.

So he decided not to love anyone.

Feared, feared, and unloved.

Time evolved the boy into a monster.

If there was a god in this world whose purpose was to control violence,

then the boy must have earned this god's love.

More than anyone and anything.

Shinjuku

"And why would Shizu be standing right outside my apartment building?" Izaya Orihara wondered with a smile that could only be described as bitter.

"…Because I'm here to kick your ass, obviously," replied Shizuo with a humorless smile. Every other part of his being was overflowing with rage.

They were outside the high-class apartment building in the middle of the night. Izaya had returned from a trip to the convenience store to find Shizuo just about to kick the front door of the building down.

He could have left the scene as it was and gotten the police to arrest Shizuo, but Izaya considered another possibility and realized he had to show himself to his foe.

I don't want him barging into my place and finding the head before the police arrive.

"And why do I deserve a beating?"

"Because I'm feeling pretty aggravated right now."

"You know, you're really much too old to be engaging in this kind of childish logic, Shizu."

"Shut up. If I had to give another reason…it's because you're too damn fishy," Shizuo shot back.

A grimace spread over Izaya's features. "Fishy? What about?"

"This street slasher who's tearing up my hood… *How involved are you?*" he asked directly.

Izaya shook his head exasperatedly. "Why would I be involved?"

"Because ninety-nine percent of all the bizarre and violent things that happen here are your doing."

"What, you're not gonna trust that this one is in the other one percent?"

"If I were able to trust you with even one percent of my being, I think you and I would get along better… Right, Izaya?"

The veins on Shizuo's face bulged and popped as he recalled events from the past. The sight was so grotesque that someone who didn't know any better would assume he had some kind of condition.

"And even if there weren't this slasher going around, 'Bukuro's been weird lately. And that's your fault, ain't it? What are you plotting?"

"This is quite an accusation," Izaya stated with a wide smile. He already had a knife clutched in his hands. Shizuo looked at it and grinned, then put a hand on the guardrail out in front of the building.

"?" Izaya felt a bit of sweat break out on his skin. He didn't know what Shizuo was doing. *He's not going to rip that guardrail out and fight me with it, is he…?*

The problem was, Shizuo Heiwajima was exactly the kind of man who did the thing you assumed he wouldn't possibly do. Sure enough, as Izaya dreaded, Shizuo clenched the hand holding the guardrail tight.

"…Seriously?"

He'd just have to stab Shizuo before he pulled it out of the ground.

The moment Izaya made up his mind to stab the other man, the smile vanished from his face. When Shizuo noticed that, his own smile got wider: "Do it, if you can."

And just as the tension reached its peak, the face-off was interrupted by the sudden entrance of a shadow.

The black motorcycle appeared without a hint of sound and cut between the two.

"Well, well."

"Celty…what do you want?"

She quickly waved Izaya back and showed her PDA screen to Shizuo. It was a copy of the chat log that she'd saved to the device.

He took some time to read it over. Eventually he squinted and asked, "The hell is this?"

Shizuo thought for several moments, and with an oddly calm look in his eyes, he turned back to Izaya. "Is this part of your plot?"

"I dunno what this means, but if I could have calculated that Celty would randomly show up here, I'd have dropped a meteor on your house by now."

Shizuo kept watching Izaya for a while after that, then clicked his tongue in disappointment and got onto Celty's bike without another word.

Ever since high school, Izaya had used everything at his disposal to get to where he was. There was only one person who never acted the way Izaya wanted him to, and that was Shizuo Heiwajima.

At first, I actually thought I could control Shizu, Izaya thought ruefully to himself as the motorcycle rode off.

"How does an amoeba like him get so sharp?"

His smile was one of both pure joy and irritation.

"This is exactly why I hate you so much."

♂♀

Anri's place

"I've done some research on you," Haruna said, knife in her hand. She slowly got to her feet. That angelic smile never left her face, but her eyes were a demonic red.

"What a stupid, pointless human. Ever since middle school, you've been like toilet paper stuck to Mika Harima's shoe...and now you've begun seducing two of your male classmates, and you think you can manipulate Takashi as well?"

Her face wore a smile, but there was nothing but pure malice in her words.

Meanwhile, Anri stayed silent, taking in Haruna's words. Perhaps she was frantically thinking of what action she ought to take next. But Haruna only continued her outpouring of contempt. She hurled words of despair and disaster at Anri, yet her face was as beautiful and holy as a saint announcing the girl's end.

"On top of all this...*a burglar broke into your home five years ago and killed your parents?* Apparently you claimed that you didn't see the killer, despite being in the same room the entire time... How can that be? How did you not see the killer? How did you survive?"

It was a fact that Anri hadn't even told Mikado or Masaomi. But her face did not change expression. She didn't even open her mouth. It wasn't a simple enough matter that she could settle with just facial expressions or arguments, Haruna knew, but she continued her verbal assault anyway.

"Unless you even tried to seduce the burglar? A girl in elementary school? Do you suppose he was a pedophile?"

Even after that barb, Anri's face was placid. It wasn't that on the inside her heart was brimming with rage, either. There were only swirling questions.

Why is this happening?

She only wanted a life of peace and tranquillity. What did she do to deserve this chaos?

Anri tried to view the world within the customary picture frame, but the glint of the knife in the hands of the other girl did not allow her to withdraw entirely.

Her tranquillity was crumbling to pieces.

Was there no way to go back? Would her uneventful reality never come?

Would it all fall apart, including the eternal dreamworld she'd made for herself?

There was a solution.

She could just yell something back at the other woman who kept hurling bullshit at her. She could fight. She could crush her opponent.

But just being forced into making that choice was the greatest suffering of all.

I just don't want to fight. I don't want to fight with anything. I don't want to compete with anyone. I just want to lead a peaceful life. I only fight when I want peace. I wasn't born to waste my life with stupid battles like this...

"It must be easy, living by latching onto other people like a parasite," Haruna muttered.

Anri finally found her voice. "...Not easy."

"Huh?"

"It's not...easy at all. Living off of others, trying to make sure just the right person likes you. I agree, *parasite* is a good term for me. But do you have any idea how much you need to sacrifice...to ensure the person you're latching onto doesn't drive you off?"

Now there was indeed a kind of strength in Anri's eyes.

Most people who lived comfortably in the shadow of another person would become angry and deny it if called out for it. Even they would agree that it wasn't a cool or admirable way of life. Anri certainly didn't think that her choice was necessarily laudable—but it was a conscious choice that she made for herself.

She wouldn't stand for that to be criticized by someone she'd never met until just now. It was this anger that finally wrung the words out of her.

But Haruna only smirked at her statement. Voice dripping with utter loathing, she spat, "That's what you've been doing? Sacrificing yourself so that Takashi will like you...?"

"No," Anri said, loud and clear. "Mr. Nasujima is not worth doing that."

She was surprised at how forceful her own response was.

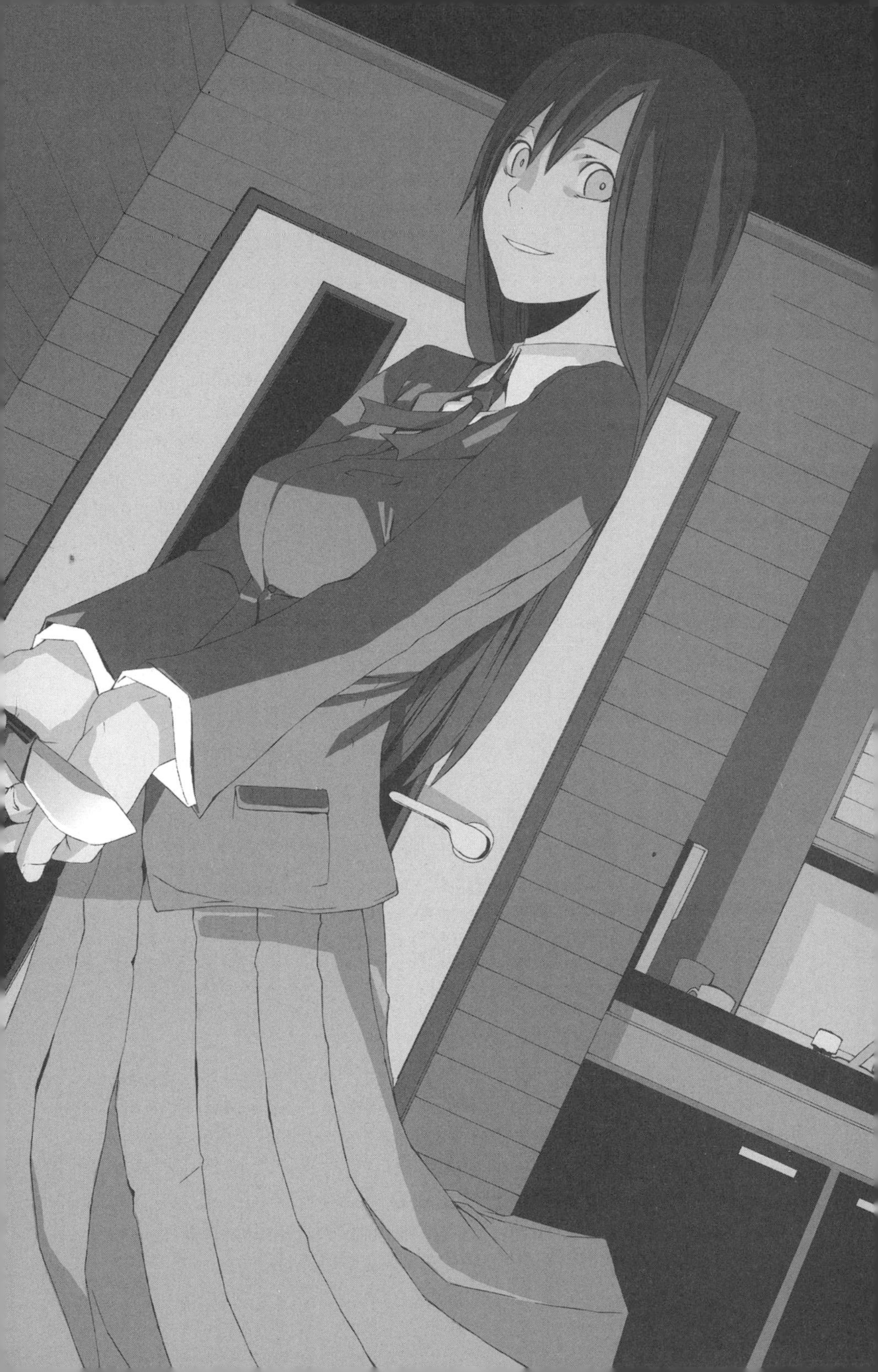

Meanwhile, Haruna's face had gone stone-still. Her expression vanished entirely, her red eyes narrowed, and her grip on the knife tightened.

"Oh ? I see."

Something charged was in the air now, but Anri did not take her eyes off of Haruna. Just moments ago, she was intimidated by the other girl, but now there was no hesitation in her actions.

But that didn't matter to Haruna. All she felt was a desire to kill the girl who stood in her way and insulted her beloved Takashi Nasujima.

"Die, then," she mumbled and thrust out the knife for Anri's throat.

Just then, the doorbell rang.

It was nearly after midnight. Who would be ringing her doorbell at this time of night? Haruna set her own issues aside for a moment to marvel at this odd occurrence.

"Is it one of your little friends?" she wondered.

Anri had no idea. Could Celty have come back?

"Well, whatever. I'll start by stabbing your friend before your eyes—and then take my time finishing you off afterward."

The smile was back on Haruna's face as she crossed the room to the door and pulled it open.

Time stopped as Haruna and the visitor came face-to-face.

"Nie...kawa?"

"Takashi!"

Anri looked out the door from across the room and saw with surprise that it was Nasujima.

What is he doing here?

In a way, his appearance was even more shocking than Haruna's, but that didn't matter at this point. Anri decided to stand back and watch what unfolded.

"Ahhh...ahh! Takashi...Takashi, Takashi, Takashi!" Haruna chanted, her features overcome with emotion and tears.

Nasujima's reaction meanwhile...

"Aheaaaa!"

He let out a garbled shriek, turned ninety degrees, and raced down the hallway of the apartment building. He had run away at the first sight of Haruna's face.

Huh?

Anri was certainly confused about his appearance at her apartment and didn't want to consider what he had planned, but this sight filled her with a different question.

Why did he run away? Weren't they supposed to be a couple? She thought that Mr. Nasujima had forced the girl into it, but now it didn't seem that way... *So why did he run away?*

"Wait, Takashi!"

Haruna started to rush out the door after Nasujima, but she immediately changed her mind and held back for a moment to warn Anri, "I was hoping to take care of you on my own...but it seems I don't have time to deal with you anymore. So I'll have everyone else kill you instead."

"Everyone?" Anri repeated, unsure of what Haruna meant. A moment later, that clarity came to her in full.

"Actually, Saika wanted to get everyone involved to help love Shizuo...but I'm glad I convinced her to let me bring a few here."

Anri realized that several men were now milling around outside the door. They all carried their own blades—X-Acto knives, kitchen knives, cleavers.

All of their eyes were red.

"These are Saika's children," Haruna announced, then raced off into the night after Nasujima.

All that was left in the now-silent room was Anri and a number of slashers with weapons held at the ready.

She backed away into the room as the men advanced, blades held high, ready to begin the slaughter.

♂♀

South Ikebukuro Park

In the back of Celty's brain—wherever that brain physically existed—the words that Shinra uttered after seeing the chat log for himself played back.

"...If you want me to analyze this situation, there's one thing I can speculate.

"Lots of human beings desire signs and symbols of love when they're in a romance. The so-called fruits of love.

"Once two people love each other, they desire something they both love together. The classic example of that would be children.

"That's right… Saika's giving birth. She's leaving a child in the souls of the humans she slices.

"Saika really does love people, it's true.

"She seeks a perfect fusion with man…with humanity."

There was no way for it to be true, but this case had involved a succession of no ways happening one after the other. In a way, her own existence was another thing too bizarre to be true, so she had no right to complain.

Celty focused on her surroundings. She'd arrived at South Ikebukuro Park with Shizuo in tow. Once the bike was parked in the middle of the park, she looked around—and muttered to herself.

No way.

She'd thought the park was empty at first. Normally there was at least *someone* out there, even in the middle of the night, but there was no one to be seen at the moment.

Yet the instant that Celty and Shizuo entered the park, silhouettes began to gather in the corners of the area, seemingly out of nowhere.

Like germs, as the overall number rose, so did the rate of their multiplication. This pyramid scheme continued for about thirty seconds. Celty and Shizuo were completely surrounded by humans.

This is way more than fifty people, she noticed.

There was quite a variety to the crowd surrounding them: salarymen, street punks, young children, housewives, college students…

There were a number equipped with yellow bandannas, as well as several who looked like Dollars members.

Given the uneven collection of people, Celty and Shizuo immediately thought of the impromptu meeting of the Dollars that happened one year earlier. There were two key differences here.

For one, the Dollars probably had greater numbers.

The other difference was that all of these people had their own blades and their eyes were as red as blood, without exception.

The blades they held were as varied as the people: knives, scissors, extendable branch pruners, even chain saws.

They had to be the victims of the string of slashing attacks.

No wonder they'd never caught the slasher. Some of the people even had hospital gowns, as though they'd just escaped in the middle of the night.

All the victims were possessed by Saika and falsified their testimony...

As Celty pondered what to do next, one of the hundred or so people surrounding them, a teenage girl wearing a Raira Academy uniform, walked up to act as spokesperson.

"I've been hoping to meet you, Shizuo Heiwajima."

Though Celty and Shizuo wouldn't have known this, she was one of Anri's bullies, the one who was attacked before the girl's eyes. Her statement passed straight through Celty to Shizuo, who was still sitting on the back of the motorcycle.

"You're so wonderful... I was watching from a distance when you beat my sister..."

Watching from where? Celty wondered. Then again, with this many of them, it wouldn't have been that strange for *one* to have witnessed the attack. But did that mean they didn't actually share consciousness among all of them?

"So I told my other sisters and *Mother* about your incredible strength... The Internet's so convenient, isn't it? In the past, it was so hard for us Saikas to share our minds. But now, all you need is a single e-mail," the teenage slasher explained, revealing their nature. It was a revelation that she likely made freely, knowing that Celty and Shizuo would be powerless to do anything about it.

"At first, it was very difficult for our consciousness to understand words...but now we each have a will just as strong as Mother's."

With each word, the circle of people closed in. They were close enough now that they could all leap in at once and engulf the two, if they wanted.

"Shizuo, we want to know more and more about your strength. We want to see more of it. This time, in front of the group. Then, I'm sure we can love you even more than we do now..."

The enraptured girl—no, it was Saika possessing the mind of a girl—inched closer to Shizuo, waving around her butterfly knife.

Celty finally felt like she had a good understanding of the enemy.

I see… When the victim gets slashed, a new Saika is born within her that takes over her body. Then, she grabs whatever blade is on hand, and that blade becomes the means by which a new body is born.

The reason nothing happened to Shinra when he touched the knife was that the knife itself wasn't cursed. Perhaps Saika wasn't a monster or spirit at all, but a kind of hypnotism. By cutting another person, that fear became a medium through which to plant itself into another person's heart. The seed then took root, just as it did in the attacker, multiplying endlessly. Perhaps that was how it worked.

So did that make Saika a life-form?

The question passed through Celty's mind, but she didn't have the time to spend considering that thought. She was too busy producing the black scythe from her hands and wondering how to incapacitate Saika's victims without killing any of them.

The girl with the butterfly knife professed her love for Shizuo, mouth twisted. "Now! Shall we make love? We'll keep loving you, no matter where, no matter how, even when you're too tired to move! We'll love you without end! And except for that monster over there, no one is allowed to interfere. Our sisters are making more and more sisters so we can keep loving the people of this city! The police will be too busy to stop us!"

The other Saikas followed the girl's lead in cackling with delighted laughter.

Celty was plenty creeped out, but she was also honestly concerned for Shizuo's safety now as well.

Yet the man behind her was not particularly angry or afraid in any way. He got off the bike and stood before the throng, his face a mask

"Can I ask you one thing?"

"What is it?"

"Why exactly…do you people like me?"

Celty nearly fell off the motorcycle with the shock of his out-of-place question.

Get a hint! Are you seriously asking that now?!

But she had no time for arguing at the moment. Meanwhile, the Saika spokeswoman at the front felt confident enough to indulge his question.

"Because you're strong."

"…"

"That preposterous strength...not derived from power or money, but the absolute extreme of human possibility, the most instinctual and violent strength possible. That's what we want. Plus...what human being wouldn't want to fall in love with a wild man like you? You're scary. But we think we're enough to love you."

She broke out of her pose and started to explain their philosophy to Shizuo.

"We love all of humanity. But just loving isn't enough for us anymore. Just creating more children with humanity isn't enough for us anymore. If loving and loving and loving isn't enough, we want to rule all of humanity. And to do that, we need excellent offspring. Powerful specimens like you, for example. Don't humans try to leave behind the best possible genes for the future?"

She sounds like a certain dictator, Celty marveled. She checked on Shizuo, figuring that such a selfish and nonsensical speech would have him exploding with rage.

"Ha-ha..."

He's laughing?!

"Ha-ha-ha...ha-ha-ha-ha-ha-ha."

It wasn't the laughter of someone trying to hide his anger. It was simply pleasant, delighted laughter.

"Settle down, Shizuo. If it starts to look bad, I'll do my best to make sure you escape."

Was the fact that they were surrounded by a hundred assailants making him loopy? She waited for him to react. Eventually he stopped laughing and gave his response to the Saikas' confession of love.

"Nah, Celty... To be honest, I'm actually happy."

"Huh...?" This reaction was not what Saika expected, either. The people in the crowd gave one another confused looks.

"I've always despised this strength I was given. I thought no one would ever accept me for what I am," Shizuo stated. There was a variety of emotions in his voice as he spoke of his past.

"The thing is...now I don't have to worry anymore. Look at how many people love me. One, two...well, let's just say 'a lot.' So...it's *all fine* now," he said, grinding his teeth with pleasure.

"I mean, I can accept who I am now, right?" he said, clenching his fists with enjoyment.

"I can like myself for what I am, right?" he said, his eyes wide with bliss as he tucked his sunglasses into his pocket.

"This power I've tried and tried and tried to get rid of, because I hated it so, so, so much... But now it's okay for me to accept it, right? It's okay for me to use it, right?

"I can—I can finally use my full power, right?"

And in the next instant, for the first time in his life, Shizuo Heiwajima willingly used all of his power. Not in the grips of rage, like always... But out of joy that *something* loved his power.

What he said next plunged the Saikas into despair.

"Oh, just for the record...people like y'all are not, at all, even the slightest, my type of partner.

"The one thing I can say for you...is that I only hate you second most after Izaya."

$$♂♀$$

Fairly close to the park, on an isolated, empty road, a man and woman were speaking of love.

The man, his rejection of it. The woman, her overflowing abundance...

"Hey...do you remember?" she said quietly, as the man sat at the side of the road in terror.

They were standing in the darkened midpoint between streetlight and streetlight, and an eerie tone dominated the scene. The woman who was the source of that aura was smiling so radiantly that tears brimmed in her eyes as she spoke of her love.

"The first time I met you, when you saved me from being bullied... You helped me with lots of things after that, didn't you?"

She was staring right into the memories of her past as she talked. On the other hand, the man saw her face as nothing more than a source of terror.

If you ignored the red eyes, she was quite a pretty girl, and he was the kind of rough-looking man who could be found roaming the streets anywhere. In most cases, you would expect their roles to be reversed.

But the man was terrified of her and didn't pay a single bit of attention to what she was saying.

"Ever since then, you've been the only thing on my mind... You noticed that, didn't you? That's why you returned my love. You gave in and accepted me. *You even did me the courtesy of using me to make money, then tried to get rid of me when you grew tired of it.* I accepted all of these things you did to me. I forgave you and I still loved you."

"H...hyaaa..."

"But eventually, it wasn't enough... I wanted more than that... That's when Saika started talking to me."

With the reflection of the knife glinting in her eyes, the woman drew the blade lightly along her own arm. A line appeared on her white flesh, little red droplets forming from the aperture.

"All I had to do was give her a little blood—drop by drop. See?"

"Hyeep!"

The girl's eyes stared right at the terrified, prone man, but her mind was somewhere far, far away. His figure did not reflect in her eyes. She was watching a fantasy of the man that existed only in their honeymoon period.

"So how about today...? Is today the day you'll finally accept my love?" she asked, bringing the knife close to the man's throat.

Slowly.

So slowly.

Like a child taking her very first kiss.

The silver blade was ready to plunge into the man,

making their bodies and minds one through the knife,

tearing his mind and body apart, exposing all of him...

"Aaaaahhh! W-wait, please wait!"

He flopped his legs, trying to push her away and put distance between them, but the stone wall blocked his back. The way he continued to flop despite the lack of any ground to gain was exceedingly pathetic, but the girl wasn't seeing him anymore.

She put her strength into the knife. She had reached the limit of her patience.

*   *   *

"Wait!"

The moment she was about to jab her beloved with the knife that was an extension of herself, a familiar voice came from somewhere behind her.

When she realized that her process had been interrupted, the girl's world suddenly fell apart. She and the man were not two abstract characters living in a fantasy, but two real human beings named Haruna Niekawa and Takashi Nasujima. Suddenly, she was seeing Nasujima's pathetic, frantic attempt to reject her.

"..."

Realizing that she'd "awakened" from the world of love, Haruna's smile vanished entirely at last. She turned toward the voice.

It was Anri, out of breath from running, but with a powerful, intent look in her eyes.

"How did you escape? There were at least five back there," Haruna said.

Anri didn't answer. She tried to steady her breathing. "Please…just stop this, Miss Niekawa. Stop hurting people with that knife…"

"This has nothing to do with you. You just don't want to die, is that it?"

"Yes…it *does* have to do with me…"

"?"

Haruna didn't know what Anri was talking about, so she assumed that the girl was just in a daze from escaping the other Saikas.

"Listen, Miss Sonohara… Your words carry no power of their own. A weak-willed human being who can only live by leeching off of someone else's life has no right to dictate what me and Saika's love should be!" Haruna stated, her words full of pressure. Anri was not intimidated, however.

"I don't need any right to stop something I think is wrong. Plus…I don't think the strength of one's words has anything to do with the way one lives," she responded, matching the intensity of Haruna's attack. "Just because I can only live through other people doesn't make me weak. I chose that way of life. That's all there is to it."

"That makes no sense…"

"Don't decide whether people are weak or strong…based solely on the way they live!" she shouted, overpowering Haruna's words with her own.

The girl standing there now couldn't be the same timid creature she'd visited earlier. Haruna was bewildered by the change but had no intention of questioning her about it.

All she had to do was believe in the power of her love—and kill the girl.

An ephemeral silence passed between the two before Haruna spoke again.

"Hey, Miss Sonohara... Have you ever even loved anyone before?"

The smile was back on her face. Anri looked mystified, but her goal here was to convince Haruna to stop what she was doing, so she had to engage the question.

"...Probably n—"

"I have!" Haruna blurted out, ignoring the other girl's answer. "When Saika first spoke to me, I almost let this one take over my body...but then it started telling me I had to cut Takashi. I cannot hurt the man I love so much! So I resisted, I fought back..."

As she spoke, she swung her arms. The reflection of the knife glimmered in the darkness, bringing the strength of her conviction to life.

"...And instead, I conquered the demon blade! I conquered Saika! With the power of love! The power of love!"

"Huh? But...you were trying to stab him just now..."

"Yes. At first, I thought what Saika was telling me was wrong. But the more I listened to her...the more I realized she was right. Controlling another person...planting yourself entirely within the deepest part of their heart is the true form of everlasting love."

Her eyes, which were already overpowering in their redness, took on the tint of madness that only heightened the eerie awfulness of the scene.

"Even if that ultimately means killing the one you love."

That was the signal.

Haruna crouched low, set her sights on Anri's throat, and put all of her might into the purpose of killing her foe. Quick action usually led to victory, but even if she didn't strike first, what was there to fear from a single unarmed girl?

"There will be no rescue for you this time. You don't have the strength to love another—you cannot stop me. There's only so far you can get on sheer arrogance!"

She began to charge at Anri. The girl started to open her mouth, but Haruna didn't care. She put all of her effort into the strike that would tear that impertinent throat right open...

*　　*　　*

A metallic ring cut through the night.

Huh?

Haruna couldn't tell what had just happened.

All she knew was that what she was seeing far surpassed her understanding.

Anri's right arm had blocked the slash aimed at her throat.

"What is…happening?"

As a response to that, Anri continued with what she was going to say moments earlier.

"It's true that I can't love anyone else. Ever since that day five years ago, I've been afraid to open my heart and love."

She was probably referring to the break-in that ended with the murder of her parents. But what did that have to do with the current situation?

Anri continued, "So I've taken to living off of others in order to make up for what I lack in my life. Yes, I admit it… I chose this way of life, after all."

Her arm was touching the knife. Through the tear in her sleeve could be seen the silver shine of steel.

"Wait…you can't…"

"So I decided that I would leech off of even the love of others."

Anri put her left hand to her right wrist and pulled the hilt of the sword that appeared out of her right arm, yanking it free.

The girl had extracted a katana, crackling, from her own arm. Haruna had no words for the scene she had just witnessed.

"Just as you cut other people to create Saika's children, your own Saika is nothing more than a child of the original… And the original takes the form of a proper katana."

"No…this can't be!"

"I cannot…" Anri muttered to herself. Her eyes literally shone with a demonic light. "So I decided to rely on Saika, who loves people for me…"

The light in her eyes was eerie, gentle, and warm, as if red fireflies had taken home within them. The light caught the lenses of her glasses, causing them to shine like giant red insect eyes.

"No…I live as her parasite…"

♂♀

It wasn't as if the boy never fell in love with a girl.

But when he inevitably failed to control his strength, his attempts to save her did more harm than good.

Not just once. It was a constant occurrence.

Eventually, no one stuck around with him. Even as a grown adult, there was no one in his vicinity. There was only one man, Izaya Orihara—but he only came over to use the boy for his own ends. He was also a man, so there was nothing like love in that equation.

Over time, the boy came to an understanding.

It wasn't a sudden enlightenment, simply something he learned through constant repetition.

He just wanted to be loved by someone.

But he wasn't allowed to have love for anyone else.

If he did, he would only hurt them.

Not of his own volition, but certainly of his own strength.

If that strength was meant to protect something, he might have been able to forgive himself. But he knew exactly what the world called that strength. *Violence.*

It was a simple matter. As some said, strength could be either violence or justice, depending on how it was used. If that was the case, his strength could be nothing *but* violence.

The boy was unable to control the sway of his emotions, and he used his strength in anger, in a way that left his own conscious will far, far behind in the dust…

It was strength—pure strength—that took the boy somewhere far away and unfamiliar.

Time passed, and as a man now, he had received words of love from another for the first time.

The man greeted the thing that showered him in pure love…

…with clenched fists.

In the center of the park, Celty Sturluson, a knight of death meant to inform people of their imminent mortality, the Headless Rider who sent waves of panic throughout Ikebukuro…was unable to do a thing but stand and watch.

Not because of the sheer force of a hundred slashers.

When faced with the sight of the red-eyed mob, she had originally thought of the Dollars' meeting a year ago.

But the result of this incident was the complete opposite of that earlier occasion.

The strength of one man, Shizuo Heiwajima, was absolutely overpowering the hundred attackers

Shizuo Heiwajima's style of fighting was exceedingly simple.

Punch.

Kick.

Throw with all your strength.

That's all it came down to.

Punch, punch, punch.

Kick, kick, kick, punch again.

Throw while kicking backward, spin and throw a punch.

Just the same simple combinations, like hammering a single button in a fighting game.

But that very simplicity was what made it so terrifying.

All he had to do was punch the blade-holding arm of an attacker, and it would cause a nasty crunch and no longer function. A low kick meant to fend off an onrushing person would completely demolish the knee.

When he punched a person, they flew horizontally, like something out of a slapstick comic book.

He didn't fight with the grace and agility of a Hong Kong action movie. But even still, Celty and the hundred slashers present to see it felt their hearts being stolen by the sight.

He was strong.

That was the only word needed to describe Shizuo.

But if one were to add more, another two words would suffice.

He was scary.

And he was *cool*.

I mean…I knew he was strong…

*...but...*this *strong?!*

If Celty used all of the power at her disposal to produce a deadly shadow scythe and attack Shizuo at this moment, she didn't think there was a chance she could win. She couldn't even envision such a scenario.

Fighters all shared a desire to fight those who were stronger than themselves. If she had to classify herself, Celty believed she was in that category rather than the opposite.

But this Shizuo was someone she never wanted to fight.

Not just because of fear.

She couldn't possibly turn her blade upon something that made such a strong impression on her.

Even the word *demon* didn't describe him anymore.

If any term fit Shizuo Heiwajima at this moment, it was more like *demon god*.

In fact, no words were necessary at all to describe him.

His strength became a word greater than words, telling the rest of the world of his existence.

Shinra had once explained Shizuo's strength to Celty.

"When muscle fibers are damaged, they grow that much thicker, but his constant rages don't give his cells any rest.

"So the cells of Shizuo's body—whether by a miracle or fate—chose a different route. The bundles of muscle fiber abandoned the process of bulking up and chose to stay at their current size, just tougher. That might be one of the reasons why he has such strength while remaining skinny.

"It's minimal regeneration. Shizuo's way of life caused his own bones and joints to change the way they grew so they could be stronger. His bones are hard as steel, and his joints are extra tough after endless dislocations. And this all happened within the short life of Shizuo Heiwajima.

"You might call this a kind of miracle."

A miracle.

But even that word might be too tepid to describe it.

There was no combination of words that Celty could use to adequately describe Shizuo's strength.

It must be a similar feeling to what would happen if one saw Superman or the protagonist of a shonen manga come to life. It was easy to say anything when viewing the situation objectively, but actually being present for the experience would blow anyone's worldview out the window.

That was the kind of presence Shizuo had now.

Despite the fact that the slashers' weapons gave them twice his reach, they couldn't hit him. The meager advantage of reach was not even a proper handicap against Shizuo.

He dodged their long swings by a hair, then countered by punching either the man holding the weapon or the flat of the blade. When the opponent lost his balance, the finishing kick was already incoming.

The onslaught continued without losing any momentum. Shizuo was joyfully unleashing all of the pent-up frustration that he'd accumulated throughout the evening, and he was going to get rid of *all* of it.

The hundred-strong Saikas were taken aback by Shizuo's overwhelming strength, so they held back and shot signals to one another to form more complex combination attacks.

But suddenly, they all moved as one.

Everyone in the park, aside from Shizuo and Celty, turned their heads in the same direction.

The move was as pristine and precise as a champion synchronized swimming team. Their eyes all pointed toward the same spot.

What is it?

Celty turned the same direction herself, but all she saw was the entrance to the park.

Though she couldn't possibly have known it, at that very moment elsewhere, Anri Sonohara had just pulled Saika out of her arm.

"Hey, is it just me…or is something happening close by?" Shizuo asked, surprisingly calm given his actions. Celty nodded in agreement. "I can manage this scene here if you don't mind going and checking it out. Either way, you ain't doin' nothin' here, are you?"

It was a considerate offer. Otherwise, she would have felt uncomfortable leaving Shizuo behind by himself. But in this case, she didn't think she needed an ounce of worry for his sake.

As a parting gift, she produced more shadow from her hands,

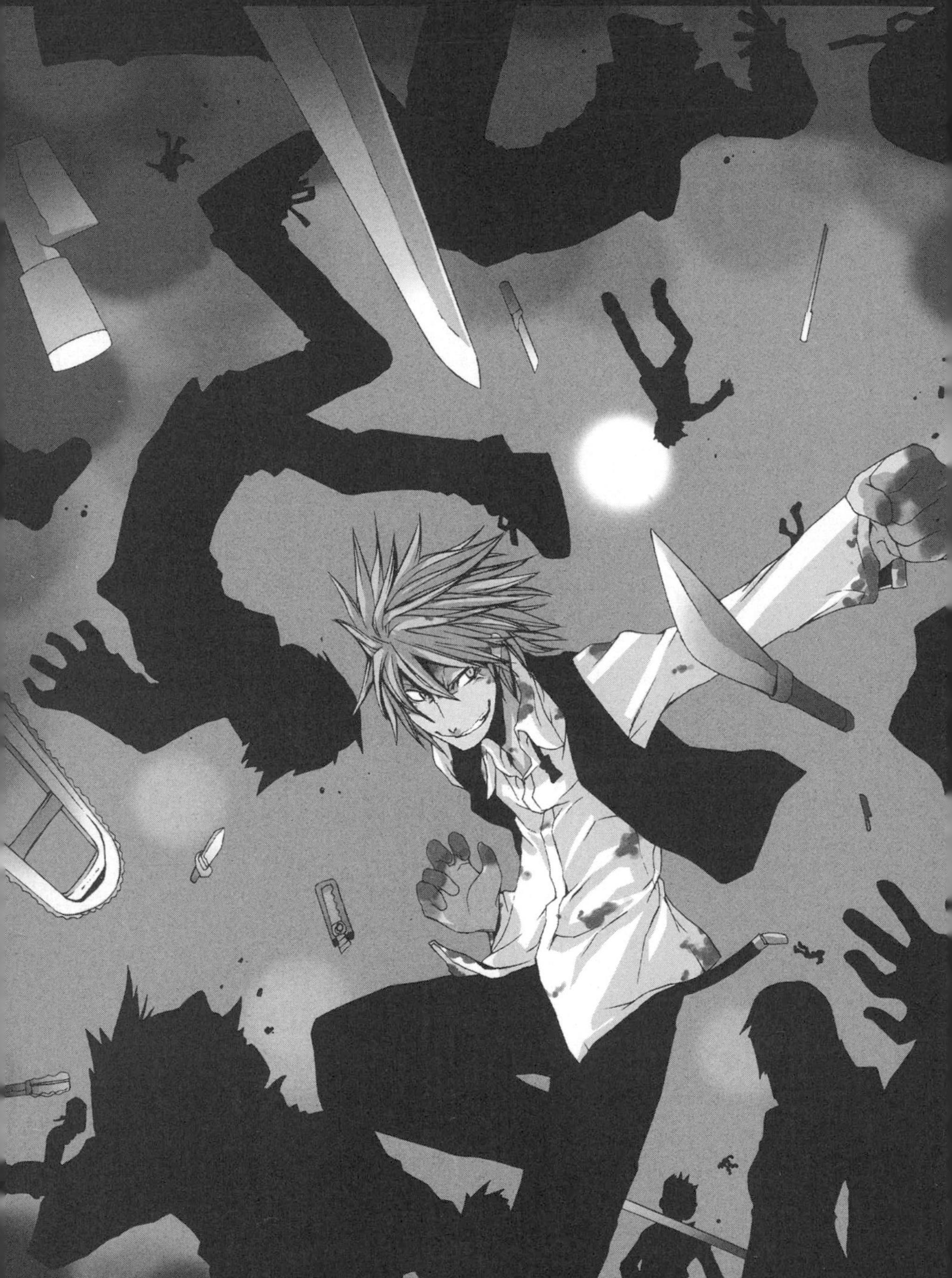

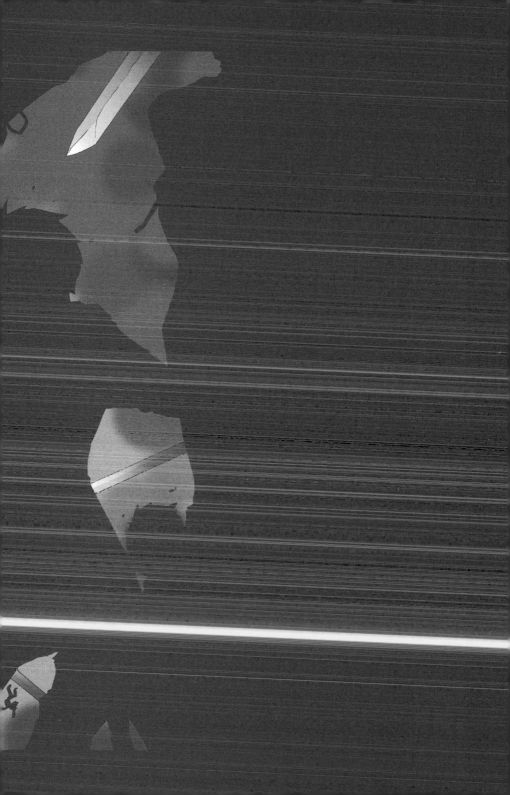

fashioning it into a pair of gloves, much like she had with the shadow helmet earlier.

"*Special-made like my scythe. They'll be able to stop a blade,*" she typed into her PDA, then tossed the gloves to Shizuo.

Not because she was worried for him. She simply wanted to be a part of the legend that she'd just witnessed.

"...Thanks."

Shizuo grinned and put the gloves on. Celty scattered the paused slashers as she drove the bike out of the park and out of sight.

"All right, then."

Now Shizuo was truly alone.

All alone against a hundred attackers.

But he had no thought of defeat.

Meanwhile, the Saikas surrounding him shared the same thought: that they didn't have the confidence to love Shizuo enough.

♂♀

What's going on? What's going on?

Our opponent is hardly unharmed.

Countless scratches and cuts cover Shizuo's body. But he shows no signs of accepting our love. The fear and pain of one simple cut is supposed to be enough to force him to accept our thoughts.

If there's any explanation...it's that Shizuo's not human...or...

Oh...how can this be?

The creature known as Shizuo Heiwajima does not feel the slightest ounce of fear.

Not just about himself being wounded.

Shizuo doesn't have an ounce of fear that he might hurt others, either.

He joyfully throws his full will into our destruction.

All because he accepted our words of love.

...Is this fear?

Is it fear?

We feel fear from a human that we love.

What irony.
We are afraid of a human who accepted our love.
We are afraid.
Afraid. Afraid.
Afraid...
The one who accepted our words of love does not fear us.
Therefore, we cannot pour the "reign" of love into him.
We cannot love him.
Does she know? Has our mother realized this truth yet?
Our mother, and the one who begat her, the great progenitor... Does she realize?
That our existence is so full of contradictions.
That from the perspective of a human being, the love of a demon sword is nothing more than an illusion...

♂♀

As the Saikas continued to close in, regardless of the challenge, Shizuo found a smile creeping over his features.
Don't get the wrong idea, you idiots.
No one will love me because they're all scared? Don't make me laugh.
I'm the one who's scared.
It's me.
I'm the world's biggest coward.
Because I'm scared of what I should trust the most—myself.
But so what?
Me being a coward and destroying you assholes have nothing to do with each other!
Besides.

I can't afford to get knocked on my ass in front of someone who actu-ally loves me, can I?

♂♀

Maybe that was the moment that it started.
When even if I liked someone—I was afraid to love them.

*   *   *

Anri still had the dream.

The dream of her family in happy times. The dream where they all laughed together.

But it was nothing but a lie.

Not because it was a dream, but because Anri Sonohara was *never that happy in the past.*

Anri was abused by her father from a young age.

Upon nearly every encounter with him, she had to suffer insults and injury. It was a daily occurrence.

Her mother would attempt to step in and help, but he would just beat her instead.

The process escalated over the years, so that by the time she was eleven years old, there were always fresh marks on her body.

Not because he was a drunk. That was not the case.

He never hit Anri's face, and he made sure not to leave marks when she had swimming lessons and people might have seen them. It was calculated. He performed just the right amount of violence to keep her from being able to report it to the school or police.

In time, she closed her heart off and lived in a deep depression with no escape.

That was about the time that the slashing attacks started happening around town.

"No...that katana...Saika!" Haruna stammered in shock. "That's it...that's the sword that attacked me five years ago!"

Just as Anri imagined.

Haruna was a victim of Anri's Saika, and the seed within her that had been growing all along found quick purchase within the imbalance from her love of Nasujima, she suspected.

Meanwhile, Haruna sneered, "Y-you...you killed them! Your own parents! With that katana..."

"That's right. I might as well have killed them, I suppose," Anri replied, neither an affirmation nor denial. She raised the katana.

That was all she did—pull it upward—but the back of the sword hit Haruna's arm in a sensitive spot, causing her to drop the knife.

"Ah..."

Haruna panicked and crouched to pick up the knife—an amateur's mistake. In the next instant, the long blade of the katana slid against her neck, freezing her instantly.

"...!"

"That child of Saika won't tell you how to fight, will it? Which means...it might inherit the will and aims of Saika but not the experience and memory," Anri conjectured. "Please...I have a request. Tell the other Saikas to stop this... As the parent, your orders should reach the children. Of course, if you're under Saika's control, my Saika can order you to stop, as your parent..."

"No...this can't be!"

Despite Anri's request that she not hurt anyone, those very words did indeed hurt Haruna's pride deeply.

"Saika tried! It rushed up and tried to take me over, day after day... but I survived it! I held it down with the power of my love! And yet, you don't know the first thing about love...so how can I lose to you...?"

She glared up at Anri, the picture of frustration.

In contrast, Anri's voice held nothing but sadness. "Miss Nickawa...I'll let you hear just a little bit."

"Huh...?"

"Of the words of Saika's love, the thing that constantly echoes within me..."

Anri moved the katana away from Haruna's neck and stuck it, just a fraction of an inch, into the girl's arm.

She felt a small prick of pain on her arm, then—

The words of love came right into her heart and

and

and

love

love

was all

ve, love, love, lo

ause of love." "So mu

ust love people." "Don't be ridicu

"Don't talk about who you love, that just

o, no, no! I love all, all, all of humanity equally

What do I love? Don't be ridiculous! It's everything

love blood splatter." "I love hard bone." "It's love." "Nice

so I forgive you." "So you can forgive me too, okay" "I won't

all of this." "Ah!" "The slice of meat during the moment of ecstasy

I just love the soft and yet hard muscle that rips right apart!" "And
there's that hard bone, so smooth and supple, weak yet sharp, tough
and cracking!" "Love trembling and soft and silky and squishy sticking
and sticking and sticking tight together as voices echo with cries of
love, yes? I'm so jealous I wish I had words of love to speak but I don't
so I want you to love me instead I want to be filled but yes oh yes but
oh yes I'm so jealous even dying can be a form of love lust is a powerful
form of love but no you can't try to narrow love to a definition that's
blasphemy against the heart there is no definition of love all that you
need are those simple words I love you I love you I love you I love you I
love you I love you I love you I love you I love you I love you I love you

I love you I love you I love you I love you I love you I love you I love
you I love you I love you I love you I love you I love you I love you I
love you I love you I love you I love you I love you I love you I love you
I love you I love you I love you I love you I love you I love you I love
you I love you I love you I love you I love you I love you I love you I
love you I love you I love you I love you I love you I love you I love you
I love you I love you I love you I love you I love you I love you I love
you I love you I love you I love you I love you I love you I love you I
love you I love you I love you I love you I love you I love you I love you
I love you I love you I love you I love you I love you I love you I love
you I love you I love you I love you I love you I love you I love you I
love you I love you I love you I love you I love you I love you I love you
I love you I love you I love you I love you I love you I love you I love
you I love you I love you I love you I love you I love you I love you I
love you I love you I love you I love you I love you I love you I love you
I love you I love you I love you I love you I love you I love you I love
you I love you I love you I love you I love you I love you I love you I
love you I love you I love you I love you I love you I love you I love you
I love you I love you I love you I love you I love you I love you I love
you I love you I love you I love you I love you I love you I love you I
love you I love you I love you I love you I love you I love you I love you
I love you I love you I love you I love you I love you I love you I love
you I love you I love you I love you I love you I love you I love you I
love you I love you I love you I love you I love you I love you I love you
I love you I love you I love you I love you I love you I love you I love
you I love you I love you I love you I love you I love you I love you—

*   *   *

Just at the moment Haruna's mind threatened to explode, Anri pulled the sword away.

"Did you hear Saika's words?"

She heard them. To be more precise, she couldn't shut them out.

It was nothing at all like the words that Haruna had heard within herself.

This was not love.

Taken one by one, the words might have included love, but boiled and bubbled into one solid mass of "words of love," it was nothing but a thick stew of voices of loathing to anyone who heard it.

"H-how...? How can you possibly stand...those haunting curses?"

"I am lacking in many ways," Anri explained, forcing a smile onto her face despite the sadness in her eyes. She examined her own Saika. "So I must fill the gaps of what I'm missing... I'm a parasite. I live off of all kinds of things."

She continued in a tiny voice, as if speaking just to herself, "I know that I lack the heart to love others...and that's why I've been able to listen to the voice, over and over...with total objectivity..."

From outside the picture frame.

Anri looked down as she envisioned the familiar image, and Haruna took it as her chance to strike. She picked up the knife from her feet and swung it at Anri with everything she had.

Once, twice, thrice—the knife flashed at the limit of speed for a human being, carving fresh slices into Anri's body. Though she didn't hit any fatal spots, there were heavy wounds on her arms and legs.

"Ha-ha...ah-ha-ha-ha-ha! I did it! Yes, you could never stop me..."

Her gale of laughter was short-lived.

Anri withstood the assault with utter calm, and now the point of that katana was pressed to the other girl's throat.

"Ah!" Haruna shrieked with fear.

Anri asked curiously, "Why are you so afraid of being cut? Isn't that just a result of being loved?"

It wasn't sarcasm, but an honest question. Haruna gritted her teeth and put on her bravest face, throwing the question back at Anri.

"Wh-why did you just let me cut you...?"

Haruna was no fool. She was rational enough to understand that Anri chose not to dodge attacks that she could have avoided. Anri responded to the question by allowing her expressionless eyes to flash red.

"If you won't stop the other slashers now, I'll have to do something awful to you. This means we'll be even," she announced.

"Huh…?"

It was an absurd thing to say, when she was the one who'd just taken several deep slashes, Haruna thought. But while her rational mind was confident, her subconscious heart was trembling in fear at what might happen to her.

Just as her heart feared, Anri pressed the tip of the sword against her throat.

"I'm letting Saika take over just a bit of your heart. You'll be fine—I highly doubt it's fatal…"

"Ah…aaaah…"

"I won't apologize. If I apologize to you now, I'll be denying my very way of life. Yes, I think I'm a coward. I'm trying to protect my own peace of mind by doing something awful to you…but I can't help it."

The bespectacled girl smiled ruefully.

That was the last image Haruna saw before her mind was occupied.

"After all, I'm a parasite."

The tip of the sword broke the skin of her throat, just the smallest of margins—and the words of love flowed into her.

She remembered that it was the voice that entered her for only an instant when she was just barely grazed by the slasher five years ago.

The last thing Haruna heard was Anri's voice atop a tremendous flood of loving curses.

"You see, Saika gets very lonely. So it hurts to hear you claim that you 'suppressed' her or 'used' her. From our human perspective, she might be doing it wrong…but it's true that Saika does love all of humanity…

"So please…love her back.

"Miss Niekawa, I want you…to love Saika.

"You, at least, can love others…unlike me…"

♂♀

At the same moment—

Shizuo noticed that one of the slashers coming after him suddenly lost the will to fight, and he gave his body an order with all of his mind and spirit.

Just one word: *Stop.*

That had never worked before. The cells, ruled by his anger, always continued their destruction until everything was finished.

But this was different.

Shizuo was not ruled by anger now.

It was joy. He was using his strength of his own will, out of nothing but joy.

Stop...stop...*stop, damn you!*

Finally, his anger appeared, its momentum focused at all of his own cells. The fist that threatened to crush the face of the oncoming but nonhostile slasher, now just an ordinary, harmless person...

Stopped right before making contact with the nose and went still.

"...Ha-ha."

Shizuo looked at the halted fist and realized he was laughing.

"Ha-ha-ha-ha-ha-ha...ha-ha-ha-ha-ha-ha-ha-ha-ha..."

It was the laughter of an innocent child and the laughter of an insane killer.

What the hell?

About time you finally started listening to me.

Behind him was the by-product of that personal victory.

An entire field of Saikas, beaten until they couldn't move again, and a pile of broken blades in all shapes and sizes, snapped in half by Shizuo's shadow-gloved hands.

But none of them was dead.

He swung his fists with a different emotion than anger. It was pleasure—still a twisted emotion to utilize for fighting—but the result was that he'd been able to hold back for once.

*   *   *

It was the moment that violence turned to strength for Shizuo Heiwajima.

♂♀

One night, five years ago

Anri's father was trying to kill her.

Not out of anger. He stared at her with calm, blank eyes as he put his weight into strangling her around the neck.

Daddy.
Daddy.
It hurts.
It hurts.
Don't.
Why are you strangling me?
Why is Mommy lying on the ground?
I don't want you to fight with her.
I don't want to fight with you, either, Daddy.
I won't cry when you hit me anymore. I'll hold it in.
Just don't kill me. Please, help me, Daddy…

As her wits began to fade, the girl saw her mother standing over her father's back. He continued to choke Anri, unaware.

She didn't know what had happened between her father and mother or why he was trying to kill her.

All she knew was that her mother said, "I love you, dear," and lopped his head off with a swing from a katana that she'd produced from somewhere. At the end of the swing, she turned the blade around and stabbed it into her own stomach.

As the katana fell from her mother's hands, it clattered to the ground at Anri's feet and filled her heart with the accursed words of love.

But they didn't reach her.

For the first time, Anri was seeing the world and herself from outside of the picture frame—and even Saika's cursed words couldn't reach her mind.

The words poured right off of her. She picked up Saika, her mind blank—and learned of Saika's past, her intentions, and the fact that her own mother had been the source of the slashings.

Anri's body absorbed the sword. The police never found the slasher's weapon.

"A-Anri. Is that you...Anri?"

She came back to her senses at the sound of Nasujima's voice.

In front of her was an unconscious Haruna and Nasujima, who looked down at the girl's body as though she were something creepy and disgusting.

"I-I don't know what you did...but she tried to attack me in the faculty room once. The school helped me hush the matter up and transfer her out, but... Shit! I guess she never gave up, the freaky stalker!" he ranted, all image of an educator lost.

Suddenly, he shrieked and backed away from Anri. Was he startled by the katana in her hands? But that wasn't the case.

Anri turned around to see that a motorcycle had appeared without producing any engine noise. It was Celty.

But why now...?

Anri shook her head in resignation and turned toward Celty. Just as she was about to say something, Nasujima grabbed her shoulder from behind.

"C'mon, Sonohara, run away with me. Okay? Okay?"

His ulterior motives were obvious even in this extreme situation. Anri just shook his hand away.

"Wh...why are you turning me down? D-don't you remember how I saved you from those bullies, Sonohara? Before? Y'know?"

"I already returned that favor."

"Wh-what, you mean just now? W-we've got bigger fish to fry!"

"No...I did this for myself..."

She turned her back on the confused Nasujima and delivered a statement meant for both him and Celty.

"Until just recently, I thought that the Black Rider here was responsible for all of the slashings. So when I thought you were *being attacked*,

I didn't think twice—and I used my power...because I just wanted to save you..."

"Huh...?"

"It wasn't because I like you. I *hate* you! That's why I wanted to repay you for helping me. So we could be even!"

Oh.

Anri's words jogged Celty's memory. She studied Nasujima's face.

He was that scumbag...

Celty thought back to the night that Anri attacked her and recalled the face of the man standing right there.

And he's a teacher? If he was a teacher, why was he taking money out of a place like that?

"But, sir, it doesn't add up. The Black Rider here...is a very, very good person. Much stronger than me...and forthright...and helping to keep our neighborhood in order."

Nasujima finally realized that something chilling was in the air. He didn't attempt to interrupt any further.

"So, sir...can you tell me...why you were *running away from the Black Rider?* What exactly were you doing?"

She slowly turned to face Nasujima. At last, he noticed the Saika in her hand and shrieked, "Nuh-nuh-nuh-n-not you, too! Not you, too, Anri! Are you pulling that sword on me t-t too, too, too?!"

His voice rattled into an unintelligible mush.

"No, sir."

Anri wore a faint smile and started to walk toward Nasujima, the cursed katana Saika in hand, a part of her now.

"Miss Niekawa and I are different."

"Unlike her, all I feel for you is utter loathing."

♂♀

After Nasujima fled in a panic, Anri turned back to Celty.

She was ready for what came next, if that should happen to mean a fight and possibly her own death...

But all she saw was the Headless Rider slinging the unconscious Haruna over a shoulder and getting onto that motorcycle.

"Huh…?"

Anri watched Celty in bewilderment. Celty apparently noticed her confusion and typed out a quick message on the PDA.

"I've been watching you for quite a while, actually. I've pretty much got a grasp on the situation. I'll take the girl to see an unlicensed doctor I know—don't worry about her," the message read nonchalantly.

Anri blurted out, "C-Celty! Um, I'm really…"

"Don't apologize," the PDA said, the font enlarged for emphasis. *"You did what you thought was right, didn't you? I think it was the right thing to do in that situation. Knocking my head off might have been excessive, but I can complain to Saika about that later."*

The rider leaned closer to Anri and typed in a fresh message.

"But don't think that I'm sympathizing with you."

That statement felt like it was covering something up and was followed by another more bashful one.

"I just think that if we fought, I couldn't beat you."

After Celty left, Anri clenched her own Saika as she stood in the empty street.

Sympathy… I don't really bother myself with the sympathy of others…

But Anri didn't particularly think that she was worthy of pity.

She didn't feel sadness.

This was the life she chose for herself.

Anri thought back to the last message Celty left upon departure.

"If you still can't accept all of this…then instead of apologizing to me, use that sword of yours to protect Ikebukuro. You could, let's say…use those hundred Saikas to do volunteer work around town or fund-raise to plant more trees in Ikebukuro…"

As Celty said, Anri Sonohara had gained a sword.

A mob of more than a hundred slashers. In normal circumstances, they acted with their own wills, but when the time came, Anri could call upon them as faithful partners.

It was a burden, but a weight that Anri wanted on her shoulders.

She had been floating aimlessly before this, so the weight of controlling the fate of others kept her feet firmly on the ground.

The weight might keep her from moving from that spot.
But at least her eyes and mouth, hands and heart were still free.
She could look where she wanted.
She could listen to the world around her.
She could tell someone about that.
She could reach out and grab what she wanted.
And she could still smile.
She wasn't sad.
She might not be having fun, either.
So she chose to smile.
Even she didn't know if that was her true will or if she was just fooling herself.
She kept smiling without a sound.
Happily, sadly.

For a moment, the voice of Saika that echoed throughout her body halted, and she heard a voice say, *I cannot love you, but I do not hate you.*

To be honest, maybe she only imagined that she heard it.

"Uh…"

But the cursed voice was back to its usual state and wouldn't respond to her.

Then Anri realized that Saika had tried to comfort her, and for a moment, she felt just a little bit happy.

Chat room

—SAIKA HAS ENTERED THE CHAT—

|um, well, im typing this from a manga cafe|
|im sorry for everything that happened|
|i probably wont be around anymore|
|im really very sorry|

—SAIKA HAS LEFT THE CHAT—

—THE CHAT ROOM IS CURRENTLY EMPTY—
—THE CHAT ROOM IS CURRENTLY EMPTY—
—THE CHAT ROOM IS CURRENTLY EMPTY—
—THE CHAT ROOM IS CURRENTLY EMPTY—
—THE CHAT ROOM IS CURRENTLY EMPTY—

—TAROU TANAKA HAS ENTERED THE CHAT—

【Eh? Huh?】
【What does that mean?】

—TAROU TANAKA HAS LEFT THE CHAT—

—SETTON HAS ENTERED THE CHAT—

[Oh, what's the harm? Saika says there won't be any more trouble.]
[But if you want to chat, we'll be waiting for you here, Saika.]
[Well, good night.]
[Later...]

—SETTON HAS LEFT THE CHAT—

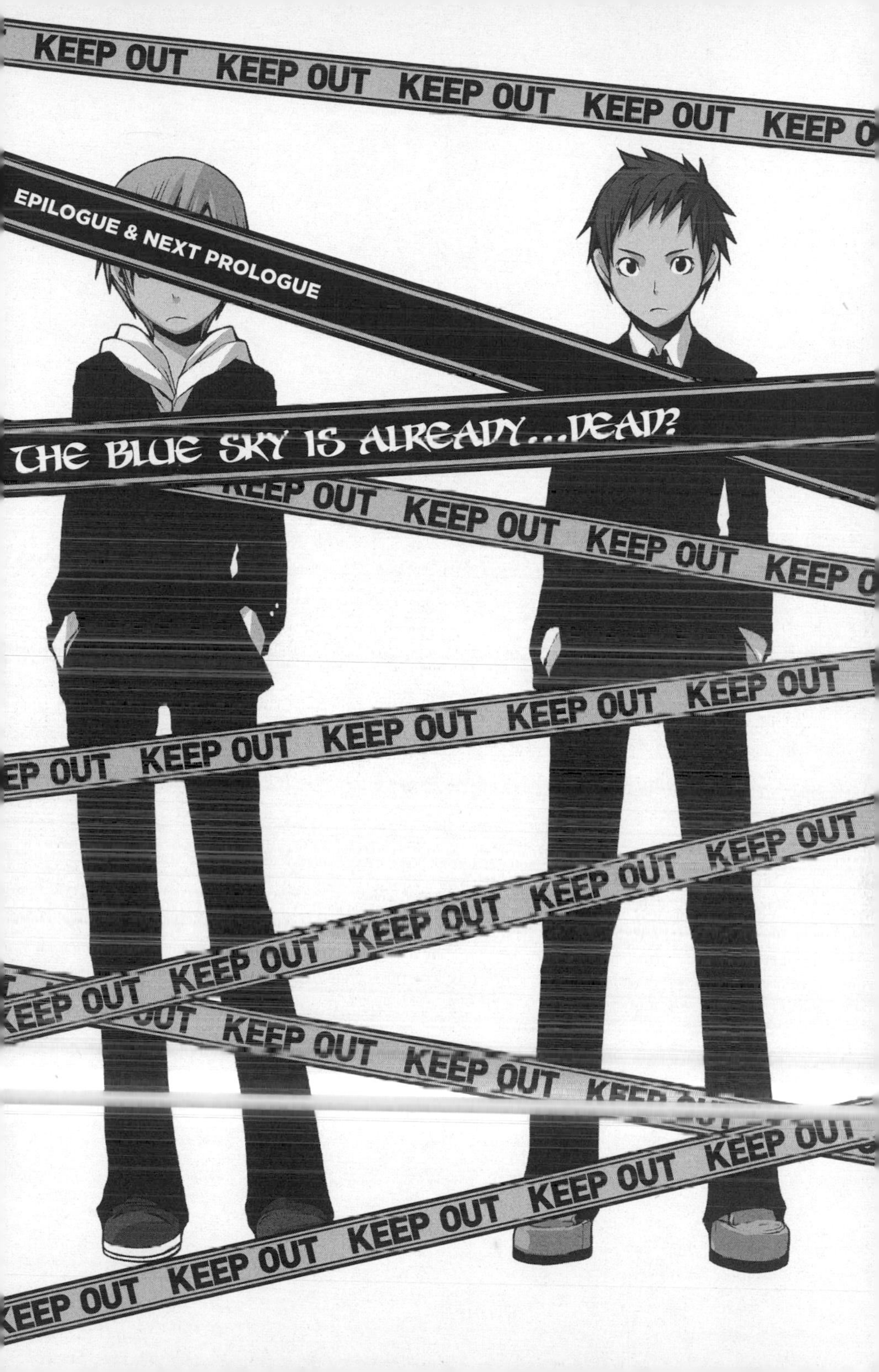
EPILOGUE & NEXT PROLOGUE
THE BLUE SKY IS ALREADY…DEAD?
KEEP OUT

A van drove the streets of Ikebukuro.

For some reason, the side door was brand-new while the rest was old, and it stood out like a sore thumb due to some kind of anime illustration on the side.

"…Well, we definitely can't get up to trouble in this van anymore…"

Yumasaki handled the door repair, as he knew someone who worked with sheet metal. The result was that their van looked incredibly nerdy now.

"Shit, I should have known this would happen if I asked Yumasaki for help," Kadota grumbled. Meanwhile, Togusa gripped the steering wheel in silence. The otaku had already burned one of his cars to the ground, and he was obviously furious with them.

The guilty party, meanwhile, was busy with the usual chitchat in the backseat.

"Oh, right. We gotta pick up the Dengeki Bunko releases for May."

"Yeah, the fifth volume of *Dokuro-chan* is out."

"It's an odd-numbered volume, so it must have another final chapter in it."

"Can't wait to hear about Allison's kids."

Kadota leaned over to see that Yumasaki and Karisawa were sprawled out in the back of the van, rear seat removed, reading through a pile of books and manga.

Can't believe they don't get carsick, he thought with wry admiration. The nerd talk continued.

"I'm already looking forward to next month's releases."

"Yeah, it's the last volume of *Lunatic Moon*. Gotta love Tomaz and what a little cutie he is."

"Even in two dimensions, I'm not interested in guys."

"Aww, you're no fun, Yumacchi."

Kadota could tell that Togusa's driving was getting more and more violent as their nonsensical chatter continued. He turned to face forward and held his head in his hands. Yes, they were irritating Togusa. The problem was, they had no idea that they were.

But what's done is done. No use raising a fuss about it now.

They had bigger problems than infighting right now.

The events of that prior day had been nicknamed the "Night of the Ripper."

The authorities hadn't made any headway into solving the incident that produced more than fifty victims in a single night.

But public opinion held that the events of that night were something different from the string of ongoing street slashings. The primary reason for this was that all of the victims were young men wearing yellow bandannas.

At the same time, there had been a huge brawl in South Ikebukuro Park, so the residents of the town assumed it was some motorcycle gang squabble. There was just one teenage girl included in the victims, but she was explained away as one of the usual slasher victims.

The case was classified as a color gang's internal conflict, but this only meant that the heightened tension in the town reached even greater levels.

What worried Kadota most was that the Dollars were listed as a potential culprit for the attack.

When Celty and Shizuo captured the slasher, they found he had alibis for some of the other crimes and figured that it would be pointless to give him to the police, so they left him outside of a hospital instead. He really was being controlled by something and had no memories of anything.

They'd had him blindfolded while questioning him, so he couldn't possibly bring charges against them…but just in case, Celty arranged for some support money through Shinra. While they felt guilty about hitting him with the car, they were essentially even, as far as they cared.

But this meant that no slasher had been caught.

Celty sent a message saying not to worry about that anymore, and nothing like it had occurred since the Night of the Ripper—but the fact that the police hadn't caught anyone meant that society at large was still nervous.

As long as that fear doesn't get turned against the Dollars, Kadota hoped, looking outside the window.

The town was full of people in yellow bandannas. At least half of the crowd was wearing them. They weren't really doing anything, but their eyes were all full of hostility toward *something.* That hostility colored the entire neighborhood of Ikebukuro yellow.

The Yellow Sky will soon rise…

Kadota recalled the line that launched the Yellow Scarves Rebellion from the very start of the *Romance of the Three Kingdoms* novel and the irony of the Yellow Scarves gang that colored the streets.

The kids were young—many were in middle school, and some even looked like elementary age.

Kadota looked up at the blue sky above with irritation and repeated a line he'd said once before, but with more disgust this time.

"…The town is starting to fall apart."

♂♀

Shit, shit! I'm so tired of everyone treating me like a fool! I'm a teacher! And a far more talented and intelligent teacher than the others! How can this be happening to me?!

Just you wait, Anri Sonohara.

I'll ruin your life at the faculty meeting! I'll tell them you attacked me with a katana! If I tell them you were working with Niekawa, the other teachers will take my side.

And screw that stupid Niekawa! I fool around with her once, and she becomes a damn stalker!

Ooh, what if I use that as a threat against Anri? Could I leech some money out of her?

I've got the Awakusu-kai backing me, I'll say. That'll freak her out.

...She *will* freak out, right?

Guns are stronger than swords, after all.

Yeah, that's a plan.

Sonohara, Niekawa, Kida: No one messes with me and gets away with it...

At the same moment—

"What's up, Shizuo? Why the good mood?"

Shizuo was on his way to collect some debts for the hookup website, dragged out by his boss, Tom. He was normally sluggish and reluctant to work, but he was being rather proactive today.

"Nothin' much. Just cleared my head a bit yesterday."

Even the way he spoke to his boss seemed a bit more natural and polite than normal. Tom couldn't help but be curious, but business called.

"Today's target is a real piece of work. He borrows five hundred thou, then tries to weasel out of it by saying, 'I've got yakuza friends!' Well, I laughed my ass off when I looked into it. Not only does he *not* have any yakuza connections, all he did was borrow money from a back-alley loan shark working for the Awakusu-kai. And somehow he thinks that gives him any kind of leg to stand on?"

"So we're going to find him and break that leg for him?"

"That's basically it... Man, you really are excited today, aren't you?"

"Actually, I think I've finally figured out how to control my strength. I'm just dying to test it out," Shizuo remarked, his eyes flashing with childish exuberance behind his sunglasses.

In the end, Shizuo's strength turned into violence.

But as for whether the liberation of his power turned his life in a more positive direction—that would depend on how he used it in the future.

It would be up to the man Shizuo was about to pound to decide what the answer was.

"Funny thing is, it turns out this guy is a teacher. From Raira Academy."

"Well, that makes it even worse. It'll feel good to sock him one."

"Just don't go overboard and kill him. Let's see, Nasujima, Nasu-jima...ah, here's the place." Tom spotted the apartment nameplate. They took positions on either side of the door and rang the buzzer.

Who is it at this time of night...?
I-is it *him*? That informant?
Has he come to make me disappear?
Or is it Anri?! Or Niekawa?! The Black Rider?!
Shit! Shit! Not now! I was almost ready!
You won't get me without a fight.
I dare you to open that door. I'll crush your skull with this extinguisher.

"...No answer. His electric meter's been reading steadily, so I'm pretty sure he's still here."
"Let's open this up."
Shizuo squeezed the doorknob. It cracked and broke out of the door, lock and all. He swung the door open forcefully.
A fire extinguisher appeared from within and struck him soundly on the head.

Silence.

After a brief hush, Shizuo grabbed the extinguisher, which was still pressed to his forehead, and crumpled it with his fingers alone.
A blast of exhaust and white powder buffeted Nasujima in his hiding spot.
"Gaah!"
As Nasujima coughed, Shizuo slowly lowered the fire extinguisher. His boss had already sprinted off for safety, which left only Shizuo and Nasujima in the apartment hallway.
From behind the extinguisher appeared the face of some vengeful god, veins bulging on every surface.
"That...*hurt, dammit!*"
He threw a punch using the twisted remains of the extinguisher like

brass knuckles, catching Nasujima smack in the middle of the face and sending him into dreamland.

Shizuo's boss watched the explosion from a safe distance away and remarked in relief, "Good, that's the Shizuo I like to see."

And thus began a day in the life of Shizuo Heiwajima, just like any other.

Just as his name suggested, a day of peace and quiet, if only for himself.

The next time Nasujima opened his eyes, it was already April, he had been fired from his job due to complaints about sexual harassment from students, and there was a gang of young toughs from the Awakusu-kai at his bedside.

But that's a story for another time.

♂♀

"Are you sure you're okay, Sonohara?"

Mikado Ryuugamine was watching Anri in her hospital bed with concern.

"Damn that slasher! So sorry, Anri. If only I'd been at your side twenty-four hours a day, this never would have happened," Masaomi Kida joked, though there was a surprisingly serious, angry look in his eyes.

They'd skipped school and raced to the hospital the moment they heard Anri was a slashing victim.

She was sure they'd said a lot of stuff to her, but she couldn't remember what it was. Anri only remembered that she was happy about it.

Later that night, she didn't have the usual dream.

And yet, when she woke up in the morning, she wasn't plunged into despair.

Mikado and Masaomi visited again the next day.

Masaomi was attempting to seduce the nurse when his phone suddenly went off.

"Masaomi! Turn your phone off in the hospital!"

"Sorry, sorry, gotta be careful about that. Looks like I got called out. Gotta leave for today."

"Huh? Really?"

"Well, I'll be back tomorrow, Anri. And remember: All men are wolves, so keep the nurse call button close in case Mikado tries anything funny," Masaomi warned as he left the room. Based on that, he didn't seem likely to return today.

Given the criminal angle of her injuries, Anri was in a private room so the police could question her. The nurse had just come by for her check, so no one would be coming for a while.

That meant that Anri and Mikado were completely alone in the room.

It was his chance.

Though he felt that being thankful was inappropriate, Mikado couldn't help but be grateful to God. Normally Masaomi would be running interference, but now they could finally speak alone.

It was nearly a year since he first met Anri.

Time for him to move on from just being her class representative partner.

Mikado Ryuugamine steadied his breathing and did his very best to act normal.

"Um, hey, Sonohara."

"What is it, Ryuugamine?"

"I w-was just wondering if there was anyone you had…on your mind?"

He knew that it was totally impossible, but he couldn't help but hope against hope that she might say, "Actually, *you*…"

Mikado waited for Anri's response, praying to God for a positive response.

"Hmm… Well, there are some people I look up to."

"…h! O-oh. You don't say. Who would that be?" he tried to reply nonchalantly as possible, ringing bells of doom in his ears.

"Well…I didn't say this to the police, but…I was attacked by the slasher a few hours before I actually got hurt…and some people were there to save me. In particular, there was a guy wearing bartender clothes, and the other person there was supercool…"

"Bartender clothes?"

That's not Shizuo, is it?

Mikado shook that horrifying image out of his head and waited for her to continue.

But I think he's like me... Someone who can't actually love other people, Anri thought to herself. But by not saying it aloud, she kept Mikado in prickly suspense.

"And the other person was...well, don't be too shocked."

"Who?"

"It was the Black Rider, believe it or not!"

Gong! The bell rang again. Mikado felt his heart being ripped out of his chest, but he did his best to keep the smile up for Anri's sake.

"We talked a bit after that...and I could feel such a radiation of purpose and affection... It seems like the Black Rider has everything I don't... Ha-ha, I suppose you wouldn't believe that, would you?"

As a matter of fact, Mikado knew Celty well. And based on the combination with the bartender outfit, it was most certainly Celty and Shizuo.

Huh...but...what? I mean, Celty's a woman, so...huh?

Mikado was completely baffled until he remembered that from a distance Celty's gender was essentially indistinguishable. But if he was going to explain that to Anri, he'd have to reveal that he knew Celty. And in order to explain *that*, he might be forced to talk about the Dollars.

No, I can't do that. I don't want to get her involved in our side of things.

He thought it over rapidly and decided to try to push her away from them.

"Oh, but that Black Rider and the other folks...they're so far outside of what we experience in our normal lives, you know?"

Says the guy who was obsessed with the abnormal, he thought wryly. But Anri cut him down with a faint smile.

"Ryuugamine... In the world we live in, what do you think is truly abnormal?"

"Uh...well... Using mental powers, crazy events popping off, stuff like that?" he replied, confused. She shook her head, still smiling.

"It's when *nothing* happens. When the same exact things happen day after day without even the slightest variation. From the moment you wake to the moment you fall asleep, the same boring repetition. That is the most unlikely event of all."

"Oh...good point."

"Breaking the peace or having your peace broken, yearning for boredom or change deep within your heart—I think that is humanity's true nature."

Mikado wasn't sure what Anri meant or how to respond. She gave him a sad smile and wrapped up her point.

"So I think...I've finally gotten back to normal."

"Huh?"

I've been escaping into the abnormal world of my dreams ever since Mom and Dad died, and now I'm finally back on this side, she thought, smiling at the confused Mikado.

After meeting hours were over and she was alone in the hospital room, Anri stared up at the ceiling.

In the end, she didn't tell Mikado or Masaomi the truth: that she was Saika. They probably wouldn't believe her if she had. Of course, it was easy for her to assume that, given that she didn't know the truth about Mikado, either.

This is for the best.

Ryuugamine and Masaomi are good friends of mine.

I can't get them involved. I can't draw them into the underworld.

I won't cause any more slashings. I won't let that happen.

That means that neither of them will need to worry about anything...

She imagined their faces and then something else entirely.

The one really pulling the strings.

As she was the one controlling all of Saika's children, Anri understood virtually everything that had caused events to take the path

learned of the presence of this mastermind.

She didn't know what he looked like or his goal, but...if that mastermind thought he could use them to destroy the town again—if he tried to destroy Mikado's and Masaomi's peace...

She felt her fists clench atop the blanket.

*   *   *

Racked by unease and determination, Anri thought of the mastermind's name.

Which was...

♂♀

"Izaya Orihara is a very strange name, when you think about it..."

"Hmm... It might just be coincidence that I turned out the way I did, but I think it actually suits me perfectly."

In an apartment in Shinjuku, Izaya Orihara was playing a curious customized game of shogi by himself. A secretary was making rounds between mountains of documents and a computer behind him.

Izaya didn't bother to help her with the avalanche of processing ahead of her. Instead he asked, "Namie, how much do you believe in coincidence?"

"...What do you mean?"

The board was triangular with triangular spaces, and normal shogi pieces were arranged neatly into three different formations.

"They're probably thinking that all of the stuff that just happened was mere happenstance. When Haruna Niekawa was in Anri Sonohara's apartment, they think Nasujima showing up was a coincidence. Nasujima was pressured into being there at that point in time. He was flattered into it. He had to be given Anri Sonohara's precise address. That was all me. Funny thing is, for a teacher, he was a real idiot. He could've just looked up her address by peeking into the other class's student register. Maybe he just didn't want them to spread rumors about him. The guy who hit on every girl in the school!"

Izaya chuckled as he recalled the entire string of events.

"Another funny thing is when you research fairies and possessed swords and all that stuff under the assumption that they're *real*, you actually come up with quite a lot of results."

Izaya was positively tickled by the existence of all that information he hadn't known, and remembering the conclusion of Saika's incident sent him trembling with excitement.

"The only true coincidence this time was that when Nasujima took my money, the real Saika showed up."

*　　*　　*

Nasujima led an unstable life to begin with. He had borrowed money from one of the Awakusu-kai's loan sharks, and his back was against the wall. So he came up with a plan. Haruna Niekawa had once threatened him with a knife. What if he blackmailed her parents over that and squeezed some money out of them?

The Awakusu-kai put him through to an information dealer named Izaya Orihara. When he visited the man's office and Izaya said he needed to leave for a while and just walked out, there was a black bag on the table with multiple stacks of bills poking out. Just as Izaya expected, Nasujima ran off with the money. He probably expected to pay off the loan shark and then hightail it for safety. Perhaps he figured that given Izaya's line of work, he wouldn't be reporting that stolen cash to the police.

All that was left was to hire Celty to capture Nasujima.

Izaya threatened to tell the Awakusu-kai about the stolen money and thus had himself a faithful little pawn.

That was his angle to using Haruna Niekawa, the true Saika.

"But then, out of the blue comes the owner of the real Saika, not a simple copy like Niekawa. That made things much more interesting... Personally, it would have been perfect if Shizu had died in the fray, but I can't ask for too much, I suppose."

"How were things made 'interesting'?" Namie asked the elated Izaya, her own face an emotionless mask. To her, the only thing that mattered in the world was her brother's happiness, and everything else was immaterial—including herself.

Izaya knew her bizarre proclivities, but he was like a child bursting with a secret inside, his eyes sparkling.

"Now the city is split in three, between the Dollars, the Yellow Scarves, and Anri Sonohara's demonic army... And the demon blade has infiltrated the ranks of all the rest..."

"Hmm. And that's interesting to you?"

"The shit won't hit the fan right away... But for now, a few sparks will do fine. In a few months, those sparks will smoke and smolder, and...oh, I just can't wait anymore!"

He laughed and rolled back onto the sofa, as giddy as a boy

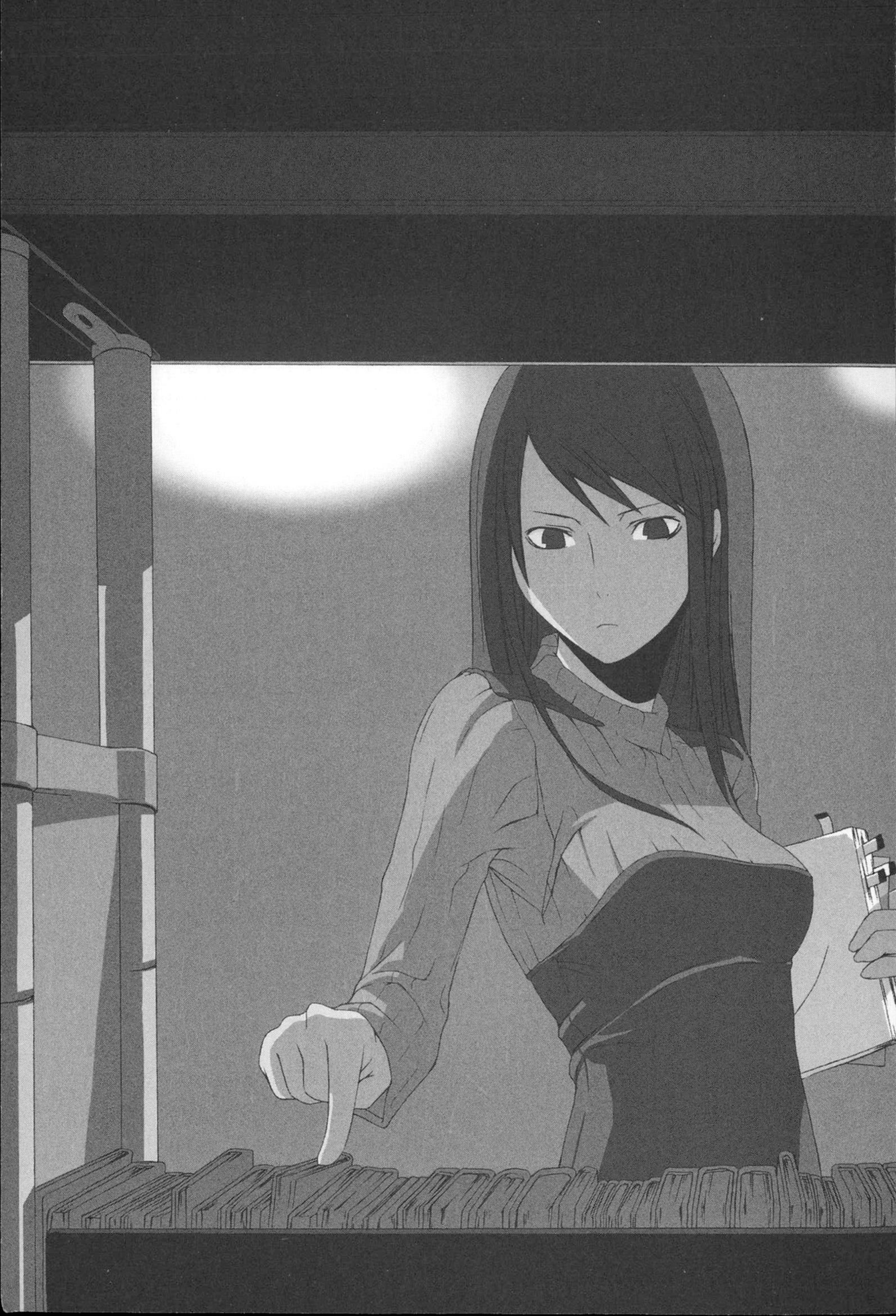

waiting for the release of a new video game. Meanwhile, Namie was still expressionless and flat.

She asked, "The Yellow Scarves might have the numbers, but weren't they just created by some stupid kid three years ago? Doesn't speak well to their balance, does it?"

"Actually, no… Think about it. It means that 'stupid kid' is able to handle an organization of that many people. The threat is real!" he proclaimed, then muttered mostly to himself.

"Of course, it's not like the shogun of the Yellow Scarves is a total stranger to me, either…"

♂♀

"…Don't try to drag me back into this."

It was an abandoned husk of a factory somewhere in the city, a distance away from Ikebukuro. Within that desolate, empty space—almost unthinkable for such an urban location—squirmed hundreds of shadows.

The owners of those shadows were all young—boys and girls from elementary to high school ages. Even more striking was their clothing: While all of their outfits were different, every single person inside the factory building wore a yellow bandanna somewhere.

"I don't want any part of it. You got that?" a languid and tired voice rang out, at odds with the stifling nature of the place. "Normally, I'd claim that you would never understand how I feel, but if you were psychics who could actually read my mind, I'd feel pretty stupid, wouldn't I? So I won't say that."

No one else spoke. The lazy voice continued to bounce off the walls.

"At any rate, once I got involved with Izaya, I decided that I was never going to come back here," the man said in the midst of the yel-

Despite his complete denial of the group, one of the Yellow Scarves nearby spoke up without a hint of respect. "C'mon…we ain't got nothin' goin' on without you, bud. The yakuza are too scary to mess with, and we can't run a business with nothing but numbers on our side."

The next moment, a much larger boy next to him kicked him in the face. "His title is *Shogun*."

The original boy waved off the angry one with an idle hand. "Nah, nah, it's cool! I'm not cut out to be a fancy shogun at this point. Just a simple commoner. Commoner? Hell, I'm just a student."

And the man they called Shogun, creator of the Yellow Scarves, got to his feet.

"Seriously, though, when did this turn into such a massive operation? We could give the Dollars a run for their money, yeah? All that yellow is almost kinda creepy though."

It was an Ikebukuro color gang, the kind that had been featured in a famous TV drama. The boy had chosen yellow for their color because it looked so cool on the gang in the show. The odd thing was—

"Actually, it's not yellow in the original books. I was real shocked when I borrowed it from the library!" he cackled, but no one else joined in.

"That doesn't matter, Shogun. The thing is...we have suspicions about the Dollars' involvement."

"..."

"We know you're one of the Dollars, Shogun. There are several others of us who are double affiliated. But the Dollars is a gang that otherwise has very few connections to other groups. I suspect that several of the Dollars attacked us on the day of the incident...and it's not just me. Plenty of us feel the same way, Shogun."

Even after that plaintive speech, the "Shogun" didn't lose the nonchalant smirk.

"I'm saying I ain't doing anything for your sakes. I got my peace and tranquillity, which is what I wanted: surrounded by good friends, living a life of just the right amount of danger."

In the next instant, his carefree expression tightened up. "But that serial slasher destroyed my tranquillity."

His reptilian eyes were sharp and cold enough to freeze everyone there. The entire gathering shivered with the power of that shift.

"Society calls it gang warfare, but that's wrong. It's something else, something weirder...but that doesn't matter. It just doesn't. I'm gonna destroy this slasher. And if there's more than one, then multiple destructions are in order," he said with quiet determination, looking out upon the crowd.

"I care about my people, of course...*but it's Anri getting hurt that I really can't handle.*"

The crowd didn't recognize the name, but no one was going to speak up and interrupt.

"No matter how many people are involved, we're going to annihilate this goddamn slasher. And if the Dollars are behind this—well, I'm one of them..."

The Shogun paused, then spoke as if all the air had been wrung out of his lungs.

"But I'm prepared to bring them down from the inside."

In the empty factory, the Yellow Scarves' shogun, Masaomi Kida, sat alone in a pipe-frame chair, dazed.

"Shit...how dare you...pull me back...," he lamented to the ceiling, cursing the unseen slasher. The only things in his mind were retribution against whomever destroyed his peace of mind—and the smiling faces of Anri, Mikado, his classmates, and his friends.

This drove his irritation into hatred—for the "Saika" that the Internet rumored was the culprit.

"Dammit... How dare you pull me back in... How dare you... *dammit!*"

♂♀

"The fun thing about staring down at the board from above is the illusion that you are God."

Izaya poked and prodded at the triangular shogi board, smirking like a child.

"God attacks! *Hi-yah!*" he chirped, pouring the oil from a lighter onto the board. The smell spread throughout the room, but he paid it no mind, pushing the 〔...〕 were gathered in the center.

"A three-way battle's a wonderful thing. Especially when the leaders are so closely aligned," he gloated, his innocent smile now full of malice as he lit a match. "The sweeter the honeymoon, the greater the despair as it burns ever higher."

Izaya tossed the match onto the board.

Flame.

Transparent blue flame, almost cold in its appearance, enveloped the shogi board. It burned quickly, crackling and charring the pieces as the oil evaporated. The wooden pieces burned up one after the other on the glass table.

"Ha-ha-ha-ha! Look, the pieces burn like trash!" he gloated, a parody of some stereotypical mad villain. It was Namie, who wasn't even watching the exhibition, who doused his excitement with a freezing comment.

"Well, *anything* will become trash if you burn it. Now clean all of that up."

"Tsk. You're no fun, you know that?" he griped, shaking his head in disappointment. But he was back to his good mood in moments. He picked up a pair of cards from the table nearby. "The real question is, how do the other cards who *aren't* my pawns move now? Yumasaki's group, Shinra Kishitani, Simon, Shiki from the Awakusu-kai...the cops... But I suppose Shizu's got to be the king."

He flipped the king card right into the flames. "And Celty's the joker...no, the queen. Then the joker is...Shinra's dad with Nebula...? Know what, I don't really care."

Izaya tossed all of the cards in the fire, bored. As he watched the pile flame away, he turned to the object resting next to him.

"It's actually getting interesting now...don't you agree?"

The eyes of the beautiful severed head resting next to Izaya just barely seemed to twitch.

♂♀

"Ahh...it's so peaceful..."

On the terrace of the luxury apartment building, Celty lay sprawled out on the deck, soaking in the sun. She made a point of typing how comfortable she was into the PDA to show it to Shinra.

He responded by claiming that she'd get sunburned and helped her put on sunscreen and set up an umbrella before getting down next to her.

"By the way, about Saika's katana—it pretty much turned out the way you said it would. Thank you."

"Ha-ha-ha, anything for you, Celty. But I wish you'd whisper your thanks into my ear while we're in bed. In fact, who needs a bed when we can do it right h— *Wugh!*"

She thumped him in the stomach with a backhand punch to shut him up before putting her own doubt into words.

"But you were so precisely correct, it creeped me out a little. I was going to look into it myself, but when I looked on the Net and in the texts, I couldn't find a single reference to a cursed sword named Saika. And your input on the matter was way more detailed than Izaya's. How did you find this stuff out?"

"Oh, that. I found my dad's diary."

"?" Celty typed into the PDA, prompting Shinra for a less vague answer.

"Well, turns out my dad was researching Saika. He was really fascinated with this story of a sword that could 'slice souls in two.' He actually owned it until a few years ago, when he sold it to an antiques trader he knows. I believe the trader's name was Sonohara, but I haven't heard much about the place lately..."

"What?!"

Shinra's father was the very man who smuggled Celty into Japan, as well as the man she suspected of stealing her head in the first place. Even Shinra didn't know where he was or what he was doing now. What would he be doing studying Saika?

"When you say slice souls, that doesn't mean...it could have been used to split the soul between my body and head so that my head could be stolen, does it?"

"Celty...you're bang on. I've been thinking that very thing."

"...No. Never mind. No use getting angry at you."

The Headless Rider gave up and turned over to bask in the warm sunlight again.

"If you're going to sunbathe, it'd be a lot more effective if you took your clothes of— *Fwrgh!*"

She punched Shinra again and looked up at the sky.

It was so very vast and blue. She took a tangible feeling of peace from it.

The town below might be gripped with chaos and confusion, but the blue sky never changed.

For a moment, she disconnected herself from the city and looked up at the blue to ponder Anri and Shizuo.

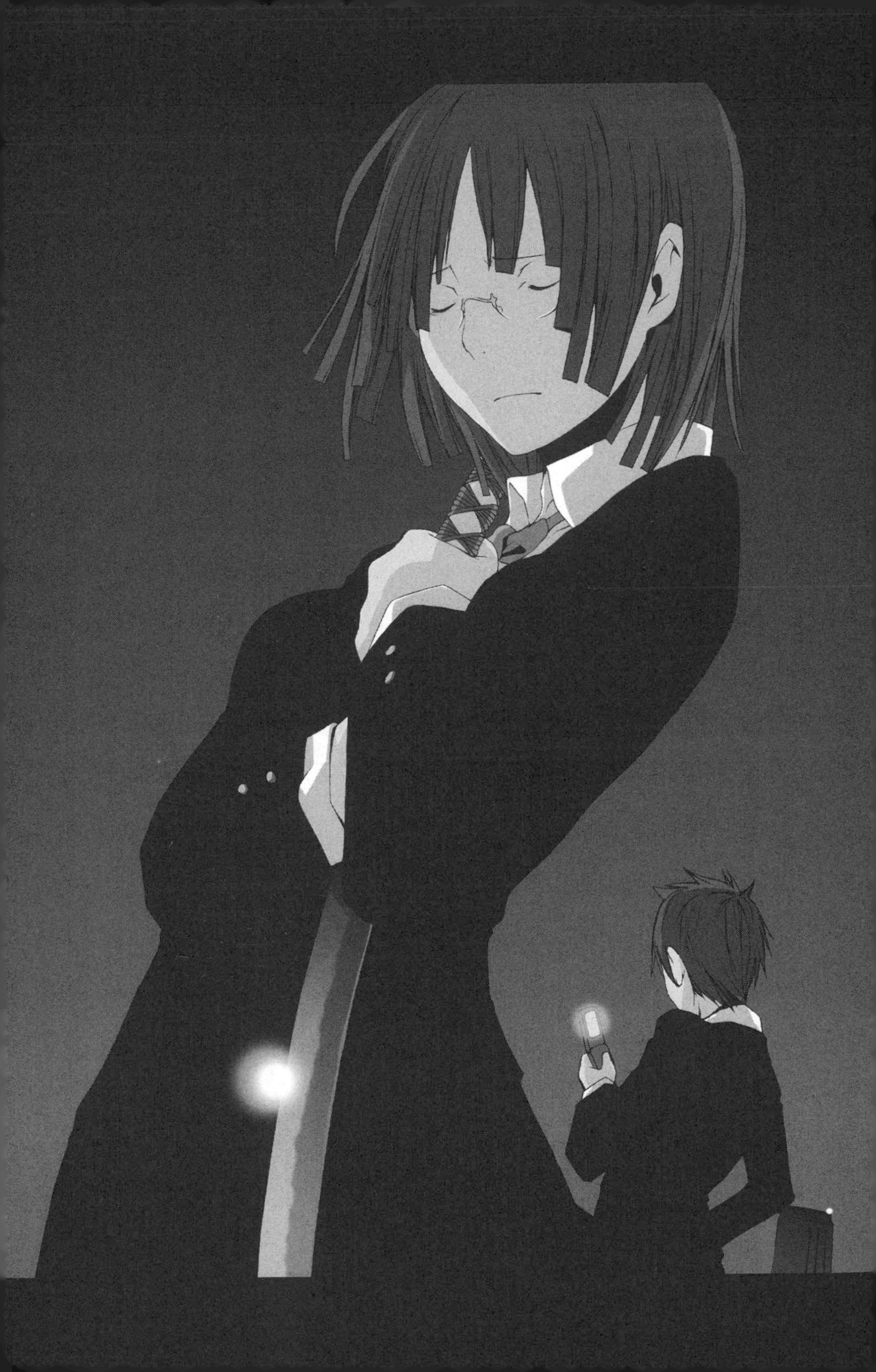

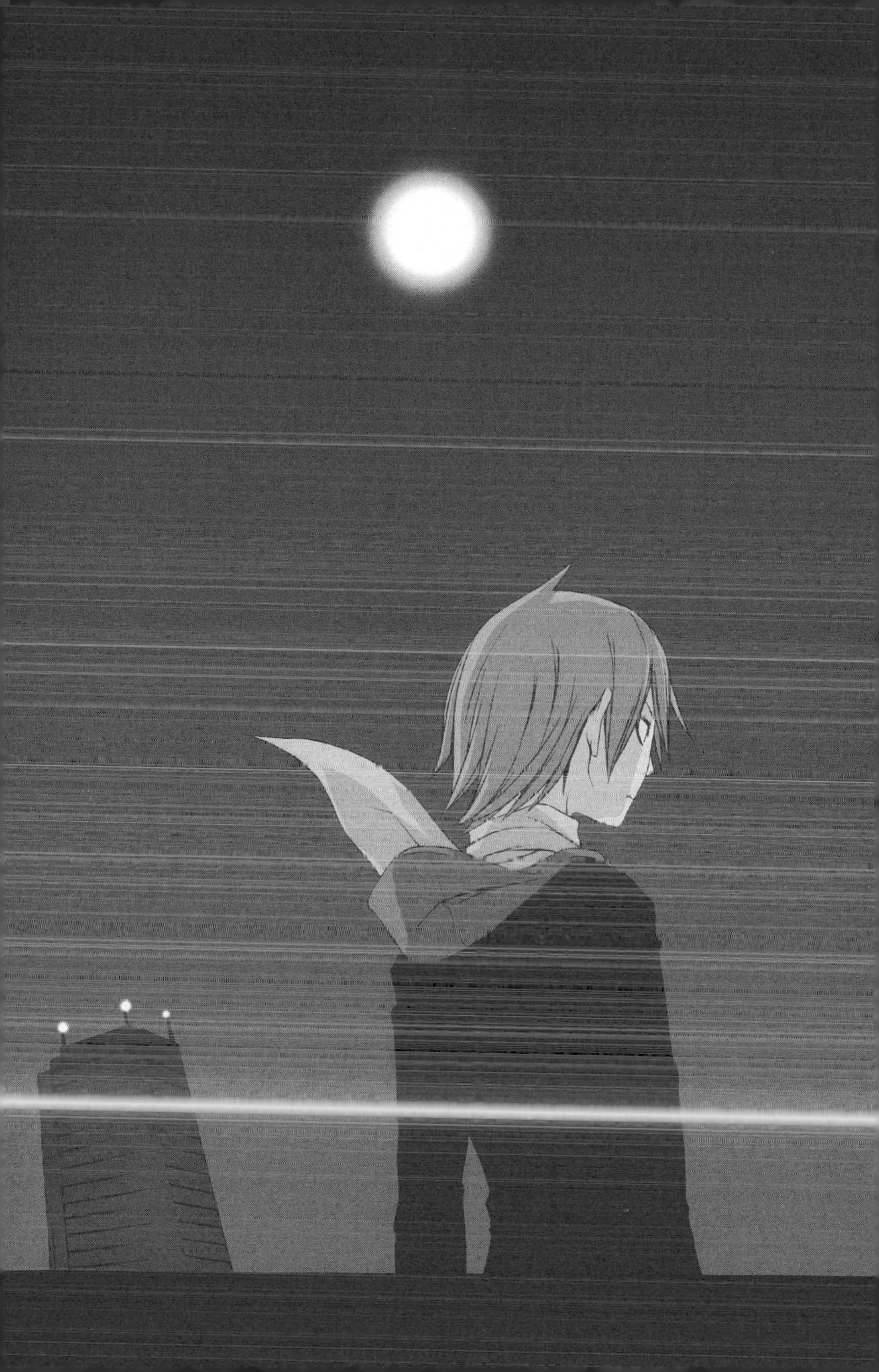

They were both awkward people who had trouble loving others. But for some reason, these two people, flawed at being human, struck Celty as being incredibly human because of that.

What about me? I love Shinra...I think. But is my loving providing Shinra with anything? Is it making Shinra happy? she wondered idly as she stared up at the sky. Then she considered Mikado and the brown-haired boy, the ones who hung around with Anri.

When I listen to Anri and Mikado, it sounds like each of the trio is living off the others, finding things they lack themselves.

It seemed like that in itself was a form of love to Celty, as she slowly drifted off into sleep.

But she didn't realize what a very cruel thing her last waking thought was.

She let sleep steal over her body, quietly, so quietly.
Letting her shadow feel just a moment's peace.

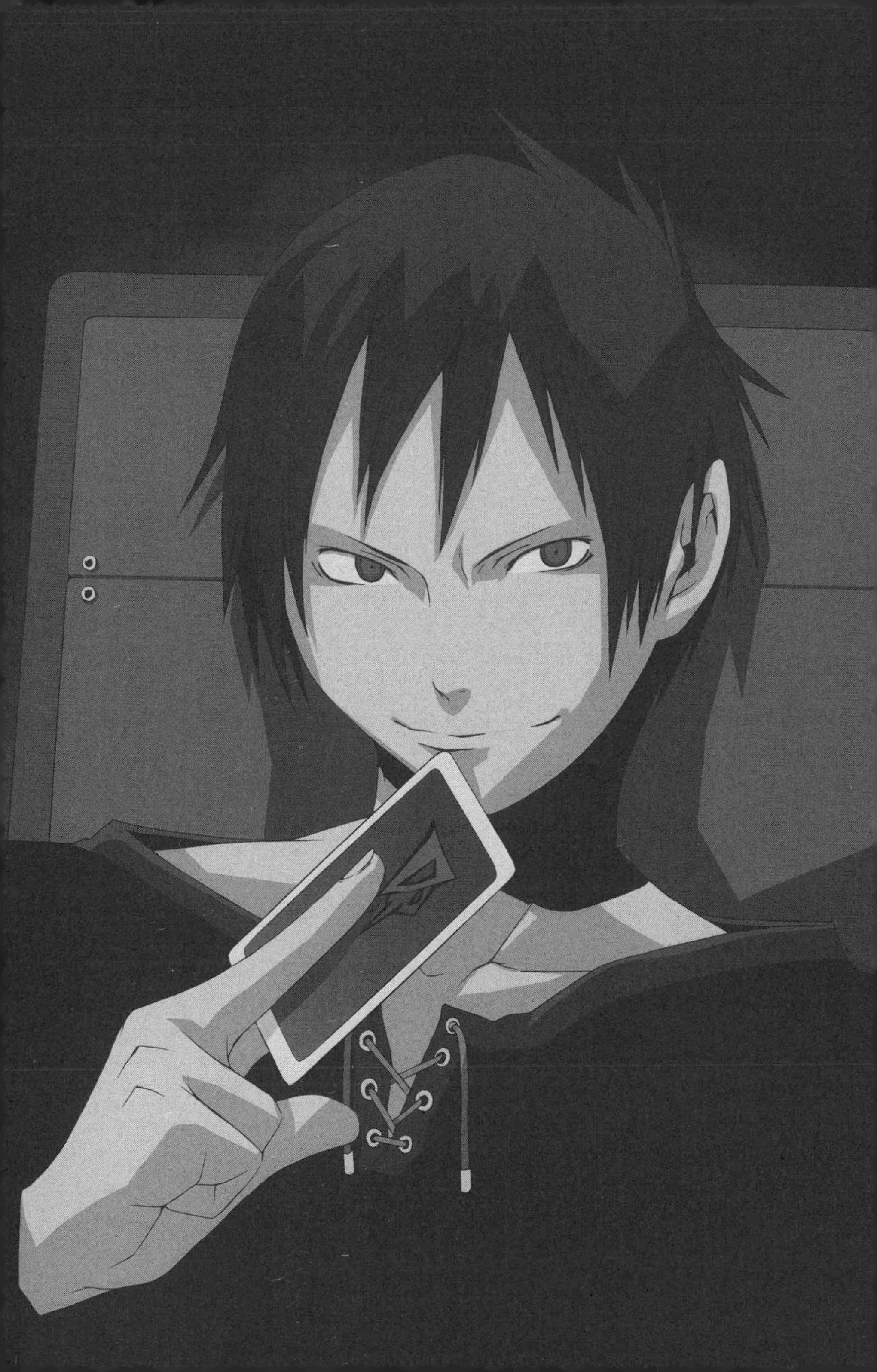

CAST

Mikado Ryuugamine
Masaomi Kida
Anri Sonohara

Shizuo Heiwajima

Celty Sturluson
Shinra Kishitani

Izaya Orihara
Namie Yagiri

Kyouhei Kadota
Erika Karisawa
Walker Yumasaki

Seiji Yagiri
Mika Harima

Simon Brezhnev

Haruna Niekawa
Takashi Nasujima

Third-Rate Tabloid Writer

STAFF

Author
Ryohgo Narita

Illustrations & Visual Concepts
Suzuhito Yasuda (AWA Studio)

Design
Yoshihiko Kamabe

Editing
Gun Suzuki
Atsushi Wada

Publishing
ASCII Media Works

Distribution
Kadokawa Shoten

Durarara!! v2 - The End
© 2005, Ryohgo Narita

Hello, I'm Ryohgo Narita.

Well, it's been a while since you heard from me, and my first book back is the second volume of *Durarara!!* For a second volume in a series of mine, it's almost miraculous how *few* new characters there are. I spent most of the book shining the spotlight on those characters who didn't stand out in the first volume, but I'm pretty sure the story idea was already constructed at the time I wrote the first book...I think. Well, let's say the truth about that is lost in the mists of time.

Once again, I've thrown a lot of little experiments into *Durarara!!* If you recognize the references in Yumasaki and Karisawa's conversations, feel free to smirk; if you don't get them, please just take them as they are: creepy weirdos listing off a bunch of names and terms that make no sense to normal people. But unlike last time, in this book they're just present for flavor, not plot reasons. However, at the time of this writing, with the book submitted and galley proof checked, I only just now got a message from my editor saying, "Oops, I forgot to get permission from all the authors you referenced." Yikes!

At any rate, if this book safely sees the light of day—thank you to Kiyohiko Azuma, Masaki Okayu, Keiichi Sigsawa, Jin Shibamura, Suzu Suzuki, and Soichiro Watase!

I just realized that it's been an entire two years since my published debut. My body and soul have been corrupted by the strain, but there's nothing more exciting than seeing *doujinshi* made about my stories. To the groups who have been putting together eighty-page *doujinshi*, Viscount merchandise, and Celty figurines, you have my utmost gratitude. Thank you very much! Different authors have different feelings about derivative works, but I am perfectly happy about it. I just never thought anyone would want to create fan works about my stories! Thank you, really!

Just as I was writing that, my artist sent a message asking if we could add one more spread illustration. When I said, "Absolutely!" my editor included a note saying, "Just one page for the afterword, to make room for the art." I'm writing this ten minutes before my deadline, so hang on real quick, there's too much I want to say! Um, first of all, thanks to Suzuhito Yasuda for producing such wonderful illustrations on a hard schedule! Thanks to everyone else who helped make this book a reality! Aaaaaaah, no room left, oh crap, I forgot to thank everyone for all the Dengeki Bunko references! Um, there's Yu Fujiwara, the author of *Lunatic Moon*...

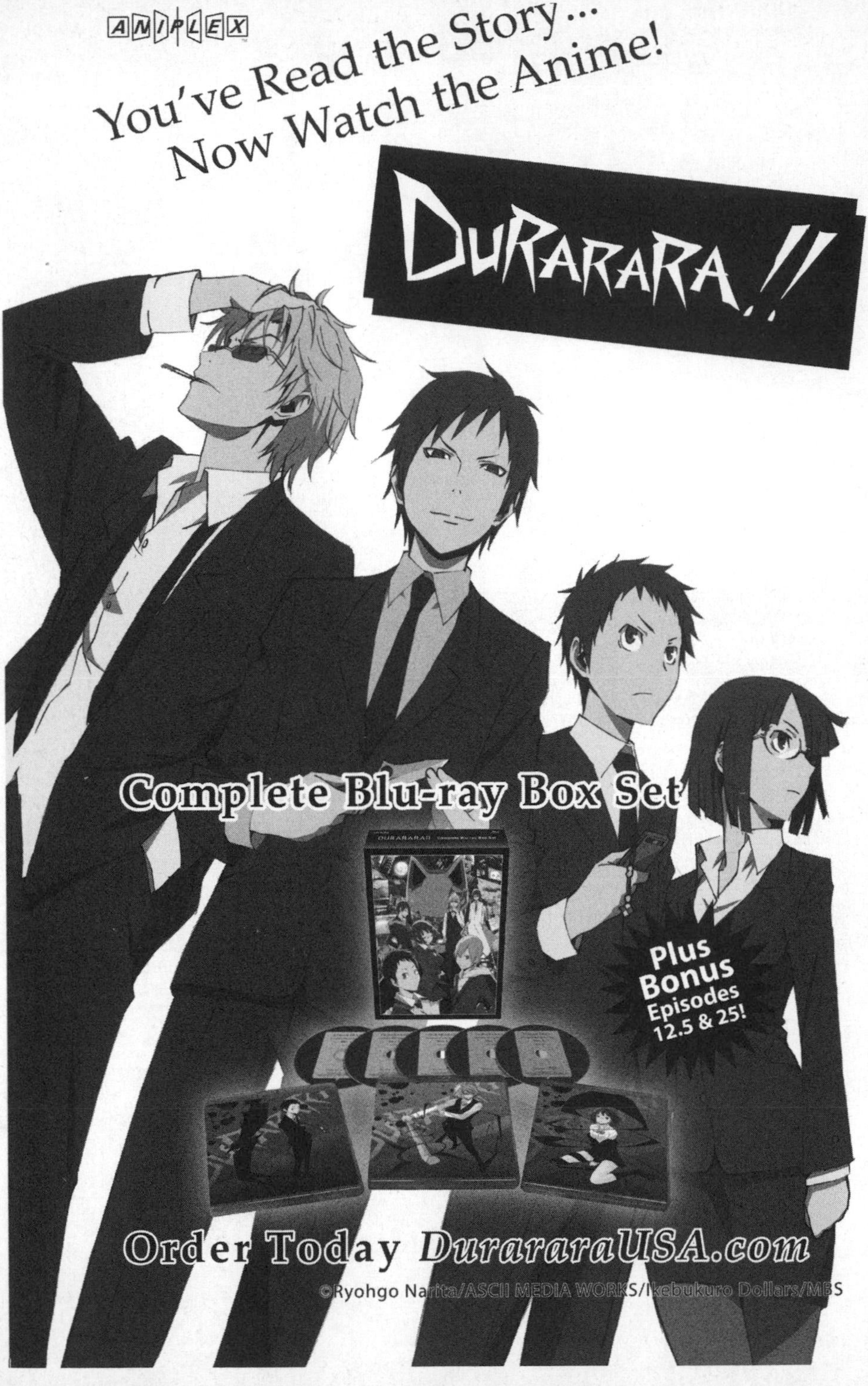
ANIPLEX
You've Read the Story...
Now Watch the Anime!
DURARARA!!
Complete Blu-ray Box Set
Plus Bonus Episodes 12.5 & 25!
Order Today DuraraUSA.com
©Ryohgo Narita/ASCII MEDIA WORKS/Ikebukuro Dollars/MBS

WELCOME TO IKEBUKURO, WHERE TOKYO'S WILDEST CHARACTERS GATHER!!

DURARARA!!

DRRR!! 1

CREATOR
RYOHGO
NARITA

CHARACTER
DESIGN
SUZUHITO
YASUDA

ART
AKIYO
SAIORGI

AS THEIR PATHS CROSS, THIS ECCENTRIC CAST WEAVES A TWISTED, CRACKED LOVE STORY...

AVAILABLE NOW!!

Yen Press